# MY BIG GREEK ISLAND
# EX-SCAPE

## SANDY BARKER

Boldwood

First published in Great Britain in 2026 by Boldwood Books Ltd.

Copyright © Sandy Barker, 2026

Cover Design by Leah Jacobs-Gordon

Cover Images: Leah Jacobs-Gordon

The moral right of Sandy Barker to be identified as the author of this work has been asserted in accordance with the Copyright, Designs and Patents Act 1988.

Every effort has been made to obtain the necessary permissions with reference to copyright material, both illustrative and quoted. We apologise for any omissions in this respect and will be pleased to make the appropriate acknowledgements in any future edition.

A CIP catalogue record for this book is available from the British Library.

Paperback ISBN 978-1-83678-028-1

Large Print ISBN 978-1-83678-027-4

Hardback ISBN 978-1-83678-026-7

Trade Paperback ISBN 978-1-80656-100-1

Ebook ISBN 978-1-83678-029-8

Kindle ISBN 978-1-83678-030-4

Audio CD ISBN 978-1-83678-021-2

MP3 CD ISBN 978-1-83678-022-9

Digital audio download ISBN 978-1-83678-025-0

This book is printed on certified sustainable paper. Boldwood Books is dedicated to putting sustainability at the heart of our business. For more information please visit https://www.boldwoodbooks.com/about-us/sustainability/

Boldwood Books Ltd, 23 Bowerdean Street, London, SW6 3TN

www.boldwoodbooks.com

*This is dedicated to hopeful romantics everywhere.*
*May we all get our happily ever after.*

# THE DIVORCED DIVA'S PLAYLIST

Into You – Ariana Grande
Bed – Raye/Joel Corry/Dave Guetta
Crush – Jennifer Page
Love You for a Long Time – Maggie Rogers
River – Bishop Briggs
These Walls – Dua Lipa
Before You Leave Me – Alex Warren
Let Me Go – Hailee Steinfeld
Tell it to My Heart – Hozier
The Door – Teddy Swims
Snap – Rosa Lin
Edge of Midnight – Miley Cyrus and Stevie Nicks
Stronger – Kelly Clarkson
Head & Heart – Joel Corry, MNEK
Back to You – Lost Frequencies
Power Over Me – Dermot Kennedy
Fall at Your Feet – triple J Like a Version – Peking Duck,
Julia Stone

Only Love Can Hurt Like This – Paloma Faith and
Teddy Swims
My Happiness – Powderfinger
La La La – Naughty Boy and Sam Smith
My Heart Goes (La Di Da) Becky Hill
Belong Together – Mark Ambor
Sucker – Jonas Brothers
Ready for Your Love – Gorgon City / MNEK
Shivers – Ed Sheeran
Ordinary – Alex Warren
Lose Control – Teddy Swims

# PROLOGUE
## THREE WEDDINGS AND A CAREER CHANGE

If you'd told me at my first wedding that I'd divorce my gorgeous husband-to-be within two years, then marry and divorce twice more before turning thirty-two, I'd have told you to shut the hell up, sit your arse down, and stop ruining my big day.

But that's exactly what happened – three weddings, three husbands, three spectacular failures.

But, despite suffering through varying degrees of heartache, my marriages made me who I am today – the Divorced Diva. Not just a blogger-turned-influencer, but a brand ambassador, break-up whisperer, and champion of divorced singletons everywhere.

Ironic, really, because once upon a time, I believed in love – head-over-heels, sweep-you-off-your-feet, happily-ever-after love.

Now I believe in sex positivity, emotional boundaries, and sleeping slap bang in the middle of the bed.

But I'm getting ahead of myself.

Before I tell you a bonkers story involving two of my ex-husbands (yes, *two*), I should probably explain how I became the poster child for divorce – make that *thriving* after divorce – and the owner of three unopened air fryers (apparently, toasters are *so* last century).

It all started with Tommy – brilliant mind, charming dreamer, sexiest man I've ever known.

We met in our final year at Oxford, falling fast and hard into the kind of love where a few hours apart felt like a lifetime. Against everyone's advice, we got married straight out of uni – because when you've found the love of your life, why wait?

Wrapped in Tommy's arms, I felt safe, cherished, and utterly adored. And we had plans – a big life filled with love, adventure, and making the world a better place. For a while, I believed we'd last forever.

But then he took a job that whisked him off to disaster zones for weeks at a time – sometimes months. At first, I missed him. Then I resented him. Eventually, I barely recognised the moody stranger who came home between projects – or myself, now a clingy, miserable woman pining for what we'd lost.

When I begged Tommy to choose our marriage over his career, he didn't. So, I chose me.

Seventeen months, three weeks, and two days after our wedding, I signed the divorce papers with a shattered heart and a shaky hand.

Which is how I ended up with husband number two: Rick – American rockstar, objectively unattractive, subjectively sexy.

Well into my post-divorce, throw-caution-to-the-wind phase, I met Rick in a London pub while his band was touring. After one night together – the first time I'd laughed in ages – I was convinced I'd found the one. Again.

Three days later, we married in the bar at the Ritz, his tour manager officiating.

But it didn't take long to realise that Rick was more into his fans than he was into foreplay, and by the end of the band's European tour (and our forty-seven-day marriage), I was done with life on the road, mediocre sex, and being elbowed aside by screeching groupies.

From rockstar chaos to silver-fox sophistication, enter husband number three: Julian – tech genius, filthy rich, fifteen years my senior.

Julian wooed me over oysters and Champagne, proposed with a vintage Cartier ring, and whisked me around the world on his yacht. I was dazzled – and, honestly, a little drunk on the lifestyle.

Then I caught him in the captain's cabin, canoodling with a gorgeous Swedish steward called Ebba, wearing a sheepish grin and trying to hide his naked erection.

I kept the ring, the car, the Chelsea flat – *and* my dignity. Julian kept the yacht and I have no idea what happened to the steward.

So, there you have it: three husbands, three divorces, and less than three years in wedlock.

And somewhere between blogging about heartbreak and landing my first endorsement deal, I ditched the PR job and started building the Divorced Diva empire.

Life was ticking along nicely – the campaigns, the causes, the blissful singlehood – until the day I came face to face with two of my ex-husbands. At the same time.

And that was just the beginning of the madness. Trust me, you're going to want to hear this.

**1**

Thought of the day...
You divorced your ex for a reason.
There is no going back, no matter how much you miss them.
(And, yes, sexual fantasies count. Do. Not. Go. There.)

I've always loved the thrum of activity in Divorced Diva HQ – AKA the ground floor of my Chelsea terrace house. There are only four of us, but even so, it has the kind of anticipatory energy that makes it feel like something incredible could happen at any moment.

It was a Tuesday morning when that 'something incredible' was a life-changing phone call. I was at my desk, deep in thought, deciding which of a dozen photos to use for the 'thought of the day' post.

To the uninitiated, it might have seemed like an easy decision – the photos *were* remarkably similar. But this wasn't my first rodeo – nor my second, nor third. A detail as simple as the angle of my chin or the look in my eyes could convey a multitude of meanings, and these factors combined resulted in precise, targeted messaging.

Chin up and to the left, eyes slightly narrowed: I have chronic PMT and will end you at the slightest provocation. Do. Not. Mess. With. Me.

Chin up and to the right, eyes lit up: I slept brilliantly and can handle any challenge you lob at me. Bring. It. On.

*Empowerment or encouragement – which would land best?* On Tuesdays, we typically favoured empowerment, a strategic way to get through the mid-week slump that comes between Motivation Monday and the lead up to the weekend.

Sticking to that strategy, I chose the don't-mess-with-me photo and started on the caption. I'd typed *Own your power* when my PA, Ruby, interrupted.

'Ally, I've got Julian for you.'

My thoughts came to a screeching halt. Why on earth was Julian calling? My eyes went to my Divorced Diva desk calendar, and I did a quick calculation. Julian and I met for lunch on the last Wednesday of the month, every other month. If he was calling to make plans, he was more than five weeks early. No, this was something else.

'Thank you, Ruby,' I said with a smile. I picked up the desk phone and spun my chair to face the wall. 'Jules...' I said in greeting, dragging his name out.

He chuckled. 'You sound wary.'

'When it comes to you and unexpected phone calls, always.'

I paused, knowing Julian would fill the silence. He hates silences.

'Well, right to it then. I have a favour to ask,' he said in his crisp public-schoolboy accent.

Julian is big on favours – I suspect half of his dealings, business or otherwise, are the giving and receiving of favours.

I mentally sifted through our 'favour ledger'. Did I still owe him for the introduction to the head of guest services at The Dorchester? No, I'd returned that favour by putting in a good word for him with Adele's people. Sure, it was the week before she announced her hiatus, but he didn't know I knew that. It counted and my debt to Julian had been cleared.

'Let's have it then,' I prodded.

'I need you to come to Aetheria. This Friday. Only for five days – maybe six.'

'Aetheria?' I asked.

'My island. In the Aegean. The one I bought the year before last. Haven't I mentioned it?'

'Er, no,' I replied pointedly. 'I think I'd remember you buying an *island*, Jules.'

'Well, I've built a resort here and it's absolutely brilliant – well, it should be, I spent squillions on it. Anyway, you're going to *love* it, Ally.'

'Hold up, you're getting ahead of yourself,' I scolded lightly. 'Now, before I agree to drop everything, what's going on?'

'Long story short: I'm in a bind and I need you to be the face of the resort.'

'The face?'

I knew what he meant, of course, but there was something rather delicious about making Julian spell it out. *And* ask for the favour properly.

'Don't be coy – you know exactly what I mean,' he retorted.

Boo – he didn't want to play. It must have been worse than I thought.

'Okay, okay,' I said with a soft laugh. 'Now, what exactly do you have in mind?'

'Just the usual. The itinerary's already been put together – all *you* have to do is be your fabulous self.'

'*And* say lots of lovely things about the resort on camera.'

'Precisely.'

'So, go on then, who cancelled on you?' I asked. There was no way Julian had left something this momentous to the last minute. He would have had someone lined up well in advance.

'One of the Emmas,' he replied.

'Ooh, intriguing. Stone, Watson, or Roberts?'

'I'm not supposed to say.'

I rolled my eyes, allowing the silence to unfurl.

Four seconds later, he said, 'Watson. But there's been a scheduling conflict. Reshoots for her next film so...'

'So, you've come to your ex-wife, hat in hand, to beg *me* to do it. And with two days' notice.'

'You make it sound as if I'm desperate.'

'Aren't you?' I teased.

'The truth? Yes. The grand opening is less than two weeks away and all this was supposed to be sorted by now. *And* I've got this business deal to—' He cut himself off, then sighed. 'Look, if you aren't up for it, I'll ask the Sexy Single.'

'Well, if that's the way you want to go... I mean, Daisy Harrigan *is* a copycat pretender and she has nowhere *near* the reach that Divorced Diva has, but it's your choice, Jules.' *That should call his bluff*, I thought, gently swinging my chair.

He chuckled down the line again. 'Sometimes I forget how well you've got me pegged.'

That hadn't always been the case, but I didn't say anything.

'Look, desperation aside,' he continued, 'you'll be wonderful – *perfect* even. I should have asked you in the first place.'

'All right, Jules, no need to butter me up. Now, just bear with...' I pressed the *hold* button before he could respond.

'Ruby, how much of a nightmare would it be to clear my calendar from Friday to... let's say Tuesday?'

'This Friday?'

'Yes.'

'I'll check.'

Unfazed as always – Ruby never reacts to any situation with more than a slight furrow between her brows – she started typing rapidly on her keyboard. Moments later, Claude beelined for my desk from across the office.

'Is that Julian?' she asked, glancing at the phone's blinking hold light as she perched on the edge of my desk.

'You know it is, and I know exactly what you're about to say.'

Her mouth bunched to one side. 'Just promise me you'll run it past me before you say *yes*.'

Claude ran operations and partnerships, so technically, I *was* supposed to check with her before agreeing. But this wasn't her being the boss – this was my big sister sliding into protective mode.

'He wants me as brand ambassador for his new resort – well, the Divorced Diva.'

She sighed, tilting her head. 'Ally, I get that you've made peace with him, but he can't just cash in on your success. Especially considering how he—'

'I'll be charging him an eye-watering amount,' I assured her, cutting her off. 'And think about it – an exclusive resort... very wealthy guests... I'm sure Julian would return the favour by introducing us to some new benefactors.'

Her gaze softened, but the frown didn't budge.

'Ally,' Ruby called out, 'if we move the podcast recording to tomorrow and I postpone the photoshoot in the Cotswolds for a week, I can easily sort everything else.'

Unflappable, our Ruby – one of the many reasons I adore working with her.

'Thank you. Maya, any glaring clashes you can see?' I asked.

Maya Wylde, the fourth member of our team, is a marketing whizz/wunderkind who I poached from my former employer when I established Divorced Diva as an LLP. She runs our social media campaigns across multiple platforms, manages our online community, coordinates a team of offsite contractors (i.e. influencers), and writes all our messaging. Well, except for the thoughts of the day – those are strictly mine.

'I can move a few things around,' she said. 'And there may be some cross-promotions and brand synergies to explore – with the resort, I mean. I'll just need a contact.'

All Maya had to go on was what she'd gleaned from eaves-dropping, and she was already strategising.

'Thanks, Maya,' I replied. I looked at Claude, arching my brows. 'Well?'

She exhaled through her nose, then nodded. 'All right. But on one condition.' She leaned in, her voice low. 'Don't let him charm you into bed.'

'As if I would,' I whispered, stung by the suggestion, even though I knew it came from love.

Claude gave me a look – the one that said I'd made worse decisions with less temptation. She wagged a finger at me. 'Don't.'

I swatted her hand away, and she returned to her desk, trailing that inescapable air of big-sister authority.

I rarely regretted bringing Claude on at Divorced Diva. It had been the perfect antidote for *her* post-divorce blues, making her too busy to wallow and paying enough to keep the wolf from the door. And she was an absolute pro – the most organised, meticulous person I knew.

But at times, the line between her role at Divorced Diva and being my sister blurred. This was one of them.

There was no way in hell I'd ever sleep with Julian again – not when I was perfectly happy on my own (taking the occasional lover when it suited me). But more importantly, hooking up with an ex went against everything Divorced Diva stood for – never go back, never repeat past mistakes.

I wasn't about to risk everything I'd built just for Julian – no matter how good he was in bed.

And Claude knew that. Or she should have.

*  *  *

Friday rolled around quickly – time sped up when you had to clear a jam-packed schedule – and I spent most of the day in transit. Not my favourite aspect of travel, but is it anybody's?

With apologies that his private jet wasn't available, Julian flew me from Heathrow to Athens in business class, then sent a helicopter to collect me from there.

And while helicopters may seem like a fancy-schmancy way to get about, they make me queasy. That day, the ride to Aetheria was particularly bumpy – crosswinds, apparently – so I was struggling to hold on to my lunch. And BA does a particularly nice lunch at the pointy end of the aeroplane. However, the journey to Aetheria also served up a visual feast that lifted my spirits *and* kept my mind off my innards erupting.

Below us, the Aegean sparkled with thousands of pinpoints of sunshine, the water an array of colours, shifting and surging as if in a dance – sapphire, midnight, teal... Every shade of blue all at once.

The pilot named the islands of the Cyclades as we passed by, his commentary in my headset another distraction from the nausea. There was Kea to the left, Kythnos right below us, Syros just ahead...

He flew us lower over Syros, giving me a proper look at its enormous port and brightly coloured buildings, the eggshell blue of a church dome capturing my eye. It was a stunning island. *Note to self: book a holiday to Syros.*

The helicopter climbed again and a few minutes later, the pilot's voice came over the headset. 'You'll see Mykonos to our left and Naxos to our right.'

I looked in both directions over the expanse of water towards their ragged coasts. Naxos was vastly larger and greener than Mykonos, but both were rather unremarkable from that high up, evidence of those iconic white boxy structures invisible to the naked eye. I wondered if Julian's island would have them.

'About five minutes out, Ms Novak,' said the pilot.

'Thank you.'

I craned my neck to see out the front window of the helicopter, hoping to get a glimpse of Aetheria. The pilot looked over his shoulder and broke into a smile beneath his aviators. 'Just over there,' he said, his arm extending to the southeast.

I leaned further forward and there it was – tiny compared to other islands we'd passed. But *beautiful*, the features of its varied topography sharpening as we drew nearer, then followed the coastline south. A jagged, curved cliff, a sliver of snow-white sand at its base, the water in the cove turquoise. Gently sloping land, strewn with stands of Cyprus trees. Jagged, reddish rock formations. And on one of the gentler slopes, an erratic grove of gnarly, thick-trunked olive trees, likely growing there for centuries.

The helicopter banked and my stomach lurched, but before I could start fantasising about returning to Athens by boat, the resort appeared, hugging the southeast coast. It was the only structure on the island and whoever Julian's architect was, they'd absolutely smashed it.

Whitewashed villas dotted the wide terraces, their flat roofs gleaming under the Aegean sun and each one cocooned in lush greenery. Stone pathways meandered through manicured gardens, where bursts of bougainvillea and oleander painted the landscape in pinks and reds, visible even from the air. Closer to the shore, sleek cabanas lined the crescent-shaped beach, positioned to gaze out over a single pier that reached into the aquamarine sea. And midway down the hillside, a long, whitewashed building commanded attention, its flagstone patio stretching beside an impossibly long infinity pool.

It was breathtaking – a sanctuary carved into the rugged beauty of the island, clearly designed for those who expected luxury.

After sweeping over the resort, we hovered above the helipad, downwash bending the tops of nearby Cyprus trees, and slowly lowered to the ground. A man was standing off to the side awaiting our arrival and it took me a sec to realise it was Julian.

He looked handsome, as always – his dark-blond hair greying at the temples, his skin bronzed save for the laugh lines around his eyes – but the Julian I knew would *never* wear head-to-toe white linen or *sandals*. Oh, the horror! But there he was, the picture of ashram chic, his hands resting in his trouser pockets and one hip slightly cocked.

This was a less buttoned-up, less *affected* version of Julian.

The pilot got out and opened the door for me, and I gratefully stepped onto terra firma. Julian came forward, smiling, and grasped both my hands in his.

'Welcome to Aetheria,' he said, leaning down to kiss one cheek then the other.

'Thanks, Jules.'

He smelled great – Julian always does – but this scent was a stark contrast to his signature spicy cologne. It was citrusy with a hint of sea salt. Or that could have been the light breeze that was catching the loose tendrils around my face.

'You look absolutely beautiful,' he said, taking a step back to look me up and down. It was impossible to ignore the flirtatious glint in his eyes, which gave me pause.

Typically, Julian respected the invisible border I'd erected when we divorced. But there was nothing typical about this (literally) unbuttoned version of Julian – Julian 2.0. My eyes dropped to his chest, most of which was on display, and when I lifted my gaze, he was grinning cheekily. Oh god, he must have thought I was flirting back. Only I wasn't.

'You cad,' I said with a laugh, adding a half-serious finger wag that would've made Claude proud. 'I'm here for work and that's *all*.'

'Well, you can't blame a man for hoping,' he said with a droll smile. His words hung in the air for several seconds, then he broke eye contact and threw his arms out wide. 'So, what do you think?'

Glad to move on to the reason I was there, I beamed at him. 'Oh, Jules. It's just magical. And it clearly agrees with you – you seem almost… *relaxed*,' I teased.

He sniggered, clearly chuffed.

'It is magical,' he agreed, 'and this is just the helipad. Come on, let me show you around.' He offered his arm, and I slipped my hand into the crook of his elbow.

## 2

Thought of the day...
Putting yourself first is not selfish.
It's self-care.
(Just tell everyone else to bugger off. But in a nice way.)

I know how privileged I am.

My life is extraordinary by most people's measure, something I'm acutely aware of. Jetting about, dining in the world's best restaurants, wearing beautiful clothes, indulging in luxurious experiences like being on Aetheria...

But that doesn't mean my life is perfect. I'm still human. I have fears and doubts; I wrestle with moments of sadness and longing. A swipe of bright-red lipstick can work wonders, giving me a bold façade of confidence, but there are days when it does little more than stain my lips.

And there's far more to Divorced Diva than what's visible on social media. Our charity partnerships typically happen quietly, behind the scenes. For every photo of me with a cocktail in hand, there's a meet-and-greet with single parents who need help finding a job or a place to live.

The outward-facing Diva funds the causes that matter, the ones that allow me – *us* – to make a difference. Just like I dreamed of back in the tiny flat I shared with Tommy when we first married and subsisted on beans on toast.

Back then, Tommy was my person, but after we split, Claude became that person. She knows the real me better than anyone – not just the Diva, but the woman underneath.

I don't know what I'd do without her.

'Well, how's it going?' she asked – as usual, no chit chat, just straight into it.

I could have gushed for days about the incredible architecture, or how the landscaping evoked tropical island resort but with a Greek Island twist. Or about my villa, which was *the* most luxurious accommodation I'd ever stayed in (which said a lot). Every minute detail had been carefully selected to strike a balance between opulence and tranquillity, from the soft furnishings to the bath products and beyond.

But I knew my audience of one and Claude was asking about Julian, not the resort.

'Julian has been a perfect gentleman,' I replied, to which she scoffed with a gentle grunt. Ignoring her, I continued. 'And it's beautiful here, Claude. We should come back for a proper holiday, just us two.'

It was a futile suggestion and we both knew it. Convincing Claude to travel overseas was about as likely as me touring with Taylor Swift as a backup dancer.

'Perhaps,' Claude replied noncommittally. 'So, have you read Maya's plan?'

She meant the marketing plan. Maya had teamed up with

Julian's PR rep – for every request from Aetheria, Divorced Diva got a reciprocal opportunity.

'I read it on the plane.'

'Good, I thought you might,' she replied. 'And look out for a package. It's supposed to be in your room.'

I cast a glance about the suite, spying a cardboard box on the coffee table. Next to it was an even larger gift basket, no doubt showcasing luxury goods that Aetheria would become known for.

But it was the box that mattered most. Inside was a carefully curated selection from our boutique-brand partners – businesses founded by divorced women and men we'd supported as they launched their dreams.

'Al?' she asked when I didn't answer.

'All good – it's here,' I replied, keeping my tone neutral.

The truth is, I loathe it when she calls me *Al*. The shortened version of her name, which is Claudia if you didn't guess, is strong, classical. *Claude*. But *Al* sounds like a pissed-off seagull fighting over sandy chips at the beach. Especially the way she says it.

'We have to make the most of this,' she continued, undaunted. 'Otherwise, with you away for nearly a week, we're at a loss and—'

'Claude,' I interjected. 'I promise I won't let *any* opportunities slip through my fingers, all right?' I wandered back into the bedroom, sitting on the edge of the bed.

'All right,' she replied with a resigned sigh.

Hang on... My forthright, sometimes nag of a sister was bowing out of a robust conversation without having the last word? Something was amiss.

'Claude, what's going on? What aren't you telling me?'

She didn't answer right away, but when she did, her voice was tight and small. 'I saw Gregory today. At Tesco.'

Gregory – AKA The Twat – AKA my sister's ex-husband.

And unlike *my* three exes, Gregory is *not* a decent bloke who just wasn't right for her. He was a total and utter twat from the moment she met him. He cheated, he lied, he treated her like shit, and eventually, he gambled away their life savings.

I disliked him from the start, spotting his wily ways immediately. Whereas Claude persisted in that shitty, shitty (bang, bang) marriage for eight years. Eight years!

'Oh, no! Claude, that's rubbish! I'm so sorry. And what the bloody hell is he doing at Tesco? I thought you got Tesco and he got Sainsbury's?'

It was an odd aspect of their division of property, but when you move into a tiny flat around the corner from your marital home, a necessity.

'I know!' she wailed, following up with a sniffle. 'That's what I said when I saw him, but he made up some excuse about Sainsbury's being out of buns.'

'Oh, for fuck's sake,' I murmured, mostly to myself.

It wasn't the first time I'd wanted to throttle my former brother-in-law. It also wasn't the first time I'd wished Claude would let me cover her share of the marital debt that *he'd* racked up without her knowledge. I'd had to settle for paying her a generous salary. Of course, she deserves every penny of what she earns.

With the sound of her increasingly louder sniffles, an idea popped into my head.

'Claude, what if you came to Aetheria? Now, I mean. The official opening is still more than a week away, so there's plenty of room. You could relax, have some spa treatments... I'm going on a sailboat tomorrow – we're sailing around the entire island. And you *love* to sail. What do you say?'

Having proposed the near-impossible – Claude not only shies away from travelling, she's rarely impulsive – I waited patiently, willing her to say *yes*.

'No, it's all right. I'll just run a bath and watch something cheery. Maybe *Happy Valley*. Everyone's been on about it for ages.'

I didn't correct her – she'd find out soon enough that *Happy Valley* was about as cheery as a migraine. And disappointed that she'd turned me down, I tried to sound upbeat. 'Good plan, Claude. Call you tomorrow?'

'Okay. Bye.'

She ended our call halfway through me saying *I love you*.

I flopped backwards onto the enormous bed, sinking into the luxurious linens, my eyes drooping. The queasiness from the helicopter ride had receded but fatigue was advancing fast. I could easily have drifted off – *if* there weren't the pressing matter of my job!

I heaved myself off the bed and wandered over to my tote where I retrieved my laptop. I searched for the WiFi password, finding it on the large oak desk, and was soon logged in.

I scanned Maya's marketing plan again, then opened the itinerary from Julian's team – it was packed to the brim. Between photoshoots, filming sessions, excursions, activities, and product promotions – some of them to be live-streamed – I would barely have a moment to catch my breath.

It was probably a good thing Claude wasn't coming. It had been naïve of me to think there'd be any time for R&R.

'This isn't a holiday, Ally,' I reminded myself.

'It never is,' I replied.

Wonderful – not only was I talking to myself, I was replying.

But I had a point. When *was* the last time I'd been on a proper holiday? I ran through my recent trips, crossing them off one by one when I recalled the work angle.

Six days spent at a resort in Cabo San Lucas: a conference for female leaders. Two days sailing along the coast of Croatia: a photoshoot for an up-and-coming swimwear designer. Three nights in a treetop lodge in Thailand: trialling a yoga retreat for newly single women. I was the only one who didn't cry the whole time – even the woman running the retreat was in a bad place emotionally. I told so many sobbing women *You'll get through this* that it sparked inspiration for a line of merchandise.

Amazing experiences, each one – but they were far from holidays.

And then I remembered: the last time I'd been on a proper, read-by-the-pool, get-a-daily-massage, sip-cocktails-at-sunset holiday was with Julian aboard his super yacht two and a half years ago. The trip where I caught him in the captain's cabin with Ebba.

It turns out that catching your husband with another woman tends to take the shine off a holiday.

As I sank onto the plush linen sofa, a realisation landed. It was *me* who needed time on Aetheria to decompress, to rest, to *heal*... Well, Claude did too, but I was always telling our followers that self-care is not selfish. Maybe it was time I started taking my own advice.

Only when I eyed my laptop again, I sighed. I may have needed a holiday, but Aetheria was not it. I was there to work. Full stop.

So, I tore into the box and started decanting products onto the coffee table, then set up my travel tripod and clipped in my phone. Divorced Diva mode activated, I broke into a wide smile, held up a delicious-smelling beeswax candle from one of our partners, and pressed record.

\* \* \*

'My god, Ally, you're *breathtaking*.'

There's something you need to understand about the Divorced Diva. She's *hot* – a total smoke show, as the Americans say.

She wears figure-hugging dresses to dinner, low-cut jumpsuits with tailored jackets to work, matching crop tops and booty shorts to the gym, and bikinis by the pool.

Her body is sculpted by Pilates, her skin smoothed by treatments, and her platinum-blonde hair kept silky and lush thanks to £600 salon appointments. Makeup flawless, accessories on point – bags, shoes, jewellery – and she smells divine, as if anointed by Aphrodite herself.

And yes, I'm aware that describing oneself in the third person is almost as troubling as talking to oneself, but I've come to think of the Diva as a persona – someone separate from the real me. A *brand*.

When it's just me – no cameras, no followers about – I'm happiest in old trackies, an oversized hoodie, and Uggs, my hair in a messy bun and zero makeup.

But Wonder Woman has her gold tiara and lasso of truth, Black Widow has her leather catsuit and pistols, and the Divorced Diva? She's armed with a bold red lip, a slinky dress, and killer stilettos.

So, when I say I showed up to Julian's island ready to work, I shouldn't have been surprised that I took his breath away. But I couldn't have him hyperventilating whenever he saw me – *espe-*

*cially* after that flirtatious greeting. Maybe our well-established boundaries would need to be reinforced.

I gave him a friendly smile as he pushed my chair in, then reached for the menu, salivating as I scanned the offerings.

'This all looks incredible, Jules,' I said, my eyes not leaving the menu.

'It *is* incredible. The chef – she's a genius – she has *two* Michelin stars. I had to pay her an obscene amount of money to convince her to leave Athens.'

That drew my attention and I lifted my gaze. 'You always did know how to throw money at a problem, Jules,' I said, though not unkindly.

'Ouch,' he said, clasping his chest with both hands.

'Oh, don't pretend to be insulted – *or* wounded. You know you're proud of that.'

He sniggered, tilting his head in concession, and I dropped my eyes back to the menu. But the fatigue I'd felt earlier was settling in and deciding what to have for each course was suddenly too much.

'Any chance we can ask her to craft a menu for us?' I asked.

'Chef's choice? Absolutely.'

He discreetly raised his forefinger and an Adonis with jet-black hair, tanned olive skin, and the kind of physique that adorns the covers of romance novels appeared.

'Christos, let Dimitra know we're happy to leave the menu up to her. And bring a bottle of the Assyrtiko, will you?'

The Adonis – Christos – nodded with a polite smile, his eyes darting to meet mine before he turned and strode towards the kitchen.

'So,' I said, shaking off the brief exchange and smiling at Julian, 'you bought an island.'

He laughed. 'I did. Are you *sure* I didn't mention before?' he asked, his eyes narrowing playfully.

'Positive. So, what prompted such an extravagant purchase?'

'Oh, I don't want to bore you with all that – not on your first night here. Let's save that for another time, shall we?'

Sensing a wistfulness beneath Julian's casual brush-off, I debated probing further, but he'd tell me when he was ready, so I let the topic drop. Besides, the hot waiter had returned with the wine.

Christos made quite the show of presenting the bottle, which was from Santorini, then uncorking it with short, sharp twists of his beautiful hands. My eyes drifted to his forearms, which bulged with each twist, then up to his chiselled face. Actually, calling him an *Adonis* didn't do him justice.

He expertly poured two glasses, then set the bottle in an ice bucket. But before stepping away, his dark-brown eyes met mine again, his lips lifting slightly at the edges. It was obvious that if I wanted, I could have a very handsome Greek man in my bed that night.

But as I'd only just reminded myself, I was on Aetheria to work, not to hook up. And if I *did* feel randy, I'd packed enough toys to scratch that itch.

When I looked back at Julian, he was watching me curiously. 'He's a handsome bloke, isn't he?' he asked.

'You think so?' I quipped with a nose scrunch. 'I hadn't really noticed.'

He chuckled softly. 'You know, you're very welcome to—'

'*Jules*,' I said, cutting him off.

'What? Isn't it part of your brand, being sexually empowered?'

'It is, yes, but that's mostly about supporting my followers – helping them reclaim that part of themselves post-divorce. It doesn't mean that I'm out there bonking every Tom, Dick, and Harry who looks my way.'

'Or Christos,' he interjected.

'Or Christos – exactly. It's not about promiscuity, Jules. It's about agency, confidence, and *pleasure* – without losing sight of who you are.'

He regarded me thoughtfully. 'Have you always been this clever?'

I laughed. 'God, no. But that's the beauty of growing older, isn't it?'

'Mmm,' he murmured, giving nothing away. Just then he looked past me and broke into a wide smile.

'Oh, here's someone you should meet,' he said. 'Our trusty skipper – an excellent sailor and a top bloke to boot.'

I turned and looked over my shoulder.

*Oh. My. Fucking. God.*

It was Tommy.

## 3

> Thought of the day…
> If you ever run into your ex unexpectedly, remain calm and
> hold your head high.
> (Let's be honest, they're probably in more of a tizz than you
> are.)

*Oh my god, oh my god, oh my god.*

There's a reason I chose not to see Tommy in person: his presence wielded a destructive power that not even the Divorced Diva could protect me from, triggering heart palpitations, perspiration, shortness of breath…

And then there were the spine tingles, the heat pooling between my thighs, my sodden knickers.

Tommy was what you'd get if you blended heartbreak and lust into a smoothie.

And until that night, I'd limited our contact to occasional text messages and very rare phone calls. Call it self-preservation.

But there he was, in the flesh, so incongruous with his

surroundings that at first, I couldn't make sense of what was happening.

Then it hit me like a boulder dropping on my head. Tommy was on Aetheria. With me. And Julian. Two ex-husbands in the same place. And they knew each other! It truly was a waking nightmare, my compartmentalised worlds colliding.

Next thing, I'd discover that Julian had booked Rick's band as the entertainment!

Tommy walked closer, looking smart in fitted navy shorts, tan boat shoes, and a white Polo shirt with Aetheria's logo – a teal wave with a yellow rising moon – sitting over his left pec. The shirt moulded to his still-impressive physique, the short sleeves showing off his tanned forearms, and his dark-brown wavy hair was slightly longer than I remembered. It suited him.

*Why does he have to be so fucking sexy?*

*And more to the point, why does he have to be so fucking HERE?*

Contemplating the answers to these questions made it so loud inside my head that I almost missed Julian introducing Tommy as *Tom*.

*Tom?*

Thomas – absolutely, it's his name. And to me, he's always been Tommy. But never just *Tom*.

He smiled as he approached the table and I couldn't look away. I *wanted* to. In fact, I wanted to *run* away – go hide in my villa under the covers, my hands clapped over my ears.

But I was stuck there, frozen to my chair.

When Tommy finally clapped eyes on me, his smile didn't just fall away, it tumbled off his face like snow tumbles down a mountain during an avalanche. We stared at each other for a thousand years until Julian's voice broke through our shared fugue.

'Tom, this is my ex-wife, Ally. She's joining us for the week –

she's an *influencer*,' he added, imbuing the word with pride. I am much more than that, but I didn't have the presence of mind to be offended.

'Uh, hi, Ally,' Tommy stammered. He jutted his hand out so forcefully, his fingertips poked my right boob. We both recoiled and I redirected my gaze to the tabletop.

'Sorry,' he muttered.

'That's okay. Hi,' I replied, flapping my hand in a half-hearted wave. I didn't dare look at Julian, who must have been wondering what the bloody hell was going on.

'Hi,' Tommy said again.

So, he was as taken aback as I was.

More questions swarmed inside my head like midges at dusk.

*Why is Tommy skippering a sailboat? Isn't he supposed to be off building wells in a remote village or something? Is this him shaking up his life? When did I last speak to him? What did he tell me then? And how does he know Julian? Oh god, does Julian know I used to be married to Tommy? But he just introduced us as if we were strangers. Is Julian pretending? Is this a trap?!*

I couldn't stand it any longer. I looked at Julian. Yep – completely baffled. At least that answered some of my questions. Julian was clearly clueless that Tommy and I had a history.

*Had a history.* Now *that's* a loaded term, alluding to passion and desperation and heartache, something I was hyper aware of with Tommy standing only a couple of feet away.

'Uh, sorry,' said Tommy again, drawing my gaze. He hitched his thumb in the direction of the staff quarters, small bunga-lows by the beach. 'I should get some sleep. Big day tomorrow.'

'Goodnight,' Julian said.

I stayed mute.

When Tommy left, I suddenly put two and two together. I was supposed to spend tomorrow circumnavigating the island on a sailboat – with Tommy skippering! There would be others on board – Julian's PR team, other guests – but the excursion had been organised for *me*. And I'd been promised the full VIP experience.

Did that include shagging the skipper below deck while everyone else *oohed* and *ahhed* over the scenery?

I shook my head, grasping for a sliver of sanity, but all I found was suffocation. I had to get out of there.

'I should probably get some sleep as well,' I said, standing abruptly.

'Oh, but what about dinner?' asked Julian, looking hurt as well as confused.

'I... I'm really sorry, Jules. It must be jetlag or something, but I suddenly feel...' I waved my hand about, hoping to convey general malaise.

'Oh, of course,' said Julian, standing – always the gentleman when it comes to manners. 'We can have dinner tomorrow night – after your sailing trip,' he added. He moved closer and kissed my cheek.

'Sounds lovely. And I really am sorry – please send my apologies to Dimitra.'

'Will do,' he replied with a concerned frown. 'Rest up, Ally. A busy weekend ahead.'

I gave him a quick smile, then left, scurrying up the hill towards my villa. It was in sight when a hand reached out of the darkness and grabbed my wrist. I yelped as I was pulled behind a potted olive tree.

'Shh. Ally, it's *me*.'

I glared up at Tommy. 'You scared me half to death,' I said, my voice a harsh whisper. I rubbed my wrist where his hand had been.

'Did I hurt you?' he asked contritely.

'No, just... What the fuck are you doing here?'

'I was about to ask you the same thing.'

We glared at each other in the dim light, and I fought the overwhelming impulse to stand on tiptoes and bite his lower lip. Instead, I bit my own, and his eyes dropped to my mouth.

Forget about shagging below deck. How about against the wall behind a massive topiary?

*Lust is just a shield, Ally. The heartache's still there underneath.*

*So what? If I'm headed for disaster, I might as well enjoy the ride.*

'*Ally*...' he said, cutting into my internal argument.

A random thought leapt into my head. 'I didn't know you could sail.'

He shook his head at the non sequitur. 'I learned last year. When I was living in Sicily.'

'You lived in *Sicily*?'

'Briefly.'

'Briefly, yet long enough to learn how to sail so proficiently that you've taken a job at an exclusive resort in Greece, which just happens to be owned by my ex-husband? Like that?'

'I didn't know that—' He stopped himself and let out a long breath. 'Look, there's obviously a lot to catch up on.'

'Oh, you don't say.'

*Such as why, when your job was the biggest barrier to us being together and you've clearly quit that job, you didn't come back for me?*

'And we *will* catch up, I promise,' he continued. 'But can we please keep this between us? For now, at least?'

I assumed that by *this* he meant our marriage, but I couldn't decide what to make of his request, which, admittedly, was a tad unfair. *I* wasn't keen on telling Julian either.

He knew I'd been married twice before but it wasn't as if I'd broken out the wedding albums for show and tell. *Here we are, darling. Now this is Tommy. I thought I was going to spend the rest of my life with him, but alas, some things don't work out as hoped... And isn't he just the most handsome man you've ever laid eyes on?*

Instead, it was the opposite. Once a chapter was closed, once I'd learned my lesson – or hadn't – I kept moving forward, my collection of air fryers and some hard-won self-truths the only evidence of what had come before. I certainly didn't go about spilling the tea on my exes.

But standing there in the shadows with Tommy, two once-siloed chapters colliding, I wasn't yet willing to examine *my* motives for keeping quiet. I was more concerned about his.

'Why?' I asked, placing my hands on my hips. 'What do you care if Julian finds out about us?'

He started to speak, then stopped himself again. I hadn't seen this side of Tommy before, hesitant and unsure.

'There's just a lot going on right now and I— I'd prefer it if we didn't complicate matters by revealing that we were once married.'

'Right. So, I'm a complication. Got it.'

I went to leave, but he captured my wrist again.

'Ally...'

I wrenched it free and without another word, I strode towards my villa, chin up and hot tears stinging my eyes.

*Complicate matters? You know what complicates matters? Believing you found the love of your life, then him choosing his stupid job over you! A stupid job he doesn't even have any more!*

I reached my villa and shut the heavy wooden door behind

me, sagging against it as I caught my breath and blinked back tears.

Lust wasn't my only shield. A low hum of anger had been guarding my heart for years. But now we were being forced together, neither shield would deflect so much as a stray eyelash – especially if it was Tommy's.

*Maybe I should just leave.*

But I'd promised Julian. And it wasn't his fault he'd accidentally hired my personal Kryptonite.

I pushed off the door and walked further into the villa.

Someone had been in for turndown service. The lights were on, casting an inviting yellow glow, music played softly – acoustic guitar, which sounded more Spanish than Greek, but still calming – one side of the duvet had been turned down, and a small gift box sat on the pillow.

My stomach rumbled. It had been stupid of me to lie about not being hungry, especially considering what was on offer, and I crossed to the pillow and snatched up the small box. Expecting chocolate, I tore it open. A silver bangle fell to the floor and I stooped to pick it up, turning it in my hand so it caught the light.

I looked inside the box, and there was a note. I slid the bangle over my wrist and took it out.

*Dearest Ally,*
   *Just a small token of my appreciation.*
   *With love,*
   *Julian*

Could the night get any more bizarre? Or ironic? A gift from one ex when the man my heart still longed for – because who was I kidding about siloes and moving on? – wanted to keep our history under wraps.

I plopped onto the bed, spinning the bangle around my wrist. A glint of light caught my eye and I held my wrist up to the bedside lamp. This wasn't a silver bangle, I realised on closer examination. It was platinum and set with tiny diamonds.

I read the card again. *With love, Julian.* Oh god, was this a *romantic* gift? If so, it complicated matters (to borrow words from hubby number one).

'Oh, Jules,' I sighed wearily. 'Are you trying to win me back?'

I took off the bangle and set it on the bedside table. Regardless of Julian's intentions, I'd need to find a gentle way to return it.

My stomach rumbled again and I got up and went to the minibar where I conducted a quick inventory. There were all sorts of delicious Greek goodies. Hooray, I wouldn't starve to death before morning!

I was just about to open a packet of dried figs when there was a knock at the door. I froze. Hubby number one or hubby number three? I drew in a breath and held it, keeping perfectly still, which was ridiculous. Whichever husband it was knew I was in there.

'Just answer the bloody door, Ally,' I chastised myself.

I crossed the room and swung it open, something that took considerable effort. But it wasn't a husband. It was Christos, the Adonis from the restaurant.

'Oh, hello,' I said, unable to keep the surprise from my voice.

He presented a tray with a silver cloche on it. 'Mr Cushing asked me to deliver this. He thought you might be hungry after travelling for most of the day.'

I lifted the cloche and eyed the assortment of food – a bowl brimming with plump olives, a plate of creamy dip sprinkled with chopped parsley, and a stack of pita that, from the aroma, was fresh off the skillet.

'That's *melitzanosalata*,' he said, pointing at the dip.

'Which is?'

'It's made with smoked eggplant.'

'Ah, well it smells delicious.' I lowered the silver dome and stepped aside. 'Come on in.'

He hesitated for a sec, then entered. As I closed the door behind us, he walked over to the sitting area and placed the tray on the low coffee table. *God, he has an incredible arse.*

He straightened and turned, catching me checking him out – something I probably wouldn't have done if it weren't for the shitty, *shitty* luck of running into Tommy.

Sex with a stranger can soothe a heart that's held together with Pritt stick, tape, and chewing gum. But seducing the hot waiter would have been little more than a consolation prize – gorgeous as he was, Christos wasn't Tommy.

'Well, enjoy,' he said, his grin lingering a fraction too long to be professional.

I saw him out, and he gave me one last look before the door clicked shut. I turned to the tray of food. Forget Tommy, forget Christos – what I really needed was dinner. Easier to feed a growling stomach than mend a broken heart.

## 4

Despite being well-fed (I devoured every morsel on that tray), exhausted from the day's journey, *and* wrung out from the emotional upheaval brought on by Tommy's appearance, I barely slept that night.

I simply couldn't get Tommy out of my mind. And I tried every trick in the book.

I even tried counting sheep, but that just reminded me of the Hebridean sheep that Tommy and I saw in the Scottish Highlands during a mini break.

Wide a-fucking-wake.

I tried meditating, but every time I cleared my mind, Tommy came marching back into it. Tommy on our wedding day, beaming as I walked down the aisle towards him. Tommy asleep on a lazy Sunday morning, rumpled but so, *so* handsome. Tommy charming the old women at the bus stop with silly made-up stories about treasure hunting in Peru. Tommy stopping to help a young mum get her pushchair down a set of steps. Tommy coming in from a run, shirtless and sweaty, and chasing me around our flat trying to rub his sweat off on me, making me scream with laughter.

With each memory of him, the seams of my stitched-together heart started straining, some of the threads barely hanging on. And I knew there was no way I could spend even a minute more with Tommy without them coming apart entirely. So how was I supposed to spend an entire *day* with him?

I finally fell into a restless sleep around 3 a.m., my eyes popping open a mere four hours later. I got up and made myself a double-shot espresso with a heaping spoonful of sugar, drinking it on the porch of my villa, staring numbly at the view down to the water. I should have been awestruck by how beautiful it was on Aetheria, but I was too fraught to take it in properly.

Coffee drunk, the question of what to wear arose. I went back inside and studied the outfits I'd unpacked when I arrived, settling on a pair of white tailored shorts, an off-the-shoulder Breton top, and espadrilles. Casual, yet cute and perfect for PR photos and footage aboard a sailboat. Nothing at *all* to do with wanting to look my best for Tommy.

I applied sunscreen and a touch of blush, waterproof mascara, peachy lip gloss, and enough concealer to make me look human, then gathered my hair into a low ponytail. I packed my navy bikini, a sarong, sunscreen, a small makeup bag, and a book into my beach tote and slung it over my shoulder. On the way out the door, I stepped in front of the full-length mirror, slid on my sunglasses, and scrutinised my appearance.

I was aiming for just-a-workday-in-paradise casual and no matter how I felt on the inside, at least I looked the part. Now it was time to face the music. Or, as it were, the man who broke my heart into a thousand pieces.

I waited outside my villa at the designated time and was collected in a golf cart by... you guessed it, Christos. Aphrodite was clearly having a laugh, parading him in front of me again.

'*Kalimera!*' he called out enthusiastically, his teeth even whiter in the morning sunshine.

'And to you too,' I replied. I climbed into the back of the golf cart, and we headed further up the hill to collect the other guests for the sailing trip.

'So, you're a driver as well as a waiter,' I asked out of curiosity.

'We all have multiple roles on Aetheria,' he replied without elaborating.

*If last night was anything to go by, he's looking to add 'guest services' to his duties.*

'Did you sleep well?' he asked, pulling me from my thoughts.

'Yes, thank you.'

No one ever wants the real answer to that question. They're either asking to be polite or they want to tell you how *they* slept. Julian used to do that all the time. 'How did you sleep, darling?' he'd ask, and before I had a chance to answer, he'd commence a lengthy monologue, including a recap of his dreams.

If I hadn't caught him repeatedly sticking his penis into other women, I may have divorced him for that alone. No one wants to hear about another person's dreams either. And if they say they do, they're lying.

We pulled up in front of a villa, a mirror image to mine, and an older couple was waiting outside. He was tall, slim, and angular and wore pale-blue board shorts and a short-sleeved button-up shirt covered in flamingos. In contrast, she was round and soft, with a warm, smiling face and a halo of brown curls. She looked fabulous in her salmon-pink silk kaftan, and I took to her instantly.

'Hello!' she called out, waving enthusiastically as if we were a mile away.

'Hello!' I replied just as cheerily.

She climbed into the cart next to me and her husband sat next to Christos.

'I'm Trudy and that's my husband, Dale,' she said as Christos made a U-turn and we headed back down the hill.

'I'm Ally.'

'Oh, I love that name. Is it short for Alison?' she asked.

'No, just Ally,' I replied with a smile.

'Well, I was lumped with Gertrude, which is an awful name. And Trudy's only marginally better.'

'I think Trudy suits you,' I said. 'It's cheerful.'

'Oh, you're a sweetheart, you are,' she replied. 'So, going by your accent, you're from England?'

'Yes. A Londoner, born and bred. What about you, where are you from?'

'We're Canadian – from Ottawa,' she replied. 'I was a teacher – I taught the third grade for thirty-five years – and Dale was in tech. But we're both retired now.'

'And how did you end up on Aetheria?'

'Julian invited us.'

'Oh, so you're friends of his?' I asked.

When Julian and I were married, I only met a handful of his friends. Most of the people we socialised with were his business associates and their wives. The wives didn't care for me much, which in retrospect doesn't surprise me. I was fresh-faced and largely optimistic about life, whereas they were predominantly jaded-but-pretending-to-be-happy women who were obsessed with one-upping each other and, without exception, hated their husbands.

It's no wonder I never fit in.

'Hmm, kinda,' Trudy replied. 'He and Dale did a project together late last year.'

She left it at that, and I got the sense that Trudy was not particularly keen on Julian.

'So, what do you do?' she asked. 'Your job, I mean.'

'I run my own company – supporting people who are going through a divorce,' I replied. If pressed, I would explain further but I found that this usually satisfied people's curiosity, and I certainly didn't want to come off as braggy.

'Wow, that's fantastic – good for you, hun,' she said, which could have sounded patronising but didn't. 'And are *you* divorced?' she asked with the kind of head tilt that signposts pre-emptive sympathy.

'Er, yes actually,' I replied, leaving it at that.

Trudy didn't seem to know that Julian and I were once married, but I wasn't going to volunteer that information. She and Dale were Julian's guests and he could tell them if he wanted to.

'Oh, that's too bad,' she said, shooting me the pitying smile I'd expected.

People often commiserated when they found out I was divorced, but I was content with my life – and proud of what I'd built.

With women and men looking to the Diva for inspiration and support, hoping to emerge empowered from one of the most difficult times of their lives, I had a responsibility – one I took very seriously.

That's why I focused on self-care, saying *no*, and setting boundaries – and yes, sex positivity. Never underestimate the power of reclaiming your sexual agency.

'Though, lord knows I've contemplated divorcing Dale a dozen or more times over the years,' Trudy confided, drawing me back to the conversation. 'But that's marriage, isn't it? Most of the time you love 'em to bits, but every once in a while, you fantasise about being single.'

She laughed to herself, then sighed wistfully as she gazed at the back of Dale's head. It was a good thing he and Christos were deep in conversation – something about golf. I doubted he'd be thrilled about Trudy's take on marriage. 'Yep,' Trudy continued, 'Dale can be a real pain in the ass, but I love him. I'm not going anywhere.'

That was a lot to unpack. Not the least of which was that even happily married people, which I suspected Dale and Trudy were, fantasised about being single sometimes. But for those people, divorce wasn't a serious option. They worked through it and found a way to stay.

With Rick and Julian, staying married would have been disastrous. I knew that with total certainty – I still do. But with Tommy...

Had we given up on us too easily? Or maybe it was all my doing – had *I* given up too easily? I'd been so sure we could only be happy living in our London flat and doing London things with our London people. What if I'd been willing to compromise, joining Tommy in far-flung places and working remotely instead of going into the office?

This was the big, bad, hairy question rattling around my

head as I rode in a golf cart on a tiny Greek island, seated next to Trudy from Ottawa.

But nothing good could come from conducting a deep dive into my marriage with Tommy. Not right then, anyway. Besides, we'd arrived.

The three of us climbed out of the golf cart and I hitched my beach tote onto my shoulder and looked around.

'Oh wow,' I whispered to myself. Docked beside the pier was the most beautiful sailboat I'd ever seen. Not that I knew much about sailboats, mind you, but everything on it gleamed – the hull, the chrome, even the polished teak.

'Have a wonderful day,' said Christos, flashing that brilliant smile of his. He drove off, and Dale, Trudy, and I wandered down the pier towards the sailboat.

'She's a beauty,' said Dale with obvious appreciation.

'Good morning! Welcome!'

We turned at the sound of the voice and bustling towards us was a woman around my age, with an olive complexion and the most glorious long, dark, curly hair. She was dressed in navy shorts and a white tailored shirt, the Aetheria logo adorning the pocket. A young Asian guy trailed behind her, wearing the same uniform and lugging a camera bag.

'Hi, everyone, I'm Niki Fragoulis,' she said in a broad Australian accent, 'guest services director.'

Trudy and Dale said *hello* and Dale introduced them both.

'And I'm Ally,' I said, stepping forward. 'You've been liaising with Maya from my team.'

'Great to meet you, Ally,' she said. '*Really* excited about working together and if you haven't guessed, I'm wearing two hats – I'm also heading up PR. That's what I did back in Brissie. But when this opportunity came up... I couldn't say *no*. You know, thirty-something Greek woman, living at home with

Mum and Dad, and your cousin's cousin hears about this great job in the Cyclades and your family's from there – way back, I mean. So, it's a no-brainer, right?'

'Absolutely,' I agreed.

She was certainly... *effervescent*. Maybe before working in PR, Niki was one of the Wiggles.

'Oh, sorry,' she said, slapping her forehead dramatically. 'This is Minh, Aetheria's photographer and videographer.'

Minh nodded. 'Hey, everyone,' he said quietly, his accent American.

'Right,' said Niki, 'now before we chuff off, let's get some footage of you arriving at the boat.'

Minh may have been the total opposite to Niki – softly spoken and with considered gestures – but he was clearly experienced. Without hesitation, he directed us into position, explaining precisely what he needed.

Now I'm used to this sort of thing – photoshoots, filming – but Trudy was a deer in headlights from the onset. We had to film our approach to the boat several times because she kept flubbing her one line, *What a beautiful sailboat!*

In the end, Niki gently asked Trudy and Dale to step aside and for me to deliver the line, which I did – perfectly in one take.

'Great job, Ally!' said Niki. 'Now, let's go aboard.'

I was still basking in the glow of Niki's praise when Tommy called out, 'Hello, everyone!'

Only two words but they hurtled straight at me, obliterating any hope of breezing through the day with cool-headed professionalism.

Hah! I was further from cool-headed professionalism than a newsreader doing shots on air.

But I had a job to do, and I could not allow myself to get

distracted by Tommy's voice. Or any other part of him. *Especially* other parts of him.

Only, then I caught sight of him and my remaining shreds of self-control flew out the window.

*Gah! Get it together, Ally!*

It would be challenging, that was for sure – like climbing Mount Everest in stilettos. For one, that uniform really suited him, the bright white of his shirt offsetting his tanned skin and dark hair. And he was barefoot, and Tommy has beautiful feet. Even the statue of David has ugly feet compared to Tommy.

But most of all – *worst* of all? – he looked so at home on that boat, it was as if he'd always sailed. Whatever was going on with him – whatever reasons he had for this dramatic lifestyle change – he seemed to be on to something. It clearly agreed with him.

He stopped in the cockpit, regarding us with a broad smile.

'You must be Trudy and Dale. I'm Tom,' he said, flashing that smile at Trudy. I swear, she almost swooned and I readied myself to catch her.

'Hello, Ally. Nice to see you again,' he said, as if we were acquaintances who'd only met last night. Which was exactly what we were pretending to be.

'Hi, Tom, good to meet ya,' said Dale. 'Shoes off, I'm assuming?' he asked as he undid the buckles of his sandals.

'That would be great.'

Trudy and I exchanged a look, then stepped out of our shoes, letting them dangle from our fingertips. Dale climbed aboard, then Trudy stepped closer to the boat, eyeing the gap between it and the pier.

'I've got you, babe,' said Dale, reaching for her hand.

Trudy placed her hand in Dale's and peered at him adoringly. I thought back to what she'd said on the golf cart, about

Dale driving her mad sometimes – that she'd even fantasised about divorcing him from time to time. Yet here they were after decades of marriage, and he still called her *babe*.

'Ally, need a hand?' asked Tommy.

I didn't want to fall between the pier and the boat either, but I also didn't want Tommy to hold my hand. I mean, I *did* but I also didn't.

'All good,' I replied brightly, carefully stepping aboard. *Do not fall. Do not fall. Do not fall.* I made it, prouder of myself than I should have been.

Tommy reached out his hand, which confused me for a sec – I was already aboard – but he was asking for my shoes. Feeling foolish, I handed them over and he put them away with the others under a bench in the cockpit.

'So, let's just go over some safety procedures,' he said, indicating that we should sit. We all sat except Minh, who scampered over the deck snapping photos. Tommy lifted his hand, commanding his attention.

'You'll need to hear this too, okay?'

Seeming chastened – or perhaps even embarrassed – Minh plopped down next to Niki. Then Tommy took us through the safety briefing. Believe me, I *tried* to pay attention. But with Tommy being all 'skippery' – i.e. in charge and sexy as fuck – I kept getting distracted.

He showed us where the lifejackets were and how to put them on.

Me: *God, his biceps look good in that polo shirt.*

He instructed us to shout out *person overboard* if anyone fell into the sea.

Me: *His voice is so commanding. He could literally command me to do anything right now and I'd do it.*

He demonstrated how to toss the lifebuoys if someone fell overboard.

Me: *Stuff the lifebuoy. If I fall overboard, I want Tommy to rescue me, wrapping me in those strong arms of his.*

On and on it went. I was ridiculous. I was crushing on my ex-husband. *Hard.* I just hoped there *wasn't* an emergency. I'd be about as useful as a screen door on a submarine.

Still, crushing *on* him was far better than being crushed *by* him – which I would be if I let my guard down.

'And that's about it,' he said, concluding the briefing.

I came back to the present when a woman appeared from below deck carrying a tray of plastic cups filled with something fizzy.

'Hello, everyone. I'm Elsa,' she said in accented English. 'Who would like some sparkling wine?'

It sounded like a friendly offer, only Elsa had a very *un*friendly air about her. The word *frosty* came to mind and I watched her closely. Maybe she was having a bad day. Or maybe she was one of those people who had no business working in tourism.

She handed around the cups and I accepted one – it's never too early for champers, especially when you're trapped on a boat with your ex for the day. But just as I was about to take a sip, something caught my eye – something that soured my stomach more than Elsa's pinched demeanour.

As she slipped past Tommy to return below deck, they exchanged what I can only describe as *a meaningful look.* Then Tommy's mouth lifted slightly at one corner – a gesture that would have been invisible to the untrained eye, but one I knew well. *Very* well.

Something was going on between Elsa and Tommy.

And I did not like it one bit. Not one fucking bit.

# 5

Thought of the day...
At times, you will need to put on the bravest face that ever
was in the history of humanity.
(Even if inside, you're screaming.)

As we motored away from the pier, Tommy at the helm, I kept a close eye on him and Elsa, scrutinising every nuance of their interactions. Mostly he issued instructions – to untie the buoys, or coil a rope, or raise a sail – and she deftly complied.

But the two times she approached him, they murmured, heads close together, their voices inaudible. Although Tommy's heart-melting half-smile didn't reappear, so I started to doubt myself. Maybe they *were* just colleagues.

*But even if they aren't, what business is it of mine?* That stung, but I had no claim over Tommy. Not any more.

'Isn't it just incredible?' Trudy asked.

I tore my eyes away from Tommy, who was hoisting the mainsail, the muscles in his forearms bulging as he expertly cranked the winch.

'Er, yes,' I replied. She was admiring the scenery, not the distracting sight of my ex's muscles rippling. But both were incredible.

Trudy tipped her head to the sun and inhaled deeply. 'And I just love the smell of the sea air, don't you?'

It was a timely reminder of where I was and why. And neither had anything to do with Tommy. Taking Trudy's lead, I inhaled deeply, the briny air filling my lungs. It was like taking a broom to the corners of my mind, sweeping away the cobwebs and dust.

'I really do,' I replied. 'It's invigorating.'

'Ooh, good word. Yes, *invigorating*.' Trudy was quiet for a moment, then said, 'So...'

Uh-oh. It was obvious I was about to be in the hotseat.

'Sorry to interrupt,' said Niki, suddenly appearing before us. Not that I minded – she was saving me from an impending inquisition.

'No problem,' I said. 'What's up?'

'Now that we're under sail, it's time to get some pics of you in your togs.'

'Togs?'

'Yeah, your swimmers.'

'Oh right, yes.' I rummaged in my beach tote and took out my bikini. 'Where can I get changed?'

'Oh, um... Actually, we've got some for you downstairs – in one of the cabins.'

'Okay. And they're in my size?'

She nodded. 'I spoke to your assistant. It's for the collab with Solari Swimwear,' she explained, her pitch rising at the end.

'*Oh*, that's right,' I said, recalling the marketing plan. I broke into a warm smile. 'Let's go see, shall we?'

Less than a minute later, as my eyes adjusted to the low light below deck, I started questioning the whole 'collab' thing. These weren't bikini tops. They were pasties held together with string. And the bottoms weren't much better.

'Erm... Are there any other options?' I asked, picking up one of the bottoms from the bed. What I presumed was the front was the size of a corn chip.

'Oh yeah, for sure,' she said. 'They also sent over lime green and a floral design. But we figured these colours work best with the Aetheria logo. And you can choose.'

Having missed my point entirely, she gave me an encouraging thumbs up and left me to get changed. There were three bikinis laid out on the bed – identical, save for the colour – so with a sigh, I chose the aqua-coloured one and put it on.

There was a full-length mirror on the back of the cabin door and I turned this way and that, regarding myself with apprehension. The top barely covered my nipples – forget 'side boob', I had 'all boob' – absolutely *nothing* left to the imagination. And my arse was completely on display, the thin strip of fabric flossing my cheeks. Oh, and the corn chip? Well, let's just say it was a good thing I was freshly waxed.

I've never been shy about showing skin, but there's body confidence and there's full-frontal insanity. I was essentially wearing dental floss with delusions of grandeur.

'It's just a few photos and then you can put your clothes back on,' I told my reflection.

The boat lurched, tilting from one side to the other. We must have been tacking – or jibing – I couldn't remember which was which. Not that it mattered. Whichever one it was sent me flying, hurling me onto the bed right as Niki opened the cabin door.

'Oh, sorry!' she squealed, averting her eyes. And no wonder.

My legs were splayed and one of the nipple covers was askew. I'd shown less of my body to my waxing technician. 'I did knock,' she added apologetically, which was technically true – even though she'd knocked and opened the door at the same time. *Never* a good idea.

I clambered off the bed and righted the three triangles of fabric, then took in a deep, bracing breath. I quickly checked my reflection again, smoothing an errant lock of hair, and gave her a winning smile.

'All good. Let's get those shots.'

She returned the smile with less confidence than I was pretending to have, and I followed her up onto the deck. I pointedly avoided looking at Tommy, who was standing at the helm, but in my periphery, I caught him openly gawping for a good five seconds before he composed himself.

*Good*, I thought, *let him.* I may have been this side of nude, but he could fill in the rest from memory.

'That's quite the bathing suit!' Trudy exclaimed as I passed, unmissable admiration in her voice.

'Thanks, Trudy,' I replied over my shoulder.

Minh, who had been chatting with Dale, scrambled to keep up with me and Niki as she led the way to the bow.

'Make sure you hold on,' Tommy called out to us. 'Always have one hand on the boat. You too, Minh.'

'Aye, aye, Skipper,' I replied loudly. 'And maybe a little heads up the next time you tack – or jibe – or whatever,' I muttered under my breath.

And poor Minh – how was he supposed to take photos while holding on to the boat with one hand? Thankfully, it seemed to have levelled out, gently rising and falling on a slight swell as we cut through the water.

Minh wedged himself into the bow pulpit – think Kate and

Leo and that King-of-the-World moment – and Niki surveyed the scenery, then the deck, before her eyes settled on me.

'How about reclining here,' she said, pointing to the sun pad, 'and we'll get some pics with the island in the background.'

I carefully made my way to the sun pad, now faced with the next dilemma. How was I supposed to get onto it gracefully? Niki had already seen most of me, but I doubted poor Minh had signed up for *that* type of photoshoot. I opted for a clumsy-but-modest manoeuvre – as in, falling onto my arse, then swinging my legs around until I was reclined.

Having done this sort of photoshoot once before, I moved into position, adopting a pose that showed off (what there was of) the Solari bikini. Minh abandoned the safety of his perch, stepping around me to capture shots while Niki gave directions.

'Let's get some with you turned towards the view, Ally,' she said.

I rolled onto my side, knowing full well that my arse was on display – but by that stage not caring – and took in the scenery. Properly this time.

Bloody hell, Aetheria was even more beautiful from the water than it was from the air. We'd just rounded a point and were heading towards the white sandy cove I'd seen yesterday, the cliff rising steeply towards a glorious, cloudless sky.

I propped myself up on my elbow to get a better view.

'That's *perfect*, Ally!' Niki called out. 'Just one more there, then we'll get some of you standing.'

I rolled onto my front, my legs bent and toes pointed. Minh moved around to my left.

'Got it,' he said.

Niki offered her hand to help me stand and I took it gratefully.

'We're going to drop anchor in this cove,' Tommy shouted from the stern.

A moment later, Elsa bustled towards us, wearing her sucked-on-a-lemon expression. 'Excuse me,' she said in that surly tone that's ruder than saying nothing. Niki and I stepped back to let her pass, then exchanged a glance.

As Tommy lowered the mainsail, the boat started to slow, and on his signal, Elsa activated the anchor, which clanked loudly to the sea floor. Soon we were bobbing in place.

Tommy called out from where he was securing the mainsail. 'We'll anchor here for a couple of hours. You should get some great photographs. *And* it's calm – no risk of you being pitched into the sea,' he told me with a cheeky glint in his eye.

I wasn't sure how to take that. Was he just being helpful or trying to be charming? Either way, he was a distraction that I didn't need – *or* want. I was *working*. Or trying to.

'Excuse me,' said Elsa, shoving past us again.

'That was rather rude,' said Niki quietly.

'Maybe she's here on a trial basis,' I said.

'I doubt it. She's been here longer than me.'

'*Oh?*' I replied, unable to keep the amazement from my voice.

Perhaps Elsa was one of those people who interviewed well but turned out to be a nightmare. Julian probably had no idea she was such a sour-faced cow. But with Aetheria being high-end – *lux*, even – guests would expect nothing less than eager-to-please, approachable, and overly pleasant staff.

*Maybe I should mention it*, I thought, watching Elsa coil rope through slitted eyes.

'Should we get those standing shots?' Minh prompted.

'Oh, sorry!' I replied. 'Lost in thought. So, where do you want me?'

\* \* \*

'Having a good day?'

I had a pita chip dripping with tzatziki halfway to my mouth when Tommy appeared next to me.

'Yes, actually,' I replied, putting it back on my plate.

I was full anyway. Elsa may have been a cactus in humanoid form, but she'd served a delicious lunch: *horiatiki* (Greek salad to us non-Greeks) with the ripest, most delicious tomatoes I'd ever tasted (seriously, I'd been ruined for life), fresh, garlicky tzatziki and pita chips, spanakopita with flaky filo pastry, feta and watermelon salad with mint, and octopus salad with red onion and capers.

It only occurred to me as I set my plate down that lunch was more likely Dimitra's handiwork than Elsa's. That was some Michelin-starred dip! But entertaining trifling thoughts about who prepared lunch was merely self-preservation – or a *lifebuoy*, to use a nautical term.

Because the truth was, I'd been hyper-aware of Tommy's presence since we boarded. He was the human equivalent of an eclipse – likely to cause long-term damage if I so much as glanced at it. Or rather, *him*.

At least I was wearing my own clothes again. In my bikini and a coverup I felt far less exposed than I had during the Solari photoshoot – *and*, by extension, less susceptible to an emotional stumble.

As the gargantuan silence stretched between us, I stared out at the cove where Trudy and Dale were making a valiant attempt at paddleboarding. Dale was doing okay, but Trudy had plonked her arse on the board, legs dangling, and was going around in circles.

Tommy had done his best to instruct them from the boat,

but when it comes to paddleboarding, putting instructions into practice is something you have to figure out yourself.

'Seems like they got some good photographs,' Tommy said eventually.

*Sticking to small talk, I see.* It was a safe option, but even Elsa would have been preferable company to Tommy. Being alone with him was straining my resolve. *Bugger off, Tommy!* I willed him silently. Annoyingly, he stayed put.

'Mmm,' I murmured in reply.

'And that teeny aqua bikini...'

I swivelled my head towards him. 'Don't you dare flirt with me,' I snapped.

He lifted both his hands. 'Not flirting, merely an observation.'

*Yeah, right.*

I held his gaze a moment longer and his dark-brown eyes bored into mine. Yep – *exactly* like an eclipse.

I looked away just in time to catch Dale coaching Trudy. She nodded a few times, planted her feet, then slowly straightened.

'I'm doing it, I'm doing it!' she shouted, laughter in her voice.

'You're doing it, babe,' Dale called out proudly.

'Woohoo!' she bellowed, and I laughed, caught up in the joy of the moment.

I'd encountered happy couples before, two people in love who had gone the distance. For all intents and purposes, my parents fit into that category. They're less overtly affectionate than Dale and Trudy were, but they adore each other.

Which is why, whenever the topic of marriage comes up during family occasions, Claude and I band together. Mum, in particular, cannot fathom how both of her daughters ended up divorced. Apparently, that isn't how we were raised. And, as I've committed that 'sin' thrice, I'm on the receiving end of three times the disappointment.

But I digress.

As I watched Dale and Trudy paddle around that stunning cove – its backdrop a sheer, limestone cliff face, and the water a shade of aquamarine I'd never seen before – I felt a pang of wistful longing.

Because I'd had that once. With the man at my side.

Until I didn't.

'Looks like they're heading back,' Tommy said, gesturing towards the dinghy, which Niki was steering towards us. She and Minh had taken it to shore to get some shots of the sailboat in the cove.

When they got closer, Niki called out, 'Hey, Ally, can we get some pics of you standing on the bow?'

'Sure,' I replied, relieved to have a distraction. Reminiscing about what I once had was putting a dampener on the day.

'Back to work,' I said to Tommy, excusing myself.

There was a soft laugh at my back and I rounded on him.

'Are you mocking me?'

'Absolutely not,' he said, hands raised. 'But it's hardly a grind, is it?'

'Probably doesn't seem like it to you, but I'll have you know I'm very busy and important.'

Oops, I'd instinctually reverted to one of our in-jokes.

He smirked, that corner of his mouth hitching – this time for *me*. 'Okay, *Bridget*.'

The years since we'd divorced fell away as our eyes met. It was all very well lusting after Tommy – well, it wasn't, but you know what I mean – but there was no ignoring the impact of this well-practised routine.

These were actual *feelings* bubbling to the surface. My heart was thumping, my breath became shallow, and those stitches in my heart were no longer straining, they were starting to burst.

I couldn't say whether it was perfect or imperfect timing, but Elsa appeared on deck, seemingly impatient to have a word with Tommy. I took the opportunity to escape, leaving them to yet another whispered conversation, then carefully made my way to the bow, keeping one hand on the boat like Tommy had told us.

I was tempted to glance back to see if he was watching, but I didn't want to risk being caught. Despite the thoughts and emotions whipping through me, I was still aiming for an air of casual nonchalance.

*Oh, hey, fancy running into you on this private island that I was invited to last minute and hadn't even heard of until five days ago! What a fucking coincidence!*

I had a better chance of winning the British Lottery.

I got to the bow pulpit and parked my arse on it, my hands resting on the railing. I inhaled deeply and plastered on a fake smile.

'How's this?' I asked loudly.

'Yeah, that's great,' Niki replied.

Following her directions, I kept one eye on Tommy and Elsa. Tommy glanced over, seeming unfazed, and that's when it hit me. Maybe this wasn't as difficult for him as it was for me. Maybe to Tommy, the past was in the past and his ex-wife showing up – as he'd said last night – was simply a complication.

'Hey, Tom,' Niki shouted from the dinghy. 'Sorry to interrupt but...'

I watched closely as Elsa said something else to Tommy, then went back below deck. Perhaps she was a part-time vampire who could only tolerate five minutes of sunshine at a time.

'How can I help?' Tommy asked Niki.

'Just thinking... can we get some pics of you and Ally?'

'What?' I blurted, panic rising. My eyes darted between her and Tommy. As if it wasn't hard enough just *being* on this bloody boat, now she wanted us to *pose* together?

'Er...' said Tommy, scratching the back of his neck. Wait, was he seriously considering saying *yes*? 'It might not be the best idea. Mr Cushing really wants the focus on our special guest here,' he said, gesturing towards me.

I was part relieved, part peeved. Why did he have to say *our special guest* with such obvious disdain? It wasn't my fault we were in this bizarre situation.

'I can play with the depth of field,' said Minh confidently. 'You won't be in focus – only Ally will be.'

*No, no, no, no, no.* Until then, I'd quite liked Minh. Now I wished that the dinghy would capsize, pitching him and all his camera equipment into the sea.

Tommy considered this and agreed, making his way to the bow, sure-footed and patently not holding on – not even once.

'I thought you said to always have one hand on the boat,' I chided as he approached. Yes, I was taking out my frustration on him, but so what? He deserved at least some of it.

He shrugged, seemingly unbothered, which was even more infuriating. 'Not for experienced skippers.'

I rolled my eyes. Not that he could tell – I was wearing sunglasses – but it made me feel better. At least enough to get me through the next couple of hours.

Niki cut the motor on the dinghy and Minh lifted his camera as they bobbed nearby.

She directed us through a series of shots – me standing by

the railing with Tommy in the background, Tommy pretending to hoist the anchor while I looked on... Dull as dishwater if you asked me, but I played nice, following Niki's directions to the letter, wearing that fake smile the whole time.

I was a *pro*.

When Niki gave the thumbs up, relief coursed through me, and I tried to side-step Tommy so I could get to the stern. Dale and Trudy had returned with the paddleboards, and it was my turn.

But he blocked my path.

'Excuse me,' I said firmly.

'Ally, we need to talk. *Alone*.'

'Seriously? How many times have we been alone today and *now* you want to talk?'

'No, I meant later – tonight. It's important, Ally.'

'Whatever, *Tom*,' I said, roughly pushing past him.

But I didn't want to talk to Tommy – not then and not later tonight. I just wanted to do a good job for Julian, then get off that bloody island!

## 6

I pulled Niki aside as we sailed out of the cove.

'What else is on your list?' I asked. 'Any nice-to-haves you were hoping for?' A cunning little dodge – stay busy, avoid Tommy for the rest of the sailing trip.

She took out her phone and scrolled through a list. 'We got the paddleboarding and the shots for Solari, the cove, lots of pics on the boat...' she said to herself. She looked up. 'What do ya reckon – see how we go?'

'Okay,' I replied, disappointed. 'Let me know if something comes up.'

'Sweet as.'

She left me to go talk to Tommy, and I looked towards the coastline. That olive grove I'd seen from the helicopter yesterday was now visible, the gnarly trunks so thick that the trees must have been cultivated decades ago, possibly even longer. I imagined the people who had planted them, living on this island for generations. Who *had* owned the island before Julian?

It struck me again how unusual it was to *buy an island*. I still hadn't pressed Julian on what had prompted such a dramatic purchase, but I could bring it up at dinner.

And Julian wasn't the only ex who'd made a life-changing decision. Tommy had left his career in structural engineering to sail rich people around the Aegean. Maybe I *did* want to talk to him – if only to ask how he'd ended up on Aetheria when he'd been hellbent on saving the world. It wasn't as if there were any lifesaving wells to dig, or earthquake-ravaged dams to rebuild. As far as I could tell, the only thing broken on Aetheria was me.

As we sailed north, hugging the coast, the winds picked up and for much of that leg, the boat heeled at a steep angle. We all braced ourselves against the cockpit, holding on tight.

Even Elsa had to remain above deck. I kept checking to see if she had spontaneously combusted in the sunshine. Turned out to be wishful thinking.

When we rounded the northern point of the island, the wind behind us, the boat levelled off, returning to that gentle rise and fall. By unspoken agreement, there was little conversation. We all seemed content to soak in the scenery and sit with our thoughts.

I was wrestling with whether I should talk to Tommy later when Trudy suddenly leapt to her feet, shrieking with delight.

'Dolphins!' she exclaimed, her arm outstretched. Sure enough, three dolphins were zipping along with us, criss-crossing under the boat and riding the slipstream.

I laughed, giddy with excitement. Tommy caught my eye

and we grinned at each other, everything else falling away – our troubled history, my conflicted emotions, regret... It was simply a shared moment of pure joy.

Eventually, the dolphins left us and excitement continued to buzz about the sailboat. With a bashful but slightly proud smile, Minh passed his camera around to show us the footage he'd captured. It would be brilliant in the promos.

Not long after the dolphins swam off, the resort's pier appeared on the horizon and I settled back against my seat, sighing contentedly. There were times when all it took to fill up your near-empty bucket was an awe-inspiring experience of the natural world.

'Pretty impressive how you got those dolphins to appear on cue,' Dale said to Tommy, who laughed modestly. I sniggered along.

'If only! Those are the first I've seen since I arrived.'

'How long have you been on Aetheria?' I asked, the question flying out of my mouth.

'Three weeks,' he answered, though he seemed uncertain and looked over at Elsa. 'It's three weeks, right? Since we arrived?'

*Why's he asking her?* Then his words hit me. *Since* we *arrived.* Oh god, they'd come together.

*That doesn't mean anything,* I told myself quickly. Maybe the whole staff had started at the same time – though Niki said Elsa had been there longer than she had. And if Elsa and Tommy *had* arrived together, there was every chance they *were* a couple. Which would explain all the whispered conversations.

No, I wasn't going to talk to Tommy. Being alone with him was a terrible idea. Especially now, when I was becoming increasingly convinced that he was loved up with tart-faced Elsa. And that wasn't me being unreasonable or jealous. Even

Niki thought Elsa was surly and rude, and she seemed to get along with everyone.

Once the boat was docked – buoys lashed on and tow ropes tied off – I was the first person to disembark, stepping carefully onto the pier. I considered dashing back to my villa and pouring myself a large glass of wine, then sorting through the chaos in my head, but manners dictated that I wait for the others.

We said our goodbyes to Tommy and Elsa, who were still on duty, then trundled to the end of the pier where two golf carts were waiting for us.

As we walked, I sensed collective fatigue from such a full day – the sights, a delicious lunch, paddleboarding and swimming, *dolphins*...

There was also the Tommy Factor, turning run-of-the-mill fatigue into a dense, bone-deep weariness. If I didn't get on top of it, it would settle in and take years to shake off. Like last time.

At the golf carts, Niki got in the driver's seat of one and Minh sat beside her. 'Our office is pretty close to your villa,' she said to Trudy and Dale. 'Want us to drop you off?'

'Oh, that would be lovely,' said Trudy with a grateful sigh. No doubt she was eager to wash off the dried salt and treat those sunburnt shoulders.

She and Dale climbed into the back of Niki's golf cart and I waved them off. Which left me alone with Christos. I glanced over my shoulder towards the boat, but Tommy and Elsa must have been below deck. I didn't want to imagine what they might be doing.

'Did you have a nice day?' Christos asked as I settled beside him.

'I did. And you?'

'It was busy, but good,' he replied, driving us towards my

villa. He didn't say anything more and I welcomed the silence, content to let the world – or at least the resort – go by.

Before I knew it, we'd pulled up outside my villa. In another timeline, I might have invited him in. But adding Christos to the mix was a complication I didn't need right now.

Besides, I wanted that glass of wine and a long soak in the bath before my dinner with Julian.

* * *

I realise that my life may appear glamorous and exciting, and for the most part, it is. I promise never to complain about travelling to far-off places, attending glitzy parties, or being gifted beautiful clothes.

(And if I ever do, someone *please* give me a swift kick up the arse.)

But as well as being a lot of fun, this life I've worked so hard to build is also a business, a platform – a *brand*.

And there *are* downsides.

Sometimes all I want is to sink into a hot bath, watch some trashy TV, and get an early night. But when those moments collide with work, work wins every time.

After Christos dropped me off, I was *so* tempted to pour an enormous glass of wine and run a bath, like I'd promised myself. But after a day away from my desk, I knew I should check in with HQ. Claude would want an update and there might be other matters to attend to. So, I poured myself a medium-sized glass of wine – no sense in depriving myself entirely – then logged in.

I sped through several requests for collabs, mentally assigning them labels: *definitely*, *possibly*, and *thank you, but I'd rather not*. I was about to log off when a familiar email address caught my eye – Tommy's. Heart in my mouth, I clicked on it.

**Meet me at the boat at eleven.**

Why all this Secret Squirrel business? And what was so important? Had Tommy's sea change prompted him to reevaluate other aspects of his life? Like me and him?

*Stop it, Ally.*

It wasn't helpful to entertain those kinds of thoughts. Too much power to send me spiralling. Besides, I was the Divorced (Fucking) Diva, a woman content in her singlehood – *ecstatic* in it. And I was always telling my followers that an ex was an ex for a reason – for *multiple* reasons – and going back was going back*wards*. This was one of those times I needed to heed my own advice.

I typed a reply:

**If it's so important, just email me. I'm not meeting you at the boat.**

I read it over. *Hmm – a little curt.* Even if I was justified – Tommy had essentially sent me a directive – I couldn't shake Mum's voice in my head: *Manners cost nothing, Ally.*

'*Okay*, Mum.'

I revised it to:

**Can't you just email me? I'd rather not meet you at the boat.**

Before I could second-guess myself further, I sent it, then slammed my laptop shut and went to get ready. I was meeting

Niki and Minh at the bar before dinner – more campaign photos – and I only had half an hour.

I chose a silk jumpsuit in cobalt – a nod to the striking blue accents dotted around the resort – and strappy silver wedges. I'd been kissed by the sun that day, so kept my makeup light – a touch of shimmer across my eyelids, mascara, and lip gloss – then adorned myself with dangling silver earrings and a handful of silver bangles. I did *not* wear the platinum and diamond bangle Julian had given me, but slipped it into my clutch, intending to return it at dinner.

Before leaving my villa, I checked my appearance in the full-length mirror, giving myself a satisfied nod. I was rocking the Divorced Diva look and in the back of my mind, I knew I needed it – part of the armour. With two ex-husbands on the loose – one wooing me with expensive jewellery and the other asking for clandestine meetings – I needed all the emotional protection the Diva brings.

As I walked down the hill towards the bar, the setting sun cast a pinkish hue over the building below, turning its white-washed walls apricot. I paused for a moment, taking in the incredible view. The sky was streaked in pinks and blues, a low band of clouds lit from beneath like it was on fire.

I continued on my way, the pathways bisecting lush gardens brimming with young olive trees, aromatic herbs, and bursts of bougainvillea and oleander. I passed several villas, their doors and windows obscured by strategic landscaping, affording the level of privacy Julian's guests would expect – and that I'd already taken advantage of. The air was clean and fragrant, and I inhaled deeply, filling my lungs with top notes of jasmine and lemon and a base note of brine.

*Well done, Jules. Even the air quality is top notch.*

Soft yet lively music greeted me when I arrived at the bar, a long flag-stoned terrace bordered by the infinity pool I'd seen from the air, floating candles scattered across the surface. Overhead lanterns, suspended from beams, gave off ambient light, and overhanging branches of an olive tree were strung with fairy lights. At the far end of the bar were low-slung sofas and armchairs with plump linen cushions, and closer sat four high tables with wooden stools. Every seat looked across the pool to the view of the coastline and in the distance, the island of Naxos, just visible beneath the setting sun.

Niki was sitting at the bar, angled towards the entrance. She waved as soon as she saw me and I walked over and took the stool next to hers, setting my clutch on the polished concrete bar.

'You look great,' she said.

'Thank you,' I replied with a bright smile. 'Part of the job.'

'Right, good point.'

'What are you having?' I asked, eyeing her drink.

'It's the signature cocktail – the Aetherian Glow. I hope you don't mind, but I ordered one for you. For the pics.'

'Sounds good to me. What's in it?'

'Gin, Mastiha, a Greek liqueur, thyme syrup, lemon juice, and sparkling Assyrtiko,' said the bartender, placing a coupe garnished with a sprig of thyme in front of me.

He was dark-haired like Christos and just as handsome, only a little older, maybe late thirties.

I sniffed my glass. 'Well, it smells delish.'

'Enjoy,' he said, the corners of his eyes crinkling. I may have sworn off entanglements with the locals, but it didn't hurt to look.

'*Yamas*,' said Niki, dragging my attention from the dishy bartender.

I raised my glass to meet hers. '*Yamas*.' We sipped our cocktails. 'Oh wow,' I said, my eyes wide.

She chuckled. 'It's yummy, but potent.'

'Mmm,' I murmured. I knew a few men like that.

'Oh, hi,' she said to someone behind me.

Expecting Minh, I turned around and my smile disappeared.

'Oh hello, *Tom*.'

He looked so handsome, damn him – wearing well-worn, hip-hugging jeans and a white loose-weave shirt with the sleeves rolled up.

'Hello, Ally,' he said with a strained smile. 'I was hoping to borrow you for a minute – get your thoughts on the sailing trip, that sort of thing.'

He made it sound like the most natural thing in the world to ask of 'the face of Aetheria'. Saying *no* in front of Niki would make me look like a right cow, which I was sure was his intention.

'Er, I would but I promised Niki and Minh we'd—'

'Oh, we only need a couple of pics of you at the bar, Ally,' she interrupted unhelpfully. 'Once Minh gets here, it'll take two secs. Then she's all yours,' she told Tommy.

'Perfect,' Tommy answered, and I wasn't sure which one of them I wanted to strangle more.

# 7

Thought of the day...
At times you will be blindsided by a memory – ride out the
pain, then move on.
(Or go ahead and torture yourself because, let's be honest,
sometimes it feels good to wallow.)

Minh arrived shortly after, camera at the ready, and Tommy at
least had the courtesy to step away.

There were two set-ups I particularly liked – one of me
facing the view and sipping my cocktail with the dishy bartender
in the background looking on (a drawcard by himself), and the
second taken from the other side of the bar with me in the fore-
ground against the backdrop of that incredible sunset.

Both would be perfect for the Divorced Diva socials, but I'd
let Maya choose which to feature once we got the go-ahead
from Niki.

'I think that's all we need, Ally,' said Niki. She watched over
Minh's shoulder as he swiped through the shots on the camera

screen, then lifted her head and flashed me a smile. 'Yep, all good.'

'Thanks,' I said, returning the smile.

'She's all yours, Tom,' Niki called out, and I dropped the smile.

Tommy had been lurking down the end of the bar sipping Mythos from a bottle and the second Niki and Minh excused themselves, he wandered over. He was taking his time and I contemplated making a run for it, but I was wearing wedges. Not only would he catch me without much effort, I was at a boutique resort on a tiny island – where would I even go?

Besides, part of me was curious about what he had to say. Okay, okay, I *desperately* wanted to know. Though my plan was to pretend I didn't.

Tommy took the stool that Niki had just vacated and rather than acknowledge his presence, I stared out at the view and sipped my cocktail.

Immature? Definitely. Warranted? Definitely not. But you have to understand, this was me in self-preservation mode.

'It's quite something, isn't it?' he asked.

Now, there's pretending nonchalance to make a point and there's just plain rudeness. As I pride myself on having good manners, I answered.

'It's stunning. I can't remember the last time I simply sat and watched a sunset.'

'Remember that sunset on Santor—' He cut himself off, but it was too late. My head jerked involuntarily in his direction, my mouth agape.

The only other time I'd been to the Cyclades Islands was with Tommy – to Santorini for our honeymoon. It was only four nights but even so, we could never have afforded it ourselves. It had been a gift from his parents – his parents who, for several years, I'd called *Mum* and *Dad*.

*Oof.* Thinking about Tommy's parents was like pressing on a bruise that had never quite healed.

'Sorry,' he said sheepishly, not meeting my eye.

But what exactly was he apologising for? Dredging up one of the happiest memories of my life?

'Oia,' I replied – the name of the town on the tip of Santorini's caldera where we and hundreds of others had watched, awestruck, as the sun sank into the Aegean, drenching us all in golden light.

I'd sat on a step right in front of Tommy, ensconced between his strong thighs, my hands resting on his knees and his chin on my head. I'd felt safe and madly in love. Perhaps the happiest I'd ever been in my entire life. The chatter of a dozen languages buzzed about us excitedly. 'Aria on Air' played on a portable speaker and someone was strumming a guitar. At one point, the guitarist caught on and played along to the music.

'I love you, Ally.' Tommy's deep, resonant voice in my ear had given me chills and I'd spun around and looked up at him.

He was *bathed* in pinkish, golden light – as if it was emanating from within – and my breath had caught in my throat, tears prickling my eyes. In that moment, he was the most beautiful being I'd ever encountered and my love for him threatened to spill out of me, cascade down the steep incline, and wash away everyone between me and the sea.

I cleared my throat and took another sip of my cocktail. Tears threatened – that's how intense the memory was – and I blinked them away.

'It's a beautiful island, Santorini,' I said, finding my voice.

'Yes.'

We were quiet for some time and I wondered if, like me,

Tommy was torturing himself with the bittersweet memories of happier times.

'So,' I said when I regained my composure. 'You had something important to tell me.'

He cleared his throat, as though he wasn't sure where to start. 'I do,' he said finally. 'And it's not... *easy*.'

I swallowed hard, my eyes locked on his as he wrestled with his thoughts.

*This is it.* The moment Tommy confessed he'd missed me all these years, that letting me go was the biggest mistake of his life.

'It's about Aeth—'

'Good evening, beautiful,' said Julian, appearing out of nowhere. He came in for a cheek kiss and Tommy bristled.

*Jealousy? Hah – doubtful!* He wasn't baring his soul – this was about the island.

'Hello, Tom.' Julian reached out and they shook hands, Tommy returning Julian's warm smile with a terse facsimile.

I looked between them, a niggling thought twisting in my gut. Had Tommy known that Julian was my ex-husband *before* Julian introduced us?

I hadn't hidden my marriage to Julian from Tommy (of course not), but he and I weren't in contact much during that time and when we were, we didn't discuss Julian.

*No*, I concluded. Being stuck between a rock and a hard place – or a rocky marriage and a hard one – was pure coincidence. A nightmare that only bad luck could have conjured.

Both watched me expectantly and, for a moment, I was torn. Stay with hubby number one to find out what was behind the Secret Squirrel stuff or off to dinner with number three to return a £1000 bangle?

That long soak in a hot bath was looking better and better.

*Excuse me, husbands, but I have a prior engagement with some bath salts and a fabulous little sex toy called the Oblisserator.*

'Jules, I'm just about finished,' I said instead, holding up my nearly drunk cocktail. 'Shall I meet you at the restaurant in a few minutes?'

I could tell Julian knew he was being dismissed, which he would hate, but after a brief narrow-eyed stare, he broke into a magnanimous smile.

'Oh course, darling. And I hope you're hungry. Dimitra's planned a wonderful chef's dinner for the two of us.'

That part was obviously for Tommy's benefit. He might as well have screamed, *You're not invited, Tom!* And last night, he'd called Tommy a *top bloke.*

*What the fuck is going on with these two?*

With a curt nod at Tommy, Julian left, and I watched as he greeted a couple who were sipping drinks and enjoying the sunset. No doubt 'friends' of his who'd happily accepted a free holiday in exchange for some promo shots.

'Do you think he knows?' Tommy asked, his voice low.

I whipped around, pinning Tommy with a pointed look. 'Whatever this mystery is you want to divulge? No, I don't think Julian knows. And neither do I – which means my patience is starting to wear thin.'

'Wear th— I only just brought it up, what, an hour ago?'

'Via *email*, Tommy. And it wasn't just then, was it? No, you also mentioned it while we were at *sea*.'

My voice was getting louder and he shushed me harshly, which is a massive button pusher for me, something Tommy was well aware of. Though he was right to shush me, as the bartender was looking over and if he thought something was up, he might tell Julian and...

*Argh!*

I took in a deep breath to refocus.

'Look, I've got to go and meet Julian for dinner – just tell me.'

Tommy stared at me intensely. And you need to understand that looking into those dark-brown eyes was like stepping into the void. It's extremely difficult to save yourself, and you're not sure if you want to.

'That's not what I meant,' he said cryptically.

'You need to come with built-in decryption, Tommy,' I replied. '*What's* not what you meant?'

'I'm *asking* if you think Julian knows we were once married.'

By this stage, our foreheads were practically touching, and I sat back, then downed the rest of my drink.

'I have no fucking idea, but let's hope not,' I said through my toothy-for-appearances smile. I placed the glass on the bar and mouthed *delicious* at the bartender, who – annoyingly – was still watching me and Tommy.

'In truth,' I said to Tommy, dropping the faux smile, 'it's unlikely. Julian has his good qualities but he is a Grade A narcissist. He never once asked about you when we were married – or Rick, for that matter. As far as Julian was concerned, neither of the husbands I had before him were worth mentioning, because they'd both been superseded. By *him*. I doubt he even remembers I was married to a bloke called Tommy, let alone drawing a line between that man with you. But more to the point, *Tom*...' I began, leaning in again, 'before he introduced us last night, did *you* know about *him*?'

Something flickered in Tommy's eyes and I knew. He *had* made the connection.

'I thought as much,' I said, sliding off my stool.

I really didn't know what to do with that information – what implications it might have – but I knew I wanted out of there.

So, jumping from the frying pan into the fire, I strode off to have dinner with Julian.

'Everything all right?' he asked, standing as I approached the table.

It was in prime position with an uninterrupted view, and I paused to take it in. The sky was darker now, inky blue, and across the water, the lights of Naxos twinkled. It truly was beautiful. And if I'd been on Aetheria for any other collaboration, one that wasn't tainted by two of my exes, I would have been in heaven.

But this was *not* heaven. This was hell with good lighting and a decent soundtrack.

'Oh yes, all good,' I answered, flashing a bright smile. 'Just discussing the sailing trip,' I lied. 'It's a terrific excursion, Jules. Every guest will be desperate to get a spot. You're onto a winner there.'

I was rambling. And I'm not a rambler.

Unsurprisingly, Julian gave me a funny look.

'Allow me,' he said after a brief pause.

He stepped behind me to pull out my chair. I sat, reaching for the menu before I remembered that Dimitra was preparing a chef's selection. Instead, I regarded the view, which was changing from moment to moment, the sea between Aetheria and Naxos now a black void and those twinkling lights across the water even more prominent.

'Ally,' said Julian, drawing my attention. 'Are you really all right? Tom didn't say anything to upset you, did he?'

*Tom said ALL the things to upset me.*

'No, silly,' I said with a false laugh. 'I think I just caught too much sun – that and the time difference between here and London... I know it's only two hours but it's enough to make me feel a bit wobbly. I'll be right as rain by tomorrow.'

I was rambling again, but Julian let it go, giving me a kindly smile.

'Good to hear. Another big day planned.'

Oh, that's right, the day trip to Naxos – by *helicopter*. I should have upped my already sizeable fee. Julian was certainly getting his money's worth.

'Brilliant,' I replied with another fake smile.

*Geez, Ally, at this rate, you'll secure a sponsorship deal with Sensodyne.*

'Excuse me, Mr Cushing...'

Christos appeared, bearing a bottle of wine and slipping seamlessly into sommelier mode. He showed the label to Julian, who gave a nod, then deftly uncorked the wine and poured tasting measures into our glasses. Just like he'd done last night.

I wondered if he knew how close I'd been to inviting him into my bed. But if he did, he seemed to be playing it cool. Though I couldn't be sure – I didn't *dare* meet his eye with Julian sitting right there.

God, this was like some hellish maths problem. *If Ally is stuck on an island with two ex-husbands and a flirtatious, somewhat tempting waiter/driver, how long until Ally goes completely mad?*

'As you already had an aperitif, I thought we'd get straight to the wine,' said Julian, dragging me from my mental maze. 'It's a Kydonitsa from the Peloponnese.'

I took a sip, then licked my lips. 'It's delicious.' *Eyes on Julian. Eyes on Julian.*

'But what do you taste?' he asked.

Wonderful – Julian's (obnoxious) tasting-notes game where I would clumsily attempt to describe the wine with my limited palate, and he would coax me along until I unearthed the 'correct' answer.

'I taste Greece, Jules,' I replied, and he seemed to understand that I wasn't in the mood for playing.

Julian nodded at Christos again, and he topped up our glasses, then left the wine in the ice bucket by the table.

I exhaled – only one man to contend with now.

'To old friends,' Julian said.

'To old friends.' I clinked my glass against his, then took a large gulp.

'Ooh, here's our first course.'

I followed Julian's gaze to see Christos emerge from the kitchen, two plates in hand. Hardly ideal, him waiting on us. But, suddenly ravenous, I cared less about who brought the food and more about what was on the plate.

'Aegean lobster carpaccio,' he said, setting our plates in front of us, 'prepared with Santorini capers, shaved fennel, and citrus-infused olive oil. Enjoy.'

He left and I admired the creative plating. 'It's almost too pretty to eat,' I said, hesitant to disturb the perfect tableau on my plate.

'I could say the same about you.'

I looked at Julian, my head falling to the side. 'Jules, that's super cheesy.'

'Sorry, it's just...' He reached across the table and took my hand, and I fought the urge to take it back. 'Do you ever wonder if we made a mistake?' he asked. 'Getting divorced, I mean.'

Julian had hinted at this before, that ending our marriage was a mistake. But the biggest mistake I'd made was staying too long, forgiving him time and again for his infidelities.

Divorcing him wasn't a mistake. In fact, it was one of the most empowering times of my life, when I finally decided to put myself first. But there was no mistaking the sadness in his eyes, nor the regret. I'd have to choose my words carefully.

'No, Jules, I don't,' I replied gently, placing my other hand on top of his and giving it a squeeze. 'We're better off as amicable exes – *friends*. That's what we toasted to. And on that...' I said, releasing his hand. I took the bangle out of my clutch and laid it on the table between us.

'No, that's a gift.'

'It's the wrong kind of gift, Jules,' I replied. 'I'm sorry.'

He looked down, resting his fingertips on the bangle and tapping lightly – a tell that he was unsettled. When he lifted his gaze, his eyes searched mine.

'So, what kind of gift is the right one?' he asked.

'I already have it – a lucrative partnership with your new resort.'

He gave me a droll smile that vanished almost instantly.

'Hey,' I said, reaching over to pat his forearm, 'you're focusing on the wrong thing, Jules. You've got all this to keep you busy,' I said, gesturing to the resort, 'and it's going to be brilliant, I just know it. You don't need to take a massive step backwards with your ex-wife. This is a new chapter for you. Keep throwing your energies into Aetheria and you never know, you may just meet the love of your life.'

'*You* were the lov—'

'*Jules*...' I said, my voice just above a whisper.

He laughed gently at himself and I laughed too, the tension between us ebbing away. 'Now, can we please eat?' I asked. 'I'm about to die of starvation.'

'You always were one to hyperbolise, Ally,' he teased, picking up his knife and fork.

'*Me?*' I asked, and his laughter rang out across the restaurant.

I shook my head at him and was about to take my first bite

when he said, 'So, does that mean you'll take up with Christos then?'

I froze, my fork suspended halfway to my mouth. 'I'm sorry, what?'

'He's a handsome bloke... you're a beautiful woman... Absolutely no judgement, Ally, I promise.' He popped a bite of lobster into his mouth and chewed, regarding me thoughtfully.

My fork still hovering, I was stuck on why Julian would leap from me rejecting him to me taking Christos as a lover. Was he being magnanimous – however misguided it was to offer up his employee – or was it sour grapes?

'I told you before – I'm not planning on hooking up with Christos – or anyone for that matter,' I said, hating the defensive edge to my voice. 'This is a work trip and that's my only focus.'

*Well – that and ex-hubby number one.*

'I really don't mind—'

'Jules, I haven't even thought about it.'

A big fat lie – although a *kindly* one.

Julian seemed to take my assurance at face value, giving me a warm smile. Pleased to be back on firmer footing – amicable exes with our own special brand of friendship – I settled in for what turned out to be one of the best meals of my life.

Thought of the day...
You're now free to live life on your own terms.
Anyone who says otherwise can sod off.
(This applies, even if you have no bloody idea what your
terms actually are.)

The rest of the meal was just as extraordinary as the lobster. For our main, we had slow-roasted Cycladic lamb with fava purée and roasted cherry tomatoes (without question the best lamb I've ever had – and I may exaggerate on occasion, but not this time) and for dessert, panna cotta with honey and fig compote, the dish I'd salivated over the night before. It was just *gorgeous* – I would have licked the plate clean if I'd been at home on my own.

And after we salvaged the conversation, we kept it light, talking sports and travel and our favourite books – though between us, we'd only read seven in the past year and five of those were mine.

We even ventured into 'remember that time when...' territory. It was a daring move considering how dinner began, but worth the risk, as we ended up in fits of laughter.

It was a trip to Morocco. Julian was there for work, and I tagged along so we could spend the weekend together exploring. We got lost in the souk – as one does – and eventually, we asked one of the shopkeepers the way out. Rookie mistake. We ended up with six hand-painted bowls, three shawls, a tea set, and a bag of almond-stuffed dates. And *he* only sold shawls. Those shopkeepers saw us coming from a mile away. *And* they sent us in the wrong direction. It was two hours before we got back to the hotel.

'And you ate all the dates in the taxi,' Julian accused.

'Excuse me! I had *one* date, thank you very much. As I recall, you ate the rest because it had been a whole three hours since lunch and you were ravenous.'

He bellowed with laughter, and I chuckled along.

'Fair, fair,' he said between laughs. 'It was a bloody good trip, though.'

'Agreed.'

Our marriage had more downs than ups, but we'd had some fun times. And sitting across from Julian, looking so much like the man I'd fallen for, I reminded myself that people are never just one thing. We're layered, multi-faceted, we evolve...

Julian wasn't a bad person. He just wasn't a good husband.

'Oof,' I said when the dessert plates were cleared. I patted my (completely stuffed) tum right as Julian lifted up the wine bottle.

'You have the rest,' I said. He tipped the dregs into his glass, then downed them in one.

That was my cue to leave, and I stood, collecting my clutch

from the table. 'Thank you for an incredible meal, Jules – and the lovely company.'

He remained seated, sending me a wry look. 'No nightcap then?' he asked, once our code for after-dinner sex.

'No nightcap.'

'In that case, I promise I won't ask again,' he said, a flash of sadness in his eyes.

I released an involuntary sigh. I hadn't realised how much Julian's advances were weighing on me. I'd been aware, of course – battle-ready to fend him off – but there was a toll, having to be that guarded.

I considered kissing his cheek but decided against it, instead giving him a smile, then beelining for my villa. It was still reasonably early and despite the full day and generous meal, I was wide awake – must have been the rush of endorphins from laughing with Julian.

I glanced at the short stack of books I'd brought. I'd had that exact same stack on my bedside table for months now, carting it with me whenever I travelled. Yet none of the titles felt right for the mood I was in.

So instead of reading, I ran a bath. While I waited for it to fill, I called Claude.

'Hiya,' she chirruped, signposting she was in a good mood.

'Hiya.'

'How's paradise today?' she asked.

'It's stunning. And I've seen the whole island now – well, the coastline. Still some exploring inland to do.'

I filled her in on the day's events. Well, except that Tommy was on the island *and* that we'd spent the day together *and* had several terse exchanges. If Claude knew Tommy was there, she'd kick into concerned-big-sister mode and insist that I come home immediately.

I also omitted Julian's romantic overtures – she'd only worry about that too. Besides, I'd dealt with the matter.

So what I gave her was a glorified travel log with detailed descriptions of the food – like an episode of *Somebody Feed Phil* but with me. *Somebody Feed Ally*.

'It does sound lovely, Al. Maybe I should consider going – *someday*, I mean.'

'Ah-hah – progress!' I teased, and she laughed softly.

Sometimes it was hard to recall the girl she was before Gregory – or *BG* as we liked to call it. But in our late teens and early twenties, Claude was a bit of a wild child – sneaking us into clubs with fake IDs, late-night skinny-dipping in our neighbour's pool, even dancing on the bar once until a bouncer hauled her outside over his shoulder.

That Claude felt like a lifetime ago.

And how ironic that I'd helped thousands of people rediscover their spark, yet my own sister – the person closest to me – was still struggling to find hers. All I could do was love her fiercely for who she was, while giving her the odd gentle prod to try something new.

'So, what's on for tomorrow then?' she asked, cutting across my thoughts.

'Naxos – the nearest island.'

I heard the rustle of paper – she must have printed the itinerary.

'Ooh, a cooking class. Now try not to set the kitchen alight.'

'That was one time,' I retorted. 'And I was nine.'

'We had to call the fire brigade.'

'Again, I was *nine*.'

She laughed. If Claude outlives me, she'll probably tell this story at my funeral.

'And you're sailing there – to Naxos?' she asked, switching back to tomorrow's plans.

'Ah, nope. Going by helicopter.'

'Mmm.' A single syllable, yet it conveyed multitudes, Claude's sisterly concern crossing two bodies of water and a continent to beam into my phone.

'Perfectly safe,' I assured her. 'It's how I got here, remember?'

'*Fine*,' she relented – as if it were up to her.

I didn't care if I had to hitch a ride on the back of a seagull – I was going. Especially since Julian and Tommy weren't. Naxos would be blissfully husband-free.

I suddenly remembered the bath and went to check it. It hadn't overflowed, but it was close. I turned off the tap. 'I've got to go – my bath's ready,' I said.

'Talk tomorrow night?' she asked, and it occurred to me that, selfishly, I hadn't asked after her, not even her plans for the evening.

Although, Claude would be the first to admit that her Saturday nights were about as exciting as a trip to Tesco.

'Will do my best,' I replied, not wanting to lock something in. I had no idea how I'd feel tomorrow night. And maybe I'd be otherwise occupied with a Greek firefighter.

We ended the call and I shimmied out of my jumpsuit and slipped into that glorious bathtub, fragrant with the citrusy bath salts I'd liberally scattered into the water. I closed my eyes, releasing a delicious sigh.

It was Ally time, and anyone who dared to interrupt could bugger right off.

Even Tommy.

* * *

I woke Sunday morning well before sunrise after another fractured night's sleep. I thought I'd done everything right to sleep through the night – I stopped drinking a few hours before bed, I had a relaxing bath, I gave myself an orgasm... But alas, I was painfully wide awake at 2 a.m., a burning question ricocheting around my mind: *How the hell did Tommy end up on Aetheria?* When I eventually fell back asleep hours later, it was fitful and marred by disturbing dreams. All of them about Tommy.

Now it was nearly 6 a.m. and there was no sense in lying there stewing. I threw off the covers and drifted over to the coffee machine, made a double-shot espresso, then took it out to the porch. With the resort facing west, the sun was rising behind me, but it was still glorious to behold.

And as I sipped my coffee, my eyes drinking in the pale-blue sky streaked with ribbons of clouds in fiery yellows and oranges, I thought about Naxos. I've always enjoyed exploring new places.

Plus, it would be a reprieve from the stifling proximity to Tommy and Julian.

*Only two days to go.*

It was a comforting thought and if I focused on my professional obligations and did my best to avoid the exes, I'd be back in London before I knew it, unscathed by this bizarre set of circumstances.

I finished my coffee, then went inside to get ready. Niki and Minh were coming along to capture the excursions for the campaign, including a cooking class at one of the restaurants in Chora, also called Old Town. I had to be camera ready (as always), but at least I wouldn't have to bare my boobs or arse cheeks.

I chose a pair of wide-leg cotton trousers in sunshine yellow and a gold woven-silk tank top, and because we'd be walking cobblestoned roads, sneakers. I packed my small leather backpack with the essentials and walked down to the restaurant. I had just enough time for breakfast before meeting Niki and Minh at the helipad.

'Ally!' Trudy waved vigorously from across the restaurant and I headed over, passing two other couples, who greeted me with friendly smiles.

'*Kalimera*,' I said to Trudy and Dale.

'*Kalimera*. Would you care to join us?' Dale offered.

'Actually, that'd be lovely, thanks.' I took the seat opposite Trudy. 'Ooh,' I said, eyeing her breakfast enviously. 'That looks delicious.'

'It's the best Greek yogurt I've ever had – *so* creamy. And the figs! They're to die for.'

A waiter approached, and I ordered another coffee and the same dish as Trudy.

'So, what are you two up to today?' I asked.

'Unfortunately, I've got some pressing work matters to attend to,' said Dale.

'Oh? I thought you were retired,' I replied.

'So did I,' Trudy said dryly – the only time I'd seen anything but a smile on her face.

'I told you, honey, it's just for today.' He looked over at me. 'It's a little side project I've been working on for the past six months or so. Just need to tidy up some loose ends.'

Trudy pressed her lips together as if she was supressing a retort. In solidarity, I steered the conversation away from what was obviously a contentious topic. But I was fully on Trudy's side when it came to a husband who worked too much – *particularly* while on holiday.

'And what about you, Trudy?' I asked as the waiter served my breakfast.

'*I'm* going to Naxos. There's a whole day planned,' she said, throwing a pointed look towards Dale. 'We're touring an olive oil farm, then taking a cooking class...'

'Well, you've got company, Trudy,' I said with a grin.

'Oh, you're coming too?' she asked excitedly.

'Uh-huh.'

'See, honey? You won't be on your own after all,' said Dale, and Trudy conceded with a slight lift of her shoulder.

'Definitely not,' I agreed. 'And don't be mad – I *will* be working, but it's just some photos and a bit of filming.'

'Oh, that doesn't count,' said Trudy with a wave of her hand.

I didn't bother correcting her. Most people think my job is ninety per cent posing in front of a camera. Although, god knows what they think I do the other ten per cent of the time. Maybe *practising* posing. Hah!

'I'm glad you'll be there,' I said. 'And the more fun we have, the better for the PR campaign.'

She beamed at me. 'Now, you go ahead and eat, hun,' she said. 'The helicopter's picking us up in fifteen minutes.'

'I'm going back to the villa – get started,' said Dale, standing and pushing in his chair. 'You two have fun now, and I'll see you when you get back.'

He dropped an affectionate kiss on Trudy's cheek. Her eyes closed for a moment, then she broke into one of her winsome smiles, peering up at him adoringly. Ooh, that tugged at my heartstrings – they really were adorable.

Trudy watched him walk away and it wouldn't have surprised me if she'd sighed out loud with contentment. Dale disappeared through the archway and her focus returned to me.

'I'm glad I have you to myself,' she said, staring at me intently. 'I have something to ask you.'

Uh-oh, it was hotseat time again. Yesterday, Niki had interrupted before Trudy could interrogate me, but she was nowhere to be seen. Not even Julian was around.

'What's that?' I asked breezily before taking a big bite of my breakfast. I figured chewing and swallowing might buy me some time if I needed to formulate a satisfying answer.

'It's about you and Tom.'

I snorted with surprise *and* tried to swallow at the same time. That did not go well – I almost sprayed my mouthful over the table. I chewed some more, pressing my palm to my chest, then swallowed.

'Sorry,' I said, my voice raspy.

'Here,' she said, pouring me a glass of orange juice. I would have preferred water but I took it and drank some. It helped. But now I wasn't about to choke, I couldn't hold Trudy's question at bay any longer.

I met her eye and put on a brave smile. 'What about me and Tom?'

'It's just... did you realise that he was watching you yesterday?'

'Watching me?' I asked. It wasn't the track I thought she'd go down.

'Oh, not in a creepy way or anything,' she said reassuringly. 'Tom doesn't seem like that kind of guy at all. But there were times when you were having your photo taken, or talking to Niki... and he'd be watching you... It was like he was *fascinated* by you, *drawn* to you even... You didn't notice?'

'No, I...' *No, Trudy, I didn't notice that my one true love was watching me intently.* 'I didn't see any of that.'

'I think he might be sweet on you,' she said, a glint in her eyes.

Bugger. Now Trudy was playing matchmaker – for me and my ex-husband. If only she knew. And I'll admit, I was disappointed. I genuinely liked Trudy, and I'd thought that maybe we could become friends – proper friends, which are rare in my world. But her well-meaning suspicions were skirting a little too close to the truth for comfort.

'Oh, I doubt it,' I said, forcing a smile and waving her off.

'Ally,' she said earnestly, 'I know what I saw.'

And it was obvious from her self-satisfied expression that Trudy believed she'd gotten through to me, she'd *convinced* me. Convinced me that Tommy was interested in me. Hah!

Any moment now, a flock of flying pigs would pass overhead.

## 9

Thought of the day…
Laughter is a salve for the soul.
Make time to laugh every day.
(And, yes, hysterical 'if I don't laugh I'll cry' laughter counts.)

'Oh, speak of the devil,' said Trudy when we arrived at the helipad. 'It's Tom.'

It took a sec for her words to register, but when I looked across the large concrete circle, there he (fucking) was.

So much for a husband-free day. And god, he looked good – well-fitting shorts sitting just above his knees and showing off his tanned calves, and a short-sleeved white shirt that was slightly see-through. The trail of dark hair that started at his chest, tapered, then disappeared beneath his waistline was every kind of hot.

'Oh, my fucking god,' I muttered under my breath.

'What's that, hun?' asked Trudy.

'Nothing,' I replied brightly.

'Yoo-hoo, Tom!' she called out.

*Please, Aphrodite, kill me now*, I wished, but no such luck.

Tommy looked up from his phone, then headed over.

If only I'd brought protection from his potent presence – but alas, my Hazmat suit was back in London.

'Hi, Tom,' Trudy said as he joined us.

'Good morning, Trudy. *Ally*,' he added, making a show of acknowledging me.

'*Tom*,' I replied, wishing he was anywhere else.

'Morning, all!'

Niki and Minh had arrived and when Trudy turned to talk to them, I stepped closer to Tommy.

'Don't tell me you're also a helicopter pilot,' I said through gritted teeth.

'You should be grateful I'm not – I'm a nervous flier, remember?' he replied. I vaguely remembered that, yes, but there was a more pressing question.

'Then what are you doing here?'

'Well, Elsa was supposed to be leading this excursion, but something came up – a work thing – so...' He stretched his arms out wide and shrugged.

'You're joking. *You're* coming to Naxos?'

'Don't sound so thrilled about it,' he said, pretending to be hurt.

'This may come as a surprise to you, but I wouldn't have agreed to come to Aetheria if I'd known you'd be here.'

This time, Tommy appeared legitimately hurt – and it cut me to the quick. I took a breath, schooling my expression.

'I only meant—'

I was interrupted by the sound of a helicopter approaching. We all looked skyward and Tommy shepherded us to the side of the helipad to safety.

It was probably best that I didn't get to finish my thought, because it would have been a lie. I *wouldn't* have gone to Aetheria if I'd known Tommy was there. With Elsa. Who I did not care for and, in all likelihood, was his girlfriend. What he saw in her was baffling, but Tommy was a big boy – he could make his own mistakes.

Besides, he was no longer mine to worry about.

It was my turn to climb into the helicopter, and I snapped back to the present. The same pilot who'd flown me to the island gave me a little salute, which I returned with a smile. But it fell away when Tommy climbed in and sat next to me, his thigh pressed against mine. I scooched over to put a few centimetres between us. If it wouldn't have been such an obvious move, I'd have asked to swap with Niki, who was across from me. But then I would have had to face him. A lose-lose situation.

Once we were all buckled in – a manoeuvre that required me to lift my arse off the seat so Tommy could fumble around beneath me to latch his lap belt – a steward closed the door and we were suddenly airborne – like the Skyscreamer at Blackpool, a ride I've been on exactly once and never (fucking) again.

Tommy nudged me with the back of his hand, but I didn't respond. Then he pressed up against me, making it impossible to ignore him. He signalled for me to lift the headset away from my ear. Curious, I did.

'Are you all right?' he asked, leaning in close. His breath tickled my skin and in a feat of terrible timing, I inhaled deeply, catching a lungful of his freshly showered scent. Both were an assault on my senses, and I wished I'd left the headset where it was.

'*Fine*,' I replied out of the side of my mouth. I let the headset fall back into place, then Tommy lifted it again.

'Do you mind?' I asked curtly.

'*You* were never a nervous flier,' he said, seeming perplexed.

'That's *planes*, not helicopters. And don't you feel queasy?' I asked, shooting him an annoyed look.

'No. Actually, it's kind of exhilarating,' he said earnestly.

'Whatever.'

Doing my best to ignore Tommy – his thigh pressed against mine, the scent of his cologne, his very existence – I watched out the front window. It was impossible not to be impressed by the spectacular sight of Naxos looming before us – queasy stomach or not. It was huge compared to Aetheria.

But just as we approached the coast, we swung in a wide arc to the north, then back out over the sea.

'Where are we setting down?' I asked, holding down the *talk* button on my headset.

The pilot pointed ahead of us and there it was – a yacht with a helipad on top. A yacht I knew far too well. Julian's yacht.

We were landing on Julian's *bloody* yacht and he hadn't even changed the *bloody* name, like he'd promised. It was still called *Ally's* (bloody) *Odyssey*.

And *no* woman wants her name plastered across the scene of her marital demise.

Next time I saw Julian, I wouldn't ask him to change it – I'd *tell* him. And if he was short on ideas, I had plenty.

Tommy must have noticed I was rattled – and why. He leaned forward to look out the front window, then sat back abruptly and fixed me with a troubled stare.

*Yes, Tommy, I know. I'm not thrilled about it either.*

From the reactions of the others, they hadn't noticed – too fixated on the view of Naxos – which was a relief. Not that I was *hiding* my connection to Julian, but touching down on a yacht with my name splashed across the bow in giant gold letters was... *mortifying*.

After we disembarked, I was grateful – as always – to be back on solid ground. Even if that 'solid ground' was bobbing about in the Aegean.

As I sucked in a deep breath of briny air, Tommy drew near.

'Nice name,' he murmured low in my ear.

I really wished he'd stop doing that, whispering in my ear. Was he purposefully trying to turn me on? And I didn't acknowledge his unnecessary jab. Instead, I strode purposefully towards the steward, who was waiting to greet us. I didn't recognise him so hopefully he had no idea that I was once the Lady of the Yacht.

'Welcome aboard,' he said in a Scottish brogue. 'I'm Scott, the chief steward' – I stifled a laugh at a Scot called Scott – 'and if you need anything, just let me or another crew member know. The tender to shore leaves in thirty minutes. In the meantime, we have some refreshments for you.'

He signalled to another steward who stepped forward with a tray of freshly poured Champagne, something Julian insisted on every time we boarded.

I took one of the offered glasses and expelled a soft sigh. From Scott's welcome, there was no way he knew that I was *the* Ally.

'This way, please,' he said, leading us down the staircase to the flybridge – just a fancy name for the uppermost deck where people like to hang out.

'Oh, I could live on this yacht in a heartbeat,' said Trudy, hooking her arm through mine and unwittingly saving me from another interaction with Tommy. 'Can you *imagine*?' she asked. 'I mean, Dale and I are comfortable – far more fortunate than a lot of people – but *this*... Oh, it's something else.'

'It would probably wear thin after a while,' I said. 'I imagine it could get very lonely.'

I didn't have to imagine it. When there were no guests aboard and it was just me, Julian, and a bloated crew – seriously, it was a five-to-one-ratio – then it was extremely lonely. There are only so many hours you can lie in the sun wishing that you and your husband had more in common.

Actually, it was often lonely when we *did* have guests. None of them were actual friends and I had to be *on* the entire time playing hostess, earning that gold lettering.

'Hmm, I suppose,' Trudy mused beside me.

She clearly thought otherwise but I wasn't about to try and convince her. That would be yet another venture into dangerous territory – and it was obvious Julian hadn't told her and Dale about our history.

Once I might have tried harder with Trudy. I don't have that many female friends – besides Claude and she's family, so she's obligated to love me. I wanted to let Trudy in, but there were already secrets between us. And that's hardly the foundation of a solid friendship.

'Oh my god, look at that!' she said, gawking at the enormous jacuzzi with its glass sides – a feature that had thrilled an exhibitionist like Julian no end. But that's another story.

And Trudy was so distracted by the opulence (some might say *ostentatiousness*) that she almost missed the next step. I caught her before she tumbled down the staircase.

'Oh, *thank* you, Ally. You're so strong for such a petite gal.'

'Pilates,' I replied, and she laughed, even though I was being truthful.

With Scott in the lead, we stepped onto the flybridge and Minh rushed ahead of us, pointing his camera at me.

'Ally? Look this way please,' he prompted.

I posed, glass tilted and poised at my lips. This excursion was becoming curiouser and curiouser. The Julian I knew would never welcome groups of strangers onto his yacht – even just for drinks on the deck. But if Minh was photographing me aboard *Ally's Odyssey*, then that must have been the plan.

Two more stewards appeared, each carrying a tray of delicious-looking nibbles, but I declined and wandered over to the railing. My eyes roved the boxy structures on the shoreline of Naxos, soaking in the atmosphere as I sipped my champers. Predictably, it was Krug – some things would never change – and the taste triggered a memory.

Julian and I had just said goodbye to ten guests – five of Julian's business associates and their (intolerable) trophy wives – who we'd hosted for a fortnight as we'd sailed the French Riviera. It had been a soul-crushing experience, despite the luxurious lifestyle and beautiful setting, and I was trying to pluck up the courage to ask about returning to London. Alone.

We were supposed to sail down to Valencia to collect a new cohort of hangers-on for yet *another* fortnight of sailing, and I couldn't stomach the thought of more inane conversations with vacuous wives. There was only so much you could say – or hear – about designer handbags and face lifts.

And it may sound implausible, but day after day of 25°C and cloudless blue skies becomes mind-numbingly dull. I missed springtime in London – sun showers and bundling up to go to the farmers' market to buy daffodils and asparagus, the joy of waking up to a crisp spring morning with its milky blue sky and frost on the ground. I *longed* for London. And I missed Claude.

I had the steward bring a bottle of Krug to our suite, aiming to ply Julian with his favourite Champagne, seduce him, then ask to leave the following day. We made it as far as his toast, *To finally being alone*, when I broke down in tears and confessed that I was miserable, that I needed real life, not this picture-perfect endless holiday.

He drew me onto his lap, where I curled up, and he stroked my hair. We talked for a long time, then he picked me up and carried me to the bed where he made love to me – tenderly, lovingly. And the next morning, a helicopter collected me from the yacht and flew me to Marseilles airport so I could return to London.

I broke free from the memory, then took a deep breath.

It was never the same between us after that. Julian needed a wife who was at his beck and call and that simply wasn't me. The cheating started soon after I returned to London, and you know the rest.

'You look deep in thought,' said Tommy. I hadn't noticed him approach, and he took me by surprise.

'Just...' I trailed off, leaving the thought unfinished.

'Brings back memories, eh?'

I tore my eyes from the view and looked at him. 'Which part are you referring to exactly? Being on Julian's yacht or spending another day with you?'

'Is that such a hardship?' he asked, a sliver of hurt in his eyes.

'Nope,' I answered lightly. 'As long as you keep your distance.'

I started to walk away but he called after me. 'Ally—'

I rounded on him. 'Yes, *Tom*?' I stared at him expectantly.

He stepped closer. 'I still need to talk to you.' He lifted his head and looked around, his lips disappearing between his teeth. 'But not here.'

'Honestly, Tommy – this is driving me mad. Can't you just tell me?'

'I *will* – I promise,' he said, his eyes returning to meet mine. 'Just... Can we meet up after we get back to Aetheria? Somewhere private. I could come to your villa.'

A big fat nope to that – I did *not* want Tommy in my villa. I shook my head sharply.

'Or I could meet you at the boat,' he offered, sounding frustrated. 'We'd have it to ourselves.'

'I notice you didn't invite me to your staff accommodation.'

'No, er...'

'Against company policy? Or is it because you're sharing with Elsa?'

'*Ally*,' he warned.

'*What?*' I replied, narrowing my eyes at him. Wonderful, I was back to being the petulant, jealous version of me – without a shred of hard evidence to justify it.

'Fine,' I said, 'just come to my villa, tell me whatever it is you're *dying* to tell me, then we can stop this... this... *dance*.'

'Dance?'

He seemed genuinely confused and I wondered if I'd got things wrong – maybe this situation was only difficult for me. Maybe Tommy and Elsa were on their way to living happily ever after and *that's* what he needed to tell me.

My stomach lurched.

'Doesn't matter,' I said, flicking my hand dismissively.

But it *did* matter.

It mattered so incredibly much that if I stood there a moment longer, I might burst into tears. I left Tommy, seeking out the others to take refuge in their cheeriness.

One of the stewards was walking Trudy through the physics of glass jacuzzis. I left that alone – I'd endured that explanation when Julian had the bloody thing installed and once was enough. And nearby Niki and Scott were chatting. Nope, sorry, *debating*: Scotland versus Australia – which had the most impressive natural wonders? I left that alone too – no way was I wandering into the fray between two passionate patriots.

Instead, I hung back from the others and sipped my Krug. *What on earth does Tommy want to tell me?* I was running through every possibility I could imagine when Scott called for our attention. The tender was waiting to take us to the island.

'Ooh, I can't wait!' said Trudy, necking the rest of her Krug.

I looked at my half-full glass and did the same. I could pretend to have fun with the best of them, but being a tad inebriated made it just a tad easier.

Thought of the day...
Sometimes you'll do something stupid – just put it behind
you and move on.
(It's always possible to make it worse by doing something
stupider, so try not to do that.)

I was on edge as we boarded the tender that would ferry us to shore. And why wouldn't I be? I'd just invited Tommy to my villa. Which was bad – *very*.

And whatever it was he had to tell me – also bad. That much was obvious and if foreboding were a person, it would have tackled me and left me for dead in the dirt. Or in this case, the sea.

Then again, I had questions – *so many questions* – and it would be as good a time as any to get answers. Killing two birds with one ill-considered ~~stone~~ meeting.

'Isn't this exciting?' Trudy shouted over the engine.

I broke out of my daze. 'Yeah, it's great!'

The yacht had been anchored just offshore, so the ride to the marina only took a few minutes. The skipper manoeuvred the tender into a berth, and Tommy jumped onto the pier and secured it with two towlines, making the task look effortless. It was as if he'd been a sailor his whole life. That bloke in Sicily must have been a very good teacher.

As I waited to disembark, I smoothed down my windblown hair, which to those who know me was a sign that I was still out of sorts. I needed to get it together – I'd be on camera soon.

I was last to disembark and as he'd done with the others, Tommy reached for my hand to help me onto the pier. But this wasn't like boarding the sailboat yesterday; this was a two-foot step up with a sizable gap between the tender and the pier. There was no way I'd manage on my own, so I placed my hand in Tommy's.

It was the first time our hands had touched since we were married.

And it was everything I'd been terrified of. *Electric*. Once I was on the pier, every instinct told me to snatch my hand away, but I kept it in his for a moment longer than made sense. I looked up but we were both wearing sunglasses so I couldn't be sure if Tommy had felt it too, the connection between us.

He finally let go and I inhaled deeply, catching my breath. Tommy cleared his throat, the only indication that this wasn't one-sided, and he seemed about to say something when a booming voice called out, '*Yia sas, yia sas.*'

We all turned together and a rotund, dark-haired man in his mid-forties was speed-walking towards us, waving.

'Hello!' he said when he got to us. He broke into a broad smile. 'I'm Michalis, your guide for the day.' He was dressed similarly to Tommy in tailored shorts and a short-sleeved white shirt, only his was stretched taut over his stomach.

'*Yia sou*, I'm Niki,' she said, stepping forward. 'We've been messaging.'

This excursion must have been her brainchild. She *was* Greek Australian and she'd got the job on Aetheria through her cousin. She probably had other connections in the Cyclades.

'Yes, hello, nice to meet you in person,' Michalis replied. They exchanged warm smiles, and Niki introduced Minh and Trudy, then Tommy.

'Tom's standing in for our colleague, Elsa,' she explained. 'She'll lead this excursion from now on, but she wasn't feeling well today.'

My eyes darted towards Tommy. He'd said that Elsa had been waylaid by work, not laid up with an illness. What was going on? I was so fixated on this anomaly that I nearly missed Niki introducing me.

'Ah, the Divorced Diva,' said Michalis, nodding at me appreciatively.

I sensed Tommy stiffen beside me. We'd never really talked about the Diva – hard to, when our contact was limited to the occasional text message – but she had come up once or twice. Tommy knew what I did for a living.

Still, I may have profited from my status as an ex-wife but unlike certain pop stars, I would never flaunt it in my exes' faces. Rick hadn't gone there either. No 'Ally, why'd you leave me after forty-seven days?' songs on Havoc's latest album.

I smiled politely and Michalis must have sensed that he'd made a slight misstep, because he clapped his hands together loudly. 'We have a special day planned,' he said. 'Follow me.'

He headed back the way he'd come, and we followed single file towards the car park. Every step I took, I was aware of Tommy's presence behind me – our connection still strong. At least, for me.

When he came to my villa later, I'd have to keep my distance. I'd insist on standing with our backs to opposite walls, calling out across the room. Or even better – we could talk on the phone, me in the bedroom, him on the sofa... That would give us privacy from prying ears, but with no chance of me accidentally-on-purpose launching myself at him.

Perfect.

Except, *not* perfect.

Because Tommy's voice had other-worldly properties. It wielded so much power that he could be calling from Timbuktu and it would *still* undo me – not just in body, but in every way that mattered.

And he wouldn't be in Timbuk-bloody-tu – he'd be in the next bloody room. Gah!

It was decided – Tommy was uninvited to my villa. Whatever his big news was, he could send me an email like a normal person. I was about to tell him, but we'd arrived at a brand-new minivan.

With a push of a button on his key fob, Michalis opened the side door. I eyed the interior. *Hmm* – a little too cosy for me and with my luck, I'd end up thigh to thigh with Tommy again. So, I opened the front passenger door, climbed into the cab, and put on my seatbelt before anyone could question me. The others got in the back and when Michalis climbed into the driver's seat, he gave me a curious side-eye.

'I get car sick,' I explained. Not entirely a lie and I'd seen those winding roads as we'd flown over earlier. Best to be up front (and as far from Tommy as possible).

But it didn't take long to forget Tommy and Elsa and all the other bizarre goings-on from the past few days, because Naxos was extraordinary.

Leaving the marina, we skirted the town of Chora, with its

energetic waterfront, densely packed buildings, and the imposing Kastro Fortress.

'It was built by a Venetian nobleman, who conquered Naxos *800 years* ago,' said Michalis as we craned our necks to see it. 'The Venetians occupied Naxos for 350 years, then the Ottomans... Then, after eight years of war, we finally won our independence in 1830.'

Call it naivety, but I hadn't realised that Greece had been occupied for much of the last millennia, nor that they'd had to fight for independence. It certainly accounted for the varied architectural styles that contrasted – *clashed?* – with the boxy white structures synonymous with the Greek Islands.

The town of Chora now behind us, we started an easy climb into the hills, the views expanding with each inch of road we covered. To the left, the Aegean shimmered, its distinct, fluid shades of blue juxtaposing against the terrain – the russet-browns and ochre-tans of rugged, untouched earth and the vibrant greens of cultivated fields and terraces.

'This is Eggares,' said Michalis as we approached a small village on the slope of a lush, gently sloping hill. 'My family is from here.'

'You were raised here?' I asked, turning towards him excitedly.

'Yes,' he replied with a puffed-out chest.

'It must have been incredible,' I said, my eyes returning to the view. 'It's so beautiful.'

I watched out the window, my eyes hungrily taking in every detail of the picturesque village. The buildings were quintessentially Greek – startlingly white, sharp angles, with archways and sky-blue domes.

The church was impressive – so imposing that it seemed almost out of place in such a small village. And as we got nearer, the ornate embellishments around the blue domes stood out – reminding me of Saint Marco's Basilica in Venice, perhaps evidence of the Venetians' lengthy occupation.

Venice – another place I'd been to only once before. With Tommy. Who would have thought that a short trip to Greece would include so many bittersweet memories of my first marriage?

God, if I'd known that ahead of time, I would have told Julian to go ahead and call Daisy Harrigan the Sexy Single – AKA Copycat Barbie.

We took a turn. 'Are we going to the church?' I asked Michalis.

'To the olive press museum. My cousin Giorgios – he will meet us there.'

Now I love a good museum, but I wasn't holding out much hope that a museum dedicated to olive presses – or was it just a single olive press? – would be particularly entertaining. But Minh and Niki would need content for their campaign, so if it was dull, I'd fake it.

It wouldn't be the first time – professionally speaking, that is. I haven't faked an orgasm since uni. If it's not happening, no sense in forcing it.

Sorry, my mind's wandering again. Where was I? Oh, yes... Eggares.

Giorgios was waiting for us when we pulled up outside the museum, wearing the exact same smile as his cousin. I looked between them twice before deciding they could pass for twins – even though Giorgios looked ever-so-slightly older. Not that I would mention it.

'*Sas kalosorízoume!* Welcome, friends,' he called out as we decanted from the minivan onto the museum's forecourt.

Minh took photos of Giorgios shepherding us inside, then

jogged off towards the church next door to photograph its impressive façade. I watched him over my shoulder, wishing I could follow. The church was even more spectacular up close.

'We will have time to see it afterwards, if you like,' said Michalis, giving me a knowing smile.

'Sorry, I'm sure this will be very interesting.' I wasn't sure – how could it be? – but I was working, and I would fulfil my obligation without complaint.

But once inside, I realised how wrong I'd been. The museum was remarkable, particularly the enormous olive press. And Giorgios was a compelling guide, not just explaining the history of olive oil production but personalising the tour with stories about their family, who had lived in Eggares and produced olive oil for generations.

'And this is *Pappoús* and *Yiayiá*, our grandparents.'

He pointed to a black and white photograph of a young couple standing side by side in an olive grove. You could tell from their slightly weary expressions that they worked hard, and there was obvious pride in the man's eyes as he stared into the camera.

But what really captured my attention were their clasped hands, fingers entwined. *We're in this together*, those hands said. My heart flooded with warmth, which was more surprising than enjoying the tour.

I'd thought my days as a hopeless romantic were long gone, that I was impervious to love – public displays of affection, happily ever afters in romcoms, even real-life epic love stories like *Pappoús* and *Yiayiá's*...

But it wasn't just Michalis and Giorgios' grandparents. Hadn't I melted – just a little – watching Trudy and Dale together?

Maybe the hopeless romantic in me wasn't gone forever.

Perhaps being confronted with my romantic history had unlocked something.

All this flew through my head in the time it took for Giorgios to move us along to the next photograph.

Reluctantly, I stepped away from the photograph of his grandparents, casting one last look over my shoulder at their hands. When I turned back around, Tommy caught my eye, his expression unreadable. A lump lodged in my throat, and I looked away.

I'd been musing about whether something had been unlocked in me? Try ripped open. Try pouring the contents of my heart onto that centuries-old stone floor.

'Ally, get a load of this!' Trudy called out. She was looking out the window, excitedly waving me over. Glad for the reprieve, I went over and looked out.

'Oh, how lovely.'

Outside was a gravel terrace with picnic tables, café sets, and pairs of beanbag chairs under olive trees. Several small groups were enjoying the alfresco dining, and just the sight of those plump green olives on a nearby table was enough to make my mouth water.

'Ahh,' said Giorgios, coming up behind us, 'you guessed the next part of the tour! Come on, we have some delicious food for you to try.'

He led us to a picnic table which was laden with several *mezé* platters – cheese, bread, hummus, olive oil for dipping, and of course, olives. I was suddenly ravenous, this morning's coffee and yoghurt a distant memory.

But I waited until Tommy sat down before taking a seat at the other end of the table. I patted the bench next to me and Trudy awkwardly climbed in – though, to be fair, if there's an elegant way to sit at a picnic table, I've never discovered it.

Giorgios signalled to a young woman, who brought over a bottle of wine.

'Our local wine,' he said, taking it from her and holding it up proudly. 'Taxiarchis.' He circled the table, filling our glasses, then showed the bottle to Minh, who was taking close-ups of the food. 'Wine?' Giorgios asked him.

'Sure, thanks,' said Minh with a smile.

Giorgios poured a fifth glass, setting the bottle down beside it. Minh took another photo, capturing the wine bottle, then sat next to Niki.

I was desperate to tuck in, but I sensed Giorgios had something else in mind, and I was right. First, he invited us to taste their *exairetikó parthéno elaiólado* – the equivalent of extra virgin olive oil. It was peppery with a slight lemony taste – absolutely delicious. Then we tried the specialty oils, infused with herbs and citrus. I loved the rosemary best, instantly knowing I'd be handing over a wad of euros once we got to the gift shop.

After tasting the olive oil, Giorgios told us about the local cheeses, how the hummus was made – with their premium olive oil and lemons from the farm – and *then* we were invited to eat.

I slathered a large chunk of bread with hummus and took a bite *right* as Trudy leaned in and whispered, 'He's watching you again.'

Note to self: do not inhale when you have a mouthful of bread. As I coughed up bread and hummus, I dared to glance in Tommy's direction, but by then he was looking off towards the olive grove.

'Are you all right, hun?' asked Trudy, patting me on the back.

I nodded, reaching for the wine, which in the absence of

water would have to do. I took a sip, cleared my throat, and inhaled deeply.

That was twice I'd nearly coughed up half a lung in front of Trudy – though, to be fair, she had terrible timing when it came to telling me things I didn't want to hear.

'Sorry, everyone,' I said. How *English* of me – apologising for choking.

Niki gave me a commiserating smile across the table and Minh held off on taking the photo he'd lined up.

'No, hun, I'm sorry. I didn't mean to shock you,' Trudy said quietly.

'Not shocked, just…' I left the rest unsaid, then reached for my wine again and took a gulp. At this rate, I'd be drunk before we left for the cooking class.

'Is it because of your conversation earlier?' she asked, dropping her voice even further.

My gaze shot towards her, then I quickly looked at the others. Minh had left the table to photograph the olive grove, Niki was chatting with Giorgios and Michalis, and Tommy seemed lost in thought. *About me?* I pondered.

Assured that no one was listening to us, I slid closer to Trudy until we were shoulder to shoulder.

'Which conversation?'

'Well, all of them – on the helipad, during the helicopter ride, on the yacht…'

'Fuck,' I whispered to myself breathlessly.

'Ally, do you and Tom have some sort of *history*?'

I dropped my gaze to the tabletop. So much for being discreet. *Do I tell her the truth or fob her off with a lie?*

I met her eye. She stared back, her openness inviting me in and slicing straight through my defences. She wasn't going to let this drop – I could tell. And even if our friendship was limited to our time on Aetheria, it might feel good to confide in someone.

I scooched even closer and whispered into her ear, 'He's my ex-husband.'

Trudy's sharp inhale was so extreme, it set *her* off on a coughing fit.

Thought of the day...
If it costs you your peace, it's too bloody expensive.
(Buy yourself some nice shoes instead.)

Trudy was unusually quiet after I told her about Tommy, her eyes darting between us as if she couldn't quite believe it, bewilderment practically stamped on her face. I regretted saying anything; there was every chance Tommy would cotton on, and I wasn't sure how he'd feel about her knowing.

*This is a farce*, I thought. *The whole bloody thing – Julian, Tommy... having to pretend...*

I suppose I could have embraced it, sat everyone down in front of a whiteboard and mapped it all out, like on *Only Murders in the Building*.

*Only Husbands on the Island.*

By this stage, it *wouldn't* have surprised me if Rick rocked up (pun intended).

Lost in thought, I barely ate anything else, although I did

finish my wine. It was delicious, but mostly I was chasing some Dutch courage. I was going to need it.

After giving us enough time to taste the wares and soak up the atmosphere, Michalis directed us to the museum's shop where I stocked up on gifts for Mum and Dad, Claude, and Maya and Ruby. Olive oil for everyone!

'Would you like to see inside the church?' he asked us when we'd finished shopping. 'We have some time.'

'Oh, that would be wonderful,' Trudy replied, and Niki seemed keen as well.

'But, Ally,' Michalis continued, 'you will need, uh...' He mimed draping something around his shoulders. 'To show respect.'

'Oh, of course,' I said, suddenly remembering. I'd have to cover my shoulders to enter the church, but I didn't have anything with me. The others were dressed appropriately, and I didn't want to be the reason they missed out, so I told them to go on ahead.

'Are you sure, hun?' asked Trudy.

'Yes, yes, go ahead,' I said with a smile, waving them off.

Tommy shot a quick look over his shoulder as he followed the others into the church, but I pretended not to notice. Instead, I walked away from the entrance, following the rough whitewashed wall. While I drank in the view, I took deep gulps of the fresh, earthy air.

Part of me wished Tommy would come and find me, press me against that wall, and kiss me.

Is that what I wanted?

*Yes.*

*No.*

*Yes.*

'Ally.'

I rounded on him, startled. Had I summoned him by sheer will?

'It's time to go,' he said, hooking his thumb in the direction of the minivan.

'Oh, right. Thanks,' I added as an afterthought.

I trailed behind him, not wanting to get too close, then climbed in the passenger seat.

Trudy seemed to have shaken off her bewildered state and was chatting animatedly to Niki about her Greek heritage. I eavesdropped as Michalis drove us down the hill back to Chora, noticing the affectionate way Niki talked about her family even though they apparently drove her bonkers most of the time.

Minh was quiet as always, only asking Niki the occasional question, and Tommy was completely silent. Like me. *What's going through his head?* I asked myself.

God, I just wanted to be back on Aetheria, hidden in my villa, and running down the clock. Less than two days to go.

And I still hadn't told Tommy not to show up later.

\* \* \*

Just like everyone, I've had moments where I wished I was anywhere else. And when we left Eggares, it felt like the day would keep heading in that direction.

But then we arrived at the restaurant owned by Michalis' family, tucked in the heart of Chora, halfway up the hill from the waterfront. That's when I met their *yiayiá*, the woman in the photograph – the one holding hands with her husband in the olive grove.

And she was *beautiful*.

She would have been at least ninety, but that was doing maths rather than judging by her appearance. She may have had grandsons in their forties, but she looked far younger than her years, standing erect with the grace of a ballerina. Her large, round dark-brown eyes were wise and kind and filled with laughter, and her salt-and-pepper hair was worn in a thick, high bun. I'm only five-foot-one, but I towered over her – she was *tiny*.

She welcomed us into her kitchen with the fuss of a mother hen, her warm smile framed by laugh lines etched like laurels, making her even more beautiful.

I was in awe.

There's something you should understand about the way Claude and I were raised. Our mum, Jenny, is the sort of mum who will do anything for anyone. She might complain about it and be a little judgey (but aren't we all sometimes?), but she is generous to a fault.

Except to herself.

Mum has never booked in for a spa day or shopped anywhere more expensive than Marks & Spencers. She doesn't wear clothes that are anything more than perfunctory. *Why would I bother with all that fancy stuff? Who's going to see me?* She and Dad never have date nights or take proper holidays, no matter how much I nag them. And she *hates* it when I buy her nice things. *What a waste, Ally. My thousand-year-old [insert item here] works perfectly fine. I don't need you spending your money on me.*

But most of all (least of all?), Mum has never been one to follow her dreams. Or even *have* dreams. Or even consider that she's entitled to them!

I'm convinced she thinks of herself solely as a wife, a mother, a friend, and a neighbour – forgetting entirely that she's also *Jenny*.

I only paint this picture of my mum – a woman I love

deeply but will never truly understand – because the day I met Maria Kouros (or *Yiayiá* as she insisted we call her), I met the woman I wanted to be.

Proud. Accomplished. Generous. And beautiful – inside and out.

She was a *force*.

And so, *so* funny.

She had very little English (which was still more than my Greek), so Michalis translated for us. Even when he appeared shocked, shaking his head at her and saying, '*Ochi, Yiayiá,*' she would scold him, prodding him to translate exactly what she'd said.

Including when she looked Tommy up and down appraisingly and said, 'You remind me of my husband, Giorgios. He was... virile.' She raised her fisted hand to drive home her point, waggling her eyebrows suggestively.

Even Tommy laughed, his cheeks colouring.

That's when our eyes met, a look that reverberated through me. I hastily looked away and caught my breath.

'Oh my,' said Trudy next to me.

'She's funny, isn't she?' I asked, sharing the joke.

'I meant you and Tom,' she replied, sobering me instantly. 'You sure there's nothing between you any more?'

*Am I sure? Why no, Trudy, there is nothing in this world of which I am less sure!*

'Oh, we divorced years ago. I've had two husbands and two divorces since then,' I said lightly. Only why did I say that? She blinked rapidly, clearly shocked. But at least it wasn't pity – that would have been far worse.

'Now, you will pair up,' said Michalis, reminding me we were there to cook rather than conduct a post-mortem on my first marriage.

I looked to Trudy, hoping to pair up with her, but she'd already chosen Niki. And with Minh taking photos...

Wonderful – reunited. *Again.*

'I hope this is all right?' Tommy asked as he rounded the bench and stood by my side.

I beamed at him. 'Why wouldn't it be?'

Across the way, Minh took a photo.

'Ahh, mate, sorry,' said Tommy. 'Just... employees of Aetheria probably shouldn't be in the promotional photos.'

'Yeah, of course. Sorry 'bout that.' Minh looked intently at his view finder, then lifted his eyes, glancing between me and Tommy, and Trudy and Niki. I expected him to ask me and Trudy to cook together but instead he said, 'I'll make sure you're not in focus.'

'Perfect,' replied Tommy.

Don't you love it when the menfolk decide for you?

Only that's not fair – I could have spoken up, asked to swap with Niki. But after deliberately dodging him all morning, there was no point denying it any more – I *wanted* to be with Tommy. And cooking together would be fun.

I mean, neither of us were exactly 'home chefs', but we'd always enjoyed being in the kitchen together. Even making beans on toast, which we'd had a fair bit when we were first married and skint. We'd grate cheese over the top and slide it under the grill, then add brown sauce, laughing about being 'super posh' when we were anything but.

The memory made me smile, but I shook it off and took in the restaurant's well-appointed kitchen. Like on *MasterChef*, the ingredients and implements were laid out across three workstations, including one for *Yiayiá*.

With Michalis translating, she started demonstrating, and

we watched intently, doing our best to replicate her precise actions.

First we hollowed out fat, juicy tomatoes and just from the aroma, I could tell they were sun-ripened. I snuck a little taste, and it was even better than the tomatoes I'd had on Aetheria.

I handed Tommy a sliver, then peeked at *Yiayiá* – I didn't want to get told off. She caught my eye, but instead of scolding me, she gave me a sly smile.

'Oh my god,' sighed Tommy. 'Is there anything more delicious than Greek tomatoes?'

'Nothing,' I agreed, soaking up the warmth of his smile.

Next up were red peppers and Tommy and I worked in unison to scoop out the seeds and pith, then set the peppers on the tray next to the tomatoes. Then *Yiayiá* held up a long, narrow aubergine, and explained the next step.

'The aubergine is a little harder,' Michalis translated. 'Hold it firmly – use *strong* hands.'

I clamped my lips shut. *Do not laugh. Do not laugh. Do not laugh.*

Sure, it was juvenile to find that funny but come on! And from that glint in *Yiayiá*'s eye and the quirk of her mouth, she knew *exactly* what she was saying.

I held it together – barely – following *Yiayiá* and slicing the narrow aubergine in half longways. She scored the white flesh in a hatched pattern, then held it up to show us, saying something to her grandson. 'Do not go all the way through,' said Michalis. Then deliberately and carefully, she used a thin-edged spoon to scoop out the flesh and gestured for us to do the same.

Tommy stooped to whisper in my ear. 'Now remember, hold it *firmly*. Use *strong* hands, Ally.'

That was it. I started cackling, my whole body shaking. I

clapped my hand over my mouth but even that couldn't stop the laughter escaping.

Tommy sniggered inaudibly beside me, the bugger. He always could make me laugh and more often than not, he'd hide his laughter while *I* got into trouble. Like at his cousin's wedding when the old man next to me let off a silent-but-deadly fart. I was keeping it together reasonably well, concentrating on the service with all my might. But then Tommy poked me hard in the thigh and started shaking with laughter, provoking a loud *hah* to burst out of me. I tried to disguise it as a cough, but several people threw me dirty looks, including the old man who'd farted.

I wasn't in trouble this time though and *Yiayiá* barked out a dry laugh, her shoulders trembling. Yep, she knew *exactly* what she'd said. Still laughing, she gestured towards the aubergine, prompting me to get back to it, which I did.

Soon enough, we'd hollowed out our vegetables and started on the filling – a mixture of cooked rice, fresh herbs, chopped garlic and onions, and the innards of the tomatoes and aubergines, sautéing them in olive oil from the family's farm. You'll have to take my word for it, but it smelled incredible in that kitchen.

After stuffing the vegetables, they went into a hot oven to bake and we started assembling a Greek salad, or *horiatiki*.

Following *Yiayiá*, we chopped the tomatoes, red pepper, and cucumber, making sure all the pieces were uniform. We stacked everything exactly how *Yiayiá* showed us, to showcase each ingredient, including the fat slab of feta we balanced on top. Then we added the finishing touches: a sprinkle of dried oregano, a generous drizzle of olive oil, and a squeeze of lemon juice. It might have only been a salad, but I was proud of that *horiatiki*. It was a masterpiece. And it was going to be delicious.

'I have never been so hungry in my life,' I whispered to Tommy, peering up at him.

He returned my gaze steadily, the air between us fizzing.

A scenario started playing in my mind – me sweeping everything off the bench, including the salad, then pushing Tommy onto it, and climbing on top of him.

Hmm, tempting, but we were *so* close to sitting down to lunch. I also doubted *Yiayiá* would appreciate us bonking in her kitchen, no matter how taken she'd been with Tommy.

So instead of acting out my little fantasy, I cleaned our workstation, taking extra care to avoid eye contact with Tommy. He worked silently beside me, and we fell into a familiar sympatico, which was both familiar and alarming. How was it so easy to slip back into Ally-and-Tommy mode after all these years? Not wanting to even *contemplate* that, I concentrated on polishing the stainless-steel countertop with a soft cloth.

When the stuffed vegetables were finally ready, *Yiayiá* zipped around the kitchen, plating our creations onto a large platter. She pointed at our salads and, with a wave, indicated that we should follow her into the dining room where a table had been set for seven. We took our seats as Minh photographed the food, then stepped back to get some shots of the restaurant.

*Yiayiá*, who was frowning, waved her hand at Minh, speaking boldly in Greek. '*Éla na fáme!*'

'She wants you to stop that now,' said Michalis. 'It's time to eat.'

'Oh, sorry.'

Sheepishly, Minh sat next to Niki and I offered him a commiserating smile. I liked *Yiayiá*, but I wouldn't want to get on her bad side. She seemed as fierce as she was funny.

We passed the food around and I filled my plate to brimming, my appetite having made a full recovery since the olive oil museum.

Beside me, Tommy bit into a stuffed pepper and groaned – a sound so familiar, so *primitive*, that I was instantly pitched into the past. My fingers buried in his thick hair, my head thrown back as he thrust into me, a guttural groan escaping his lips as he came.

I shifted in my chair.

He'd touched a nerve – unintentionally, I was sure, but that didn't matter. I'd allowed myself to drop my guard, to get too close, too familiar. I'd started entertaining thoughts and emotions that I'd buried long ago. For good reason.

Across the way, *Yiayiá* caught my eye, her lips disappearing in a sad smile. She must have understood my predicament. Not the entire story – she couldn't have known that – but her eyes told me she understood, she understood that I still loved Tommy.

But I couldn't have him. Not if I wanted to keep my heart intact.

## 12

I kept my distance after that, literally as well as figuratively, sitting as far from Tommy as I could – in the minivan, on the tender to Julian's yacht, and in the helicopter. I didn't say a word to him – not even *goodbye* when we got to Aetheria – an easy decision with Elsa waiting beside the helipad.

She rushed over as soon as his feet hit the ground, speaking to him in low, agitated tones. He frowned, murmured a reply, and they walked off together towards the staff quarters.

He didn't look back, which made my stomach gripe with uneasiness.

*You can't have it both ways, Ally.*

I only realised when I arrived at my villa that I never told him not to come. I'd have to send him away face to face. *Wonderful.*

I toed off my sneakers, leaving them in the entry, and crossed to the minibar where I poured two fat fingers of Metaxa, a Greek brandy. I lowered myself onto the sofa, half reclining, and sipped.

What the hell was I doing – *besides* playing with fire?

Claude would have my head if she discovered I was spending time with Tommy – let alone *enjoying* it. As if those countless tearful nights she'd stayed up with me, helping me recover from the Tommy-shaped void, had never happened.

My phone rang, startling me, and I jumped up to dig it out of my backpack. Claude.

Had I somehow summoned her too? If so, that was twice in one day. Maybe I'd acquired a new superpower. Too bad it wasn't teleportation – I could zap myself out of there.

'Hi, Claude,' I said, making my way back to the sofa.

'Hi. Bad time?'

'Why do you ask?'

'I don't know. You sound... odd.'

'Just been a long day,' I replied. 'What's up?'

'Umm... look, it's probably nothing and you're going to think I'm mad but...'

'*Claude*,' I groaned. 'Just out with it, please.'

'All right,' she said, clearly stung.

I was being a right shit, and it wasn't Claude's fault I'd painted myself into a romantic corner. 'Sorry.'

'That's okay. I just wondered if you've seen the photographs Niki's uploaded to the shared drive?'

'Er, no... Why?' I asked, fumbling for my laptop. As I logged on, an uneasy feeling washed over me.

Claude laughed a false, shrill laugh that sharpened my apprehension. 'Like I said, it's probably nothing, but there's a bloke in some of the photos… He's never in focus but… well, he sort of reminds me of *Tommy*.'

*Fuck, fuck, fuck, fuck, fuck.*

'Um, can you hold on a sec?'

I set down the phone and navigated to the folder we'd shared with Niki. I quickly scrolled through dozens of photos and stopped when I got to one of me and Tommy on the boat. He wasn't in focus, like Claude had said, but if you knew Tommy – and she did – it was clearly him.

The photos from Naxos hadn't been uploaded yet – we'd only been back an hour – but even if Minh stayed true to his word, doing his best to disguise Tommy's identity, Claude would figure it out soon enough. I was a fool to think I could hide something this momentous from her.

I needed to tell her the truth. Only… I wasn't ready – too many unknowns, my emotions all over the place… And without question, Claude would tell me to come home. I couldn't chance it. Not yet.

'Al? You there?' Claude's disembodied voice shouted from my phone. I picked it up.

'Sorry. I'm guessing you mean the bloke on the boat?' I asked, playing dumb.

'Well, obvs,' she said with a laugh. 'But don't you think he's a dead ringer for Tommy?'

'I suppose a little – if you squint. But he doesn't in real life – same hair colour but that's about it.' It was my first baldfaced lie.

Well, not my first lie *ever*. Not even my first lie to Claude, but really, you can't blame me for telling her that the pixie cut she got after her divorce suited her. It would have been cruel to kick her when she was down. Besides, hair eventually grows back. Self-esteem has to be painstakingly rebuilt over time, so it was a kindly lie.

'Right – okay,' she said.

I laughed – partly relieved and partly amused. 'You sound disappointed.'

'Not really, I just... I don't know... I got it in my head that maybe Tommy was there and I was worried... But you would have said something if he was, right?'

*Er, no, Claude. Turns out I wouldn't have*, I thought guiltily.

'Anyway, never mind,' she said. 'I told you it was mad.'

She sounded almost wistful, and I didn't know what to say. Maybe I'd got it wrong. Maybe if I'd told Claude the truth from the onset, she would have been a friendly ear, commiserating that I'd been trapped on a tiny island with the only man I'd ever truly loved.

But it was too late to be truthful.

'Don't you miss him sometimes?' she asked quietly, and it was as if she'd slapped me.

'How do you mean?' I stammered, fighting the lump forming in my throat.

'Just that... I know how much you loved him.'

'Claude, I...' I swallowed hard, trying like mad to shake off the encroaching gloom.

'I shouldn't have said anything. I'm sorry. Besides, an ex is an ex for a reason, right?' she asked with a faux lilt to her voice.

'True,' I agreed. It may have been a foundational principle of the Divorced Diva platform, but it was also a timely reminder that there were reasons Tommy and I were no longer together. *Solid* reasons.

Right?

Only, the primary reason I left the marriage was because he chose his job over me – a job he no longer had.

Then again, his current situation wasn't much better –

working on a remote island a day's travel from London. *And* he had a girlfriend. At least, that's how it seemed.

'*So*,' said Claude brightly. Clearly, a change of subject was imminent. 'How was today? I want all the envy-inducing details.'

Relieved to be back on steadier ground, I reached for the Metaxa, then regaled Claude with the highlights, spending the most time talking about *Yiayiá*.

'Oh, she sounds like a character,' Claude said, laughing.

It warmed my heart to hear her laugh like that – it was a rarity. She was so straightforward, so purposeful and single-minded. It made me all the more certain that Claude would benefit from time on Aetheria. And she'd love *Yiayiá*.

'You need to come here and meet her yourself,' I said.

I could easily picture the two of them together. I had no doubt that *Yiayiá* would see beneath Claude's tough shell, then do her best to crack it. She'd have Claude opening up in no time, helping her get back to the Claude she was before her marriage to The Twat.

I'd done my best to help Claude, living with the constant awareness that I hadn't succeeded. But sometimes it took a stranger, one with a big heart, to break through an emotional fortress.

'I'm considering it,' Claude replied, sounding a teeny bit closer to agreeing than she had last night.

'Excellent.'

'Mmm. Look, I'll let you go – and sorry again about... you know...'

'Not to worry,' replied my inner stoic.

We ended the call and I sipped my Metaxa, revisiting the lies I'd told my sister.

The big one had seemed unavoidable, which made the lies

by omission – skirting all mentions of Tommy – unavoidable by extension. But I regretted every single one.

I should have told Claude about Tommy the first night, but I was certain she would have convinced me that being on Aetheria with *two* exes was far too much to contend with.

I mean, it sort of was, but as I considered my predicament, I had to admit that I didn't want to leave – not before I'd had it out with Tommy. I had *so* many questions. And I wanted answers, no matter how difficult they might be to hear.

So, despite what I'd decided only hours ago, when he came to my villa, I was *not* sending him away. I'd hear him out, then I'd put *him* in the hotseat.

\* \* \*

The thing about waiting for someone when you don't have firm plans *and* the stakes are high *and* you have a tendency to over-think is that it sucks.

I was two Metaxas in and Tommy still hadn't shown up.

Meanwhile, I'd practised every style of greeting imaginable.

Nonchalance: *Oh, Tommy, I completely forgot you were coming. I was about to get in the bath.*

Curt: *I'm not inviting you in. Just say what you have to say, then leave.*

Hurt: *I can't imagine there's anything you have to say that I want to hear.*

That one was a lie, of course. I was *dying* to hear what he had to say.

I even contemplated opening the door wearing nothing but a smile, but I quickly ruled that out. Seducing Tommy was a terrible idea. TER-RI-BLE.

I glanced at the clock – 6.48 p.m. We'd been back on

Aetheria for nearly two hours. Where the hell *was* he? This waiting game was excruciating.

'Well, bugger this,' I mumbled to myself.

I stood up and gauged my level of inebriation. Could I walk an imaginary tightrope? I toe-heeled-toe-heeled across the room without swaying or losing my balance. So not drunk then. Definitely tipsy though and despite thinking I wouldn't need dinner after that enormous lunch, I was starting to feel peckish. I'd pop out for a quick dinner in the restaurant and if he came by when I was out, then that was on him.

I went into the bathroom and checked the mirror, assessing that I needed a five-minute zhuzh. I spread a dollop of tinted moisturiser over my face, tidied my brows, added some shimmer to my eyelids, and dotted on some cream blush. A swish of mouthwash and I was good to go.

I stared into the mirror. Would the tumult crashing about inside me be visible to anyone else? I smiled, but my eyes were slightly wild. I dropped the smile.

'What *are* you doing?' I asked myself.

And I didn't just mean waiting for Tommy. Why was I on that island in the first place? Why had I agreed to help Julian? I didn't owe him. If anything, it was the other way around.

And as soon as I'd realised Tommy was on the island, I should have packed up and left instead of sabotaging my own wellbeing. Julian could have found someone else if I'd insisted.

Round and round my thoughts went until a knock at the door startled me – even though I'd been expecting it.

Before answering, I gave myself a pointed look. 'Get it together, Ally.'

But when I swung open that enormous wooden door and saw him standing there, everything I'd rehearsed flew straight out of my head.

'Hi,' I said softly.

'Hi. All right if I come in?'

I nodded, then stepped aside.

He moved past me, smelling fresh, as if he'd just showered. I glanced at the nape of his neck, and his hair was damp. I didn't want to think about *why* he needed to shower, but sex came to mind. Which made perfect sense to my tipsy, catastrophising brain. His girlfriend met him at the helipad and they snuck back to their bungalow where they indulged in nearly two hours of mind-blowing sex. And, as Tommy was a gentleman, not wanting to rub his sexual conquest in my face, he'd showered before he came to see me.

'The villas are nice, aren't they?' he asked, and I came back to the room with a jolt.

'Er, yes. Did you want something to drink?'

*Look at me, being the consummate hostess. So much for demanding an explanation, then sending him on his way.*

'Um, no thanks. Wait— Actually, yes.'

Glad to have something to do – my insides were somersaulting – I went to the minibar and poured two glasses of brandy, then handed one to Tommy.

We sipped, both forgoing a toast. But what would we toast to? Old friends? Hah.

Tommy looked around, obviously stalling.

'Would you like to sit down?' I asked, already heading for one of the long sofas. I perched on its edge and Tommy sat opposite me on the other sofa, the wide coffee table between us.

This was when he was supposed to start talking, but he seemed to be stuck in a loop of sipping, licking his lips, and staring at me. No, make that *frowning*.

*Any moment now...* I thought. But I didn't prompt him and

silence filled the room – almost louder than my heart pounding in my ears.

'Sorry,' he said eventually. 'This is harder than I thought.'

I inhaled slowly through my nose, exhaling from slightly parted lips. At least the brandy was chiselling the edges off my nerves – *ish*.

'Fuck it,' he said to himself. Then he looked me right in the eye and said, 'Ally, I think you should leave Aetheria. As soon as possible.'

Of everything I'd expected to hear, this was such a left turn that my mouth popped open of its own accord. I blinked a few times, shaking my head, then finally found my words. 'I'm sorry, but what the fuck are you talking about?'

He exhaled loudly – an exasperated sigh, as if *he* was entitled to be annoyed.

'Look, I've been here several weeks now and there's something going on – something nefarious and it's escalating. And the last thing I want is for you to get caught up in it.'

My mind flew in a dozen different directions at once. It was impossible to pin down a single thought.

I set my glass down on the table. 'Get caught up in what exactly?' I asked. 'Is this to do with Julian?'

'Yes.'

'*And*? You can't just leave me hanging like that. What's going on? Is he in trouble?'

'Potentially.'

I stood and gave him a hard stare. 'Tommy, you're going to have to give me more than one-word answers.'

'I know, okay, I'm sorry. Just... Please sit down.'

I hesitated for a second, then plopped onto the sofa, glowering at him. Clearly uncomfortable under my gaze, he shot up and started pacing.

'The day after Elsa and I arrived, I was supposed to meet with Julian in his office – in the building behind the restaurant. Only when I got there, he was in the middle of a heated argument – a phone call, so I only heard his side of it. I didn't mean to eavesdrop, but the window was open and it was impossible not to. It was something about a business deal that had soured and at one point he shouted, "Don't you dare threaten me!" The call ended right after that, and I walked away, waited five minutes, and pretended to be late for our meeting, so he wouldn't know I'd overheard the conversation.'

I watched Tommy intently, picturing Julian on that call. I'd witnessed similar conversations a handful of times during our marriage. But that was just Julian's way – he was a hothead one minute, and the next, he went back to being the affable larrikin.

'But Julian would've only—' I started to protest, but Tommy cut me off.

'That's not all, Ally. There's more. A *lot* more.'

**13**

Thought of the day...
You can't control everything, but you can control who you
let in.
(And this means your heart, your door, *and* your knickers.)

Tommy's tone was deadly serious and his expression so intense that I was struck mute.

He returned to the sofa and sat, leaning forward and balancing his elbows on his knees. 'You trust me, right?'

Did I? Did I trust Tommy?

The answer that immediately came to mind was *yes*. He'd never given me any reason not to.

'Of course,' I replied in a half-whisper. 'Only...' I added – buying time for my mind to catch up. I searched my memories of Julian in similar situations. Had there ever been clues that he was involved in something he shouldn't have been? 'Are you sure it's not... I don't know, just normal business stuff?' I asked, clinging to hope. 'I've been on heated calls before and that was simply me standing my ground, refusing to be taken advantage of. Perhaps Julian was drawing a line in the sand.'

'It's more than that. Once I suspected that something was untoward, I've kept a sharp eye on things.'

'*And?*'

He paused, his lips disappearing between his teeth. 'There have been other instances – Julian leaving staff briefings to take urgent phone calls – that's happened several times now. And a few days ago, the helicopter arrived in the dead of night then left again a few minutes later. The next morning, Julian missed a meeting with me, Elsa, and Niki and no one saw him for hours. We think he was on that helicopter.'

'But there could be a reasonable explanation for that,' I said, ignoring the sick feeling in my stomach. 'Maybe you're misinterpreting things.'

'Well, it's not just me, Ally. And I have tried to give him the benefit of the doubt, but then two nights ago, he had the entire staff sign non-disclosure agreements.'

I frowned. 'Two nights ago? But you've been working here for *weeks*. That's...'

'*Odd*, right? And when I asked him about it afterwards, he was annoyed. He brushed me off with "standard procedure", which, of course, it isn't.'

So that explained the tension between them in the bar, but I was still clinging to the idea that there might be some logical explanation for all this.

'Look, I debated saying anything at all,' Tommy continued. 'I mean, you're only here for a few more days.'

'Two. It's supposed to be *two* more days.'

'Exactly.' He rolled his glass between his hands, then took a sip.

'So why bother telling me at all then? Why not let me sail

off into the sunset blindly unaware?' But before he could answer, it hit me. 'Oh god, you think something's about to implode, don't you? Is it *Aetheria*?' I asked, leaning in, my eyes fixed on his.

'I'm not completely sure, but if you endorse the resort and it all goes pear-shaped, then it could have an—'

'—adverse impact on Divorced Diva,' I said, talking over him.

'Yes.'

We were both quiet for a moment.

Tommy wouldn't exaggerate his concerns – I believed that – but there *was* the possibility he was wrong. Even he'd said he wasn't positive. But if he *was* right, then perhaps I should consider cancelling the partnership. Or at least postponing until I knew more.

This sort of thing had only happened once before, with a new fragrance line. Just after it launched, one of the founders was charged with using the fragrance company as a front for fraud. We pulled the Divorced Diva endorsement straight away, but the damage was done, and we lost a substantial number of followers – and several partners severed ties with us. I'd hate for that to happen again.

But what about Julian? If he was in trouble, I couldn't just abandon him. And there was Tommy and the other staff to consider...

'What are *you* going to do?' I asked.

'I'm going to keep an eye on things, and if it comes to it, I'll leave.'

'You mean you and Elsa, right?'

'Sorry? Oh, yes – Elsa too.'

'You know, when you said you had something important to tell me, I thought it was about her.'

He looked away, not replying.

'So, how long have you two been a couple?' I asked.

It wasn't courage asking the hardest question of all – it was masochism. Like stabbing myself in the thigh with a sharp pencil just to see if it hurt. It did.

'Ally.' Tommy sighed my name as if it pained him to utter it out loud. But that was enough – it told me everything I needed to know. The subject of Elsa was off limits. It must have been serious between them.

'Can I ask something else?'

His expression told me he thought it was about Elsa.

'No, not about *her*,' I said with a shake of my head.

'All right then.'

'Just... considering everything that's going on, there were times today when you seemed to be enjoying yourself – *genuinely.*'

'That's not a question,' he said evenly.

'Okay then, *how*? If you're so worried about Julian and Aetheria and *me*, then how can you pretend everything's right as rain?'

He stared at me. 'I wasn't pretending.'

'Then what?'

'I was momentarily distracted.'

Well, that wasn't the answer I was expecting.

'*Distracted?*' I scoffed. 'By what? A charming octogenarian and some fancy olive oil?'

'No, Ally, by you.'

I wasn't expecting *that* either.

'Sorry, I shouldn't have said tha—' He interrupted himself to expel a loud breath, then tossed back the rest of the brandy. And before I knew what was happening, he got up and strode towards the door.

'What are you doing?' I asked inanely. It was obvious he was leaving, but I didn't want him to – not before he explained what he'd meant. '*Tommy.*'

He hesitated in the entry, and I dashed off the sofa, stopping just short of where he stood with his back to me.

'What did you mean by that?' I pleaded hoarsely.

Tension rippled across his shoulders and his head dropped, but he didn't leave. I reached for him, lightly resting a hand on his broad back.

I'd never been the sort of woman to pursue a man who was in a relationship – that ethos was ingrained in me, a line I would never cross.

But this was Tommy. And if he was feeling even a fraction of what I was...

One day, I might hate myself for being complicit in his infidelity. But if I *didn't* press him for an answer, I'd hate myself anyway for the lifetime of *what ifs?* that would follow.

'Tommy?'

He spun around so abruptly, I took half a step back. He peered down at me, his eyes almost black in the dim light. They searched mine and I felt the pull of his gaze so intensely, I closed the gap between us without realising it.

'Fuck, Ally,' he said and a heartbeat later, he dipped his head, his mouth crashing against mine.

His hands landed on my waist and he pulled me closer, pressing my body against his. I stood on tiptoes and wrapped my arms tightly around his neck, my fingers entwining in his thick hair.

His kiss was hungry, as if he wanted to devour me, and every nerve ending in my body was alight with want. My tongue swirled inside his mouth, jockeying with his. He tasted of the Metaxa, like dried figs and honey and vanilla.

In a single movement, he hoisted me in the air – a move that was both familiar and thrilling – and I wrapped my legs around his waist as he carried me to the sofa. He lowered me onto it, bearing the weight of us both with one arm, our kiss still unbroken. His body hovered above mine for several aching seconds until I pulled him onto me, the weight of him almost too much, but also not enough. I wanted more. I wanted his bare skin against mine, I wanted his hand between my legs, I wanted his mouth on my nipples, I wanted him inside me.

But I'd also never been kissed like that before – not even by Tommy.

A delectable abyss of a kiss, igniting my insides, electrifying my skin, pulsing between my thighs. I'd never climaxed from just a kiss before – not without a helping hand (so to speak) – but I was close, and we were both still fully clothed. I ground my pelvis against his, feeling his ramrod erection through his jeans, every sensation, every tingle intensifying.

One of his hands slid beneath me, slipping under my tank top, his fingertips searing my skin as they dug into my flesh, clasping my body to his. My fingers still tangled in his hair, I tugged gently and he groaned into my mouth. That groan – that guttural Tommy groan that flipped my insides upside down. It was a tipping point, and I broke the kiss to throw my head back. Tommy peppered fervent kisses along my jawline, nestling just below my ear – my special spot, one he knew well. He kissed me there, his lips sending a jolt of pleasure to my centre.

'You're so close, baby,' he whispered, and shivers rippled over my skin.

I rocked my hips against him, pleasure building as he kissed and nibbled at my neck.

'Oh god, oh god, Tommy, I'm going to—'

The orgasm ripped through me, sweetly decimating me as

my body shook with its intensity. As it started to ebb away, I inhaled deeply and when my breathing steadied, my eyes flitted open to see Tommy looking down at me, his face the picture of wonder.

'Fuck, Ally,' he said again, his lips curling into a smile.

I laughed – not because it was funny, just something my body does at times from the release. He shifted lower to rest his cheek on my collarbone, his face turned away from me, then pulled his hand from under me, his fingertips trailing lazily along my thigh. I held him to me, playing with his hair.

I never wanted to let him go.

I closed my eyes again, content just to lie there with him, knowing that if I spoke, it would break the spell.

*Baby*, I mused. He'd called me *baby*. It could have been habit – it's what we called each other when we were together – but then again, that was years ago. Maybe he'd meant it, maybe this was a sign that he wanted us to start over.

I was about to suggest we move to the bedroom, take our time with each other, make love properly and let me pleasure him. But then he gulped – I felt it as well as heard it – and before I could stop it, he'd pushed himself up and climbed off me. He sat heavily on the end of the sofa, staring into space, and frowned.

I felt naked – *exposed* – even though I was fully clothed.

This meant something – it *had* to, given our history. And it changed everything between us – all the carefully constructed walls and polite discourse, all the self-preservation measures.

No wonder I felt exposed – I was. Stripped bare, emotionally speaking. Because I wanted him, not just to sleep with him, but *him*. I wanted Tommy. And now that I'd had a taste of what I'd missed – literally – I could never *un*-want him again.

But judging by Tommy's reaction, he didn't feel the same.

I stared at his profile until he finally looked at me. He smiled, but it was a sad smile.

'I—'

'Don't say you shouldn't have done that. I don't want to hear it,' I told him.

His lips parted as if he was about to protest, but he didn't say anything else. He just gave me that sad smile again, then stood and walked purposefully towards the door.

He opened it, then turned, lingering in the doorway for a moment. 'Goodnight, Ally. Think about what I said.'

Then he left.

The bastard.

*Think about what I said?*

*Which part, Tommy? The part where you told me that hubby number three might be caught up in some shady shit, or the part where you said,* Fuck, Ally, *then kissed me harder than you ever have before? Or what about calling me* baby? *Should I be thinking about that?*

'Gah!' I exclaimed to the empty room.

I sat up, planting my feet on the floor, then reached for the rest of my brandy. I downed it in two gulps, letting it burn my throat – an oddly satisfying penance for making out with my ex like a randy teen.

And one thing was for sure: I was not going anywhere. I might even *extend* my stay on Aetheria!

Because if Julian *was* caught up in something 'nefarious', as Tommy had called it, then he might need my help. It was unfathomable that he'd become an evil mastermind in the years since our divorce. More likely, he'd slipped up and the situation had escalated to the point of no return. I was not about to abandon him in his time of need.

How I raised my concerns was another matter, one I'd have

to navigate carefully. Julian was a proud man; he'd never liked asking for help. Or accepting it.

And then there was Tommy.

Whatever else was going on, I couldn't ignore what had happened between us. He might have regretted it, but it hadn't been one-sided – I was certain he'd felt it too. Which meant... *what* exactly?

I had to stay on Aetheria long enough to find out.

## 14

Thought of the day...
It's okay to disagree with your former self.
If something's not working, make a different decision.
(This is even truer if new shit comes to light.)

I slept *so* well that night. It surprised me all things considered, but when I woke up refreshed, raring to help Julian sort out his troubles, I didn't look the gift horse in the mouth.

I took my coffee out to the porch and sank into the cushioned rattan chair, sipping as I surveyed the incredible view. As I stared across at Naxos, I inhaled the herbaceous, briny air, boosting my already buoyant mood.

*It's divine here.*

I was scheduled to spend the afternoon in the resort's spa being pampered Aetherian style, something I was looking forward to. And that may seem like a no-brainer, but all spas are *not* created equal. I've endured a floatation tank with pink mould (disgusting), a pedicure that felt like sanctioned torture, and a facial that left me with an angry rash for five days.

That's why we spent weeks vetting partners for our nation-wide Spoil a Divorcee initiative – a program that gifts low-income, recently divorced women a day of pampering, fully funded by a very generous corporate sponsor. And no pink mould in sight.

But I had zero fears regarding Spa Aetheria – I was sure it would be the pinnacle of luxury. Everything else about the resort had been exceptional (if I ignored that it was haunted by two of my exes). And Julian intended for the spa to be one of the resort's biggest drawcards – he would have spared no expense.

Niki and Minh would be on hand to document the experience, but hopefully not the entire time. How many photos of a woman wearing a fluffy white robe would they need?

*Kee-kee-kee.*

I looked up to see a bird arcing across the sky – a falcon was my best guess. It seemed to be riding the air currents, turning, dipping, soaring. It was as good a metaphor as any for my situation. It was only my fourth day on Aetheria and there had been enough twists and turns to make my head spin.

And one extraordinary moment when my heart had soared. Last night with Tommy.

*Baby.*

It had been more than a make-out session – for me, anyway – and the word still rang inside my head. Only it wasn't taunting me, it was seeding hope – both electrifying and terrifying.

And I couldn't discuss it with Claude, because I'd lied.

There was also the matter of Elsa – that Tommy had cheated on her with me. I didn't want to be that woman. I didn't want him to be that man.

What on earth were we doing?

As these insistent thoughts intruded, pummelling my upbeat mood, I looked across the water again. Calm washed over me, hard-won wisdom edging out confusion.

When emotions and thoughts have twisted themselves into knots, the best way forward was to forge a plan – focus on what was within my control.

I had the entire morning to myself, which gave me ample time to seek out Julian and start delving into his mess. So that's what I would do. I drained my coffee, then went to get ready for the day.

I'd intended to skip breakfast and head straight to Julian's office, but as I neared the restaurant, the aromas lured me in. Freshly baked pastries have that power.

'Ally!' exclaimed Trudy, sat at her favourite table alone.

I headed over.

'Sit, sit,' she said, gesturing to the chair opposite her. 'You can keep me company.'

'Where's Dale?' I asked.

She waved her hand dismissively. 'Oh, Dale's with Julian, up at his villa.'

*No need to rush through breakfast then.*

I knew that Julian had accommodation on Aetheria, but this made it sound like he *lived* there. And what were he and Dale doing first thing in the morning – having some sort of meeting? Was Dale involved in this mysterious business of Julian's?

'It's nice that Julian has a friend here, that he gets to spend time with Dale,' I ventured, fishing for information.

An odd look flickered across Trudy's face, vanishing almost instantly, telling me I might be onto something.

'Trudy?' I said, pretending I was playing (I wasn't – clearly, something was up). 'Have you got a secret?'

'Not really,' she said lightly. 'Nothing as big as *yours*.'

I didn't catch on right away, but then I realised she meant Tommy.

'Oh well, yes… but that was years ago now.'

'Yes, but weren't you surprised? Seeing him here?' she asked, clearly unwilling to drop the subject.

'Oh, you have no idea! A total coincidence.'

'You know,' she said, her brows lifted, 'sometimes the fates conspire…'

'Conspire?'

'To bring people together.'

I'd have entertained that notion if I believed for one *second* that external forces were actively steering my life. No, this was blind luck – a fluke – and nothing more.

I gave Trudy the sort of smile that belied my scepticism and she seemed satisfied that she'd made her point.

'*Kalimera*.' Christos was standing by the table, ready to take my order but I'd been too distracted to even peek at the menu.

I eyed Trudy's plate. 'What are those?' I asked, pointing at half-eaten pastry.

'*Bougatsa*,' she replied. '*So* good – I might ask for another.'

'I'll have *bougatsa*, please,' I said to Christos. 'Sorry, I mean, *parakalo*.' He gave me a quick friendly smile, then headed back to the kitchen. 'And coffee, *parakalo*,' I called after him.

He sent a smile over his shoulder, letting me know he'd heard me.

I had to admire how laidback he was. I got the sense that if I'd wanted to act on our obvious attraction, there would have been zero strings attached.

With Tommy, there were so many strings, I could open a shop. Want to be tethered to your past? Need a new set of heartstrings? Like playing cat's cradle with your emotions? Then come on down to Ally's String Emporium!

I sniggered to myself, stopping abruptly when I caught Trudy peering at me curiously.

'Thinking about Tom?' she asked, a telling glint in her eye. It was clear that Trudy was invested in a romantic reunion. I mean, I was too – but I wasn't up for discussing it.

'Erm... just something my sister told me last night,' I lied, and I could tell she didn't believe me. I looked away, pretending to be mesmerised by the view.

Thankfully, Christos soon returned with my order, sparing me from fabricating more nonsense.

'Thank you – *efharistó*.'

*Geez, Ally.* I'd been in Greece several days and I was still forgetting to say *please* and *thank you* in Greek. And it's just basic manners when you're travelling – please, thank you, hello, goodbye. At the bare minimum. I'd have to remember for next time.

'So, what are you up to today?' I asked, redirecting the conversation.

'I was about to ask you the same thing. I'm on my own today.'

Dale's absence, not only at breakfast but for the rest of the day, was hardly a smoking gun. Then again, he and Julian *had* worked together in Ottawa, and they were both in tech – maybe he *was* caught up in this questionable business deal.

And poor Trudy – she probably thought she was in for a luxurious holiday with her adoring husband. Now she was spending the day alone.

'Well, I'm booked into the spa this afternoon. They could probably fit you in,' I suggested.

'Ooh, a spa day! What treatments are you having?'

'Essentially one of everything – well, all their signature treatments. There'll be an entire PR campaign just on the spa. Julian says it's world-class.'

'Do you think they *could* fit me in? Even just for a manicure,' she said, her eyes dropping to her nails.

'How about I check with Niki, then let you know?'

Trudy perked up at that, beaming at me. 'Perfect.' After a moment, her smile softened. 'You know, Ally, I didn't expect to make a friend on this trip but— Oh, sorry, that was presumptuous of me.' She shook her head at herself dismissively.

'No, no, not at all. I feel the same way. And it's very much welcomed, Trudy. I don't have that many friends,' I added wryly, careful not to sound woeful.

'*Really?* But I would have thought with your— Oops, confession time: I looked you up. Ally, you're *famous*. You're the Divorced Diva!'

'I am. And you're right, I do know a lot of people. But most of them are just that – people I know, rather than close friends.'

'Well, that makes it all the more special that we met then,' she said, reaching over to pat the back of my hand.

I returned her warm smile, and for a second, I considered sharing my predicament with her. But just as quickly, I dismissed the idea. Despite our rapport, it would be unfair to burden Trudy with my worries and woes. It was too much to lay on someone I'd only just met, *and* she knew Julian.

I was about to take a sip of coffee when Trudy said, 'I've been meaning to ask... what's your connection to Julian then? How do you two know each other?'

Ignoring the ironic timing, I set down the cup and regarded her closely. It was obvious she wasn't just fishing for a juicy morsel of gossip – she seemed genuinely curious.

She watched me, her eyes wide, as she waited for an

answer. I could have lied to her again, but what if Julian let it slip that we'd been married? He'd pronounced it proudly when he introduced me to Tommy. He might not think anything of it. There was also the possibility that Trudy would stumble upon it herself. She'd looked me up – she might dig deeper. She would only have to go back to my social media posts from a few years ago and she'd have a front-row seat at *The Julian and Ally Show*.

Besides, we'd only just talked about becoming friends – I didn't *want* to lie to her.

'Well, Trudy, I was also married to Julian.'

Trudy stared at me for a beat, then threw her head back and burst out laughing. 'Oh, Ally, you're too much!' She fanned her face, gasping for air as her laughter intensified.

Well, I'd tried. If she raised it again, I'd set her straight but right then, I had more to worry about than convincing Trudy I was telling the truth.

\* \* \*

After breakfast, I found Niki in her office and asked about Trudy joining me at the spa. She assured me it was no trouble and that she'd get in touch with Trudy herself. That sorted, I went in search of Julian, thinking he might be in his office by now.

I knocked on his door and it swung open. Elsa was standing behind the desk, rifling through a stack of papers.

Her head jerked up, her eyes flaring with annoyance. 'Is there something I can help you with?' Her tone made it sound as if *I* was the one intruding – as if it were perfectly normal for her to be going through Julian's desk.

'I'm looking for Julian,' I said, keeping my voice even.

She stared at me like I was an idiot. He clearly wasn't there – but why was *she*? And what was she doing?

'He's up at his villa,' she said eventually.

'What's that?' I nodded towards the paper in her hand. I had no real authority to challenge her – unless having been married to her boss and her boyfriend counted, which it probably didn't – but she was obviously up to no good. I had to say something.

'He asked me to check some delivery manifests,' she replied smoothly, holding my gaze. The explanation sounded plausible. *Too* plausible.

'Right,' I said, 'thanks.' I backed out of the office, pausing at the doorway, unsure whether to close the door behind me. In the end, I left it open – just a crack – and headed back to Niki's office.

'Hiya, me again,' I said, feigning cheeriness.

'What's up?'

'Just wondering where Julian's villa is? He's not in his office so...'

'Oh, uh...' She suddenly looked stricken, as if I'd asked for the password to his bank account or something – also odd. 'Is he expecting you? Did you have a meeting or something?'

Niki was gatekeeping. What the hell was going on?

'Not exactly. But Julian won't mind if I show up unannounced, I promise.'

She still seemed unconvinced, licking her lips before trapping them between her teeth.

'How about this? You give me directions, and if he *does* mind, I'll tell him I found it on my own.'

She sighed. 'Yeah, okay.'

I got the directions, but I couldn't ignore how guarded Niki had been. I hadn't known her long, but it seemed out of character. Maybe Tommy wasn't the only staff member who suspected something untoward was going on.

Well, it was time to find out.

As I walked uphill along meandering paths, I contemplated the best approach with Julian. If I came right out and asked if everything was all right, he'd likely fob me off with vague reassurances. No, I'd have to be more strategic.

Then it came to me.

I'd tell him *I* was embroiled in a professional arrangement that had sprouted more red flags than summer has dandelions. Then I'd ask for his guidance about how to disentangle myself.

Fingers crossed that Julian would see the parallels to his situation – whatever it was – and seek *my* counsel. Then I could help him. Or at least convince him to seek help elsewhere. Perfect.

At the top of the hill, I passed a sign that read *Private Property*, then Julian's villa came into view. I stopped to gawp at its magnificence, then climbed the front steps and knocked on the wooden door, a twin to my villa's.

'Come in,' Julian called out, his voice muffled by the door.

I pushed it open, peeking around it. Good god, Julian's villa was palatial!

'Ally!' he exclaimed, leaping off a sofa the size of a bus. 'Good morning!'

He broke into a sort-of jog across the expanse of the lounge room, joining me in the entry. Clearly delighted to see me – the grin and the twinkle in his eyes gave him away – he grabbed me by both shoulders and planted a fat kiss on my cheek. I searched his face for any hint of strain, a shadow of worry, but there was nothing. If Julian was on the brink of disaster, he was hiding it well.

I looked about for Dale, but he must have already left.

'Come in, come in,' said Julian, turning away from me and beelining for the kitchen. 'I was just about to make coffee – would you like one? And there are pastries from the restaurant,' he added before I had a chance to reply.

I wandered over, pulled out a stool at the breakfast bar, and climbed onto it. Not an easy feat for someone of my stature, and Julian tossed me an amused look as I slid my arse onto the seat. I studied him further for signs of stress, but he seemed genuinely relaxed.

I eyed the plate on the counter, piled high with pastries. After Trudy had erupted into laughter, incredulous that I'd been married to both Tommy and Julian, I'd abandoned my breakfast. So, now I was *very* hungry.

'Yes, please – to coffee and a *bougatsa*.'

His eyebrows leapt.

'Did I say that right?'

'You did.'

He pushed them closer. Was I just supposed to help myself or was a fork and a plate forthcoming?

*Oh, sod it*, I thought, picking up a pastry and taking a huge bite. Did flaky pastry break off into tiny bits and fall all over the counter and down my front? Absolutely. Did I care one iota? I did not.

I munched happily, taking bite after bite, my cheeks bulging like a chipmunk's.

'Jules, this place,' I said when I'd devoured the pastry, 'it's *gorgeous*. And *huge*.' At a guess, it was four times the size of the villa I was staying in. 'Is it just the one bedroom?' I asked, peering down the hallway that led off the lounge.

'The primary plus two more,' he replied.

I turned back to him. 'Why do you need *two* guest rooms

when you have all of Aetheria? Surely, if friends come with you on holiday, they can stay in a villa?'

He eyed me over the espresso machine, and realisation struck.

'Oh my god, Jules, you *are* planning on living here.'

'I was going to tell you.'

'Were you now?' I asked, surprised by the sting of hurt.

'Was trying to find the right time.'

'Now will do.'

'I'm retiring and moving to Greece. Well – I am retired, and I've already moved here.'

I nodded, giving him a weak smile. 'It's a long way to travel for lunch, Jules.'

'I'll be back in London from time to time. I wouldn't miss our lunches, Ally.'

The pain eased, but only a little. Bi-monthly catch-ups aside, it had been reassuring knowing Julian was nearby if I needed him. There was nothing nearby about living a day's travel away.

He pressed the button on the machine and it gurgled, the aroma of coffee filling the air.

'You know what this reminds me of, us having breakfast together like this?' he asked over the gentle hiss of the milk steamer.

'Uh-uh,' I replied, playing along – I could process his news later.

He turned a dial, and the hissing ceased. 'Paris.'

I gasped, then broke into a broad smile. 'That little flat in the sixth.'

'Yep. Four storeys up—'

'No lift but—'

'A sodding good espresso machine.'

'So good!' I exclaimed, bursting out laughing. 'We didn't even go downstairs to the local café!'

Julian's smile softened, a little wistful. 'We barely left the flat at all, if I recall. That bed was *huge*, remember?'

'Jules,' I chided with a shake of my head. I bit into a second pastry, wiping the corner of my mouth as I chewed.

Careful not to slosh it, Julian slid a coffee cup across the countertop, then lifted his in a toast. 'To Paris,' he said.

There was an undercurrent of melancholy behind his eyes, echoes of what had fractured between us. But his toast, a reminder of happier times, cut through the sorrow and I was overcome with affection for him – for my Jules, the man I'd once fallen for.

'To Paris.'

We'd finished our coffees and Julian was tidying up when I broached the real reason I was there.

'Uh, Jules?'

He shut the dishwasher and lifted his head. 'Yes?'

'I need your help... It seems I might be in a bit of a pickle.'

'Oh? Well, tell me. You know I'd do anything for you.'

## 15

Leaving Julian's, my mind was abuzz – and it wasn't the sugar rush from the *bougatsa*. I'd planted the seed. Now I just needed to wait.

And telling him I was in a pickle hadn't been a complete lie – I'd just left out the part where the pickle was Aetheria. Which, as it turned out, was the right move. Because Julian's advice? Cut ties with this dubious partner.

Meaning, I should walk away from Aetheria. *And* Julian.

Exactly as Tommy had said.

I was rounding a bend in the path, chewing on my dilemma, when a hand darted out, grabbing my wrist and tugging me into the bushes.

'Will you *please* stop doing that?' I hissed.

'I thought you were leaving the island,' Tommy retorted.

'Well, that was a bold assumption. I never said that. In fact, I'm extending my stay.' I glowered at him so he'd understand just how serious I was.

'Extending your st—' He stopped himself, muttering under his breath.

'You don't get to be frustrated with me. I didn't ask to be brought here – and I certainly wouldn't have come if I'd known *you'd* be here.'

From his wounded expression, the jibe had hit its mark. *Good – after his disappearing act last night, he deserves to feel a little sting.*

Looking back, that barb was me re-buckling my armour – but in the moment it felt satisfying.

'Just— just be careful.'

'*You* be careful. All this sneaking about.' I flapped my hand to demonstrate. 'Someone's bound to see you and start asking questions.'

'Oh, you don't need to worry about me,' he growled.

How was I supposed to respond to that? I mean, in a way he was right. It had been years since Tommy was any of my concern.

We stared at each other for several beats, then he broke eye contact and backed away. Like Homer Simpson disappearing into the hedge. Only hot.

I turned in the other direction, swatting at branches to get back to the path. 'Apparently, I should have packed a machete for my Greek Island getaway!' I muttered to myself.

I hid behind a branch that was bursting with pink flowers and peeked out in both directions. No one coming, so I stepped out from the bushes as if it was a perfectly normal thing to do, then headed off towards the spa.

My appointment wasn't for half an hour, but I'd happily wait – especially if I could change into a robe, put my feet up, and sip some herbal tea.

As I neared the spa, still partially in a tizz, the air grew redolent of lemon and thyme.

Some places, like Paris or Prague, have a soundtrack – melodies and sounds that follow you, marking your journey through the city. A choir practising in the cathedral, birdsong in the park, the thrum of traffic, a busker strumming a guitar.

The Greek Islands had a *scent*-track. I couldn't remember ever being so aware of how good the air smelled – whether the aromas from a kitchen, the briny sea air, the island's flora, or in this case, native botanicals.

When I pushed open the door to the spa, the scent intensified and I inhaled deeply.

The woman on reception – twenty-something, with long dark hair and a heart-shaped, perfectly made-up face – looked up as I entered, breaking into a welcoming smile.

'Good morning, Ms Novak.' Impressive considering I hadn't met her yet. 'I'm Eleni. I'll be looking after you today.'

'I'm very early,' I apologised, my English manners taking over. 'I can come back if you like.' So much for lounging in a robe and sipping herbal tea until my appointment.

'No need. You're my sole client today, so we can get started right away.'

'Oh, lovely. Wait, sorry… it's just, my friend. She'd hoped you could fit her in but—'

'Mrs Bennet? Yes, Niki called earlier. My friend Sofia is coming now. She will attend to Mrs Bennet.'

'Brilliant,' I said with a small sigh. I didn't want Trudy to miss out.

'This way, please,' Eleni said, leading me into a beautifully appointed treatment room, decorated in soft tones of cream and sage green. Across from us, next to a large picture window with a similar view to the one from my villa, was an enormous standalone bathtub.

Eleni must has caught me gawping. 'I can run the bath for you, if you like. It only takes a few minutes to fill. *Or...*' she began enticingly, her brows lifted. She stepped around me and opened a glass-and-wood door. 'There's an outside shower.' I followed her to the door and peered out. The shower was enclosed on three sides, exposed only to the view.

I turned to Eleni. 'Could I have a shower before my treatments and a bath afterwards?' I asked cheekily.

'Of course, Ms Novak.' She went to the door. 'Please take your time. There is a robe for you here,' she said, indicating the fluffiest robe I'd ever seen, 'and when you're ready, please press this button and I will return.' She bowed her head and backed out of the room, silently closing the door behind her.

'Jesus, Jules,' I whispered. It was already the most luxurious spa I'd ever been to. If Aetheria didn't come undone before it even got going, he'd make a *killing*.

I slipped out of my dress and knickers, draping them over the valet stand – a classy touch – and stepped outside to shower. I lathered myself from top to toe, then rinsed under the steamy stream, letting it wash away the morning's madness.

And just as I turned off the tap, I heard that cry again. *Kee-kee-kee*. I looked up and there she was, effortlessly riding the pockets of air.

'Hello there,' I said, watching the falcon until she flew out of sight.

* * *

'Oh, my goodness, Dale is going to have a hard time getting me back to Ottawa.'

I sniggered softly, unable to move my face, which was encrusted in a clay mask. How Trudy was able to talk through her mask was baffling.

Nearby, Minh hovered discreetly, taking photos. He'd been in and out of the treatment room all afternoon, only staying long enough to get the shot, then retreating to the waiting room. He must have been bored off his trolley.

'Oh, yes, right there,' groaned Trudy.

I cracked an eyelid. Thank god – it was just a foot massage. For a second there, I thought maybe the 'full package' came with a more... *specialised* service. Still, she wasn't wrong – it was divine. Not even Tommy, whose foot rubs were bliss after a long day in sky-high heels, could hold a candle to Eleni. She had magic hands. And from the sound of things, so did Sofia.

*Is Julian bedding one of them?* I wondered. *Or both?* I wouldn't have put it past him. He was only forty-nine and Julian had the sort of sex appeal that *could* land a twenty-something stunner. *And* her bestie. Possibly at the same time.

That had been a bone of contention when we were married. For some reason, Julian figured that having a 'young, hot, sexy wife' (his words) meant he'd be the C in a two-Vs-one-C three-some every other weekend.

When I'd calmly explained that I'd had a threesome at uni – same configuration – and that it had been grossly unsatis-fying *and* had led to the end of my friendship with the other V, he'd replied, 'So bloody what?'

I'd gone into my wardrobe and come out wearing a long, red, curly wig, and in my best Scottish accent (still terrible to this day) said, 'No need for a threesome when you've got this sexy lassie in the house.'

He'd laughed long and loud, then fucked me within an inch of my life on the sofa in the front room, the curtains open several inches to up the thrill factor.

We added 'Roleplay Sundays' to our calendar and sometimes it was *Julian* who wore a wig.

I cracked a smile at the memory, which of course cracked the mask. 'Only five more minutes, Ms Novak,' said Eleni.

I cleared my throat. 'Thank you,' I said through barely parted lips.

And yes, all right, I was a little turned on. Too bad I hadn't known about the spa's epic bathtub ahead of time – I would have brought a toy with me. *Next time.*

*If there* is *a next time*, I thought, my mind revisiting Julian's unknown dilemma.

\* \* \*

I *do* work hard – most days, most of every day – and it can take a lot out of me, always being *on*, always being *the Diva*. But as Tommy said, it's hardly a grind.

And there are certainly perks – like spending the afternoon at the super-lush Spa Aetheria. After being slathered, lathered, scrubbed, and rubbed over (nearly) every inch of my body (*definitely* not the sort of spa that specialises in happy endings), I floated back to my villa on a cloud.

I stretched out on the sofa, trying to decide what to do next. I was supposed to leave Aetheria tomorrow, but so much felt unfinished. Julian's circumstances – was he really in trouble? And what about the partnership between Divorced Diva and Aetheria? Maybe Tommy was barking up the wrong tree. It's not like this was his area of expertise; he was a structural engineer turned boat skipper.

And then there was Tommy – a walking question mark.

How could I leave without discussing what had happened between us? Besides, I'd already told him I was extending my stay.

I *really* didn't want to make a dent in my blissful state – I could easily have fallen asleep on that dreamy sofa – but there was too much that required my attention. No rest for the Diva. *Literally.*

I swung my legs over the edge of the sofa and sat up, mentally sorting the tasks I needed to tick off before dinner.

First, tell Claude I was staying on Aetheria for a couple more days. Then put the PR campaign on ice – just until I was sure it wouldn't blow up in our faces. Claude could handle that, but how was I supposed to ask without spilling the entire pot of tea?

'Figure it out as you go, Ally.' I took my phone off charge and called her.

'How was the spa day?' she asked without preamble. 'And spare no detail – I'm living vicariously.'

I laughed. 'Claude, how many times have I told you – just book in at Elysium!'

I understood Claude's desire to live a frugal life – well, sort of, but not really – but we *were* partnered with one of the best spas in London. She could go anytime for free!

She laughed at herself – unusual for her.

'You're in good spirits,' I said. 'Especially for a Monday.'

'I know, right? It might be the weather – it's *twenty* today *and* the sun is shining. I actually took my sandwich to the park instead of eating at my desk.'

'Wow. Big day!'

She chuckled again.

'And to answer your question, the spa's incredible. They have an outdoor shower overlooking the sea – like something out of a shampoo ad – and the most *delicious* treatments. Oh, and the *facial*! My skin has never looked this good without makeup.'

'You're doing a very good job of selling me on Aetheria,' she admitted.

'I am? That's wonderful.'

Only it wasn't wonderful – our partnership might be dead in the water. Which brought me back to why I'd called.

'Al?'

I'd done it again – I was in my head and not the conversation.

'Hi, sorry...' *Out with it, Ally.* 'Er, look, I've decided to stay two or three more days.'

'Oh?'

Did I worry Claude with the truth or add to the half-truths (and outright lies) I'd already told her?

'Just some matters to work out with Julian – about the partnership,' I said vaguely.

'Wait, shouldn't I be involved in those discussions?' she asked, suddenly serious.

Bugger – she was right. Any discussions about the terms of the partnership *would* involve Claude. *Gah!* Going into this conversation without a plan was stupid. I needed to be upfront.

'Actually, there's more...'

I explained, attributing Tommy's suspicions about Julian to me.

'God, Ally, that's—' I could picture her exact expression, her brows knitted as she worried her lower lip between her teeth. 'Should I come? Do you want me to come?'

'You mean now?' I blurted. 'Er, no... I can handle things here. Just... I think we should delay the launch of the PR campaign.'

'Top of my list,' she replied, all business. 'I'll set up a meeting with Maya and Niki for tomorrow morning.'

'What will you tell Niki?' I asked.

'Potential conflict of interest – with Elysium.'

'Oh, I hadn't thought of that. *Is* it?'

'No, you're allowed to endorse other spas if they're outside of London. I checked that before we signed the agreement with Julian.'

God, I loved my sister – whip-smart and exactly who I needed in my corner.

'Thank you, Claude – *really.*'

'It's my job, Ally,' she replied simply.

'And you're brilliant at it.' Would she take the compliment or fob it off like usual?

'Thanks.' It may not seem like it, but acknowledging her own brilliance was a leap forward for Claude.

She said Ruby would check with me about travel plans, then we chatted a bit longer, mostly about Mum's ongoing fixation with *The Traitors*. Last night, poor Claude had endured a blow-by-blow recap that was longer than the episode.

After we hung up, I was typing a message to Julian about having dinner when a knock sounded at my door.

It was too early for turndown service. That left two possibilities – and I'd been married to both of them. Maybe it was Julian, coming to me for help. I got up from the sofa and went to the door.

Not Julian – Tommy.

'Why, hello, Tom.'

'I need to talk to you.'

'Again? Something you forgot to mention when you dragged me into the bushes?' I teased.

'I didn't forget; it's new information.'

'Okay. Well, come on in.'

I stepped aside, sweeping my arm theatrically, as if I were ready for what he had to say. Spoiler: I wasn't.

# 16

Thought of the day...
Do not allow anger to fester – find a healthy outlet to
express it.
(Shouting at the TV – okay. Hitting a punching bag at the
gym – okay. Road rage – very much not okay.)

Tommy prowled around the lounge room like Rum Tum Tugger, turning pacing into an art form. 'Are you going to sit down?' he asked, shooting a questioning look over his shoulder.

'I'd rather stay over here,' I replied.

If I kept fifteen feet away, I wouldn't risk accidentally falling onto his cock.

He stopped pacing. '*Ally.*'

'What's this new information?' I asked, steering the conversation away from seating arrangements.

'I really think you should leave. *Tonight*, if possible.'

'Hmm. Technically, that's not information – in fact, it

sounds like a directive and last time I checked, you weren't in charge of me.'

'Fair, but—'

'Just *tell* me, Tommy.'

'I know who's been on the other end of those conversations – Julian's business partner. He's someone important – *very* – and he's coming here.'

'Ooh, should I phone the *Daily Enquirer*?' I quipped.

Humour was just a protection mechanism. As long as we were bantering, I could avoid feeling, well... *feelings*.

'You're not taking this seriously.'

'In case you missed it, Tommy, this is a *resort*. The concept doesn't really work unless people come. And most of the clientele will be VIPs. Exhibit A,' I said, pointing at myself with both forefingers.

'This is different. This person has... questionable motives – *and* ties.'

'I'm assuming you don't mean cravats.'

'Do you think you could come and sit down?' he asked impatiently.

*So, not in the mood for banter, then.*

'All right.' I crossed to the nearest sofa and plopped onto it. 'Now you sit over there,' I said, indicating the other one.

He sat opposite and looked at me intently, his elbows resting on his knees and fingers steepled. Ironically, we were in the same spots we were last night. Right before the heavy petting.

'Just tell me. And skip the cryptic clues, will you – this isn't a crossword.'

'Do you know who Ivan Kovalec is?' he asked.

'Isn't that the tech billionaire, the one from Eastern Europe?'

'Yes.'

'Ivan Kovalec is coming here?'

'It seems so.'

I'd been joking when I made the comment about the *Daily Enquirer*, but they probably *would've* wanted the scoop that Kovalec was coming to Aetheria.

'Hold on, how do *you* know all this?'

'Elsa.'

*Ah, that's why she was in Julian's office – she was snooping.*

'Is snooping something you enjoy doing together? Because most couples choose something a little less *espionage-y*. You know, like playing pickleball – which is a *ridiculous* name, by the way – *or* taking a cooking class.'

Tommy flinched at the cooking-class comment as if I'd said it to wound him. I hadn't; it had just slipped out.

'Can we please get back to you leaving Aetheria?' he asked, his tone softening.

'I'm not going – well, obviously I will eventually, I'm not moving here or anything. But not today. Or tomorrow. I'm worried that Julian needs me.'

He sat back, crossing one ankle over the opposite knee, his foot jiggling like it had a mind of its own.

'What aren't you telling?'

His eyes darted away.

'Jesus, Tommy!' I snapped. 'You're deliberately being evasive *while* trying to convince me to leave the island. You do realise you're terrible at this, right?'

I was about to kick him out – this was getting futile – but seconds later, he dropped the evasive act.

'Go on, ask me anything.'

I blinked at him. *Ask me anything.*

The thing about parameters is that they make it easier to

pinpoint what you want. Take them away, and choice paralysis sets in – like it did when I was offered carte blanche access to Tommy's thoughts and feelings. *And* his relationship with Elsa. Where did I even begin?

I searched his eyes. He met my gaze, but his expression gave nothing away. And had he really meant *anything*, or just the situation with Julian?

*Fuck it.*

'When did you and Elsa meet?'

His eyes widened – I'd surprised him. 'Er...' His gaze slid to the left as he did the maths. 'Just over a year ago now.'

'Where?'

'At work.'

*Yep, like pulling teeth.*

'Engineering work or skipper work?'

He hesitated. 'It was before this,' he replied vaguely.

'So, she's an engineer too?' I prodded.

'No, a communications specialist.'

'Hah!' My cynical laugh escaped before I could stop it, echoing through the villa. The idea of that scowling, monosyllabic woman working in communications was *hilarious*. But Tommy clearly didn't share my amusement. 'I'm sorry.' I wasn't. 'So,' I went on, 'why the left turn – the change of careers? Was it the Sicily job?'

'Sicily?'

'Where you learned to sail?' I prompted, sensing something wasn't quite right.

'Oh, right, yes exactly,' he replied.

'*So?* Tell me about it.'

As soon as I prodded him, it was like a switch had flicked, and the tension eased from his face.

'I was part of a retrofit for the Roman amphitheatre in Catania, and a colleague had a sailboat at the marina. It was a summer-long project, and on weekends he taught me to sail. When it ended, I was on my way to Singapore and had a sort-of epiphany.'

'An epiphany?' It wasn't a word I'd heard Tommy use before.

'That I'd spent the better part of ten years living and working abroad, but knew next to nothing about the places I'd been to. Sicily was the first time that life was more than just work, sleep, and repeat. I owe a lot to my colleague – Mario. Sicilian, about fifty, knows everyone... Probably more people than you,' he teased with a smirk. 'His wife was lovely – Francesca – and they had five kids.'

He grimaced dramatically, and I sniggered. When we were married, we'd talked about having one child, maybe two – but never *five*.

'They'd host these incredible lunches – half the town would show up...' He reminisced fondly, his gaze unfocused. 'And it was lively and vibrant and oh god, Ally, the *food*. Francesca is the most *amazing* cook.'

'I won't tell *Yiayiá* you said that.'

'Huh?' he asked, his focus jumping back to me. 'Oh right, *Yiayiá*. Please don't. Older European women can be quite terrifying.'

'Is that right?' I asked, amused.

Admittedly, the conversation had got away from me. I'd intended to pin Tommy down and ask the hard-hitting questions but in a matter of minutes, we'd circled back to *Yiayiá* and the cooking class and *us*. An in-joke that was barely one day old.

'A story for another time,' he said lightly.

*Another time*... Didn't he realise that alluding to the future – a *shared* future – was cruel?

'Look, all these questions... Can we please get back to Julian?' he asked.

'Yeah, yeah – course,' I replied, even though my insides were coiled tighter than a spring. 'So, to recap: your girlfriend, who is a communication specialist' – *my fucking arse, she is* – 'has discovered that one of the most famous people in tech is coming here, and *somehow* this implicates Julian in some sort of nefarious – *your* word – scheme. Which will inevitably and irrevocably destroy Aetheria as we know it. Have I got that right?'

'*Ally*,' he warned.

'No,' I said, pointing a finger at him, now cross. 'You do not get to *Ally* me. Because then I get to *Tommy* you and if you think older European women are scary, you should see just how terrifying *I've* become.'

I don't use my lower vocal register very often, but when I do, I mean business. Only Tommy started sniggering softly, which should have fuelled my fury but, instead, disarmed it.

'How do you do that?' I asked, regarding him through slitted eyes.

'I know you, Ally.'

*Oof. Why don't you just pommel me with a tin of kippers? Far less painful.*

I cleared my throat, acknowledging that Tommy was probably right – we should focus on the situation with Julian and keep well away from the topic of *us*.

Only...

'Just one more question and then we can get back to Julian.'

He remained perfectly still, fixing me with his penetrating gaze while he weighed up my request. I figured he probably knew what I was going to ask. If he did, I half expected him to say *no*. But then again, he had said to ask him anything.

After several excruciating moments of unbroken eye contact, he said, 'Ask away.'

Immediately, he dropped his eyes and his lips straightened into a line – girding his emotional loins was my best guess.

I inhaled deeply. *Here goes everything.*

'What did it mean, what happened here last night?'

He nodded, confirming that he'd expected the question.

'I don't know.'

It was a non-answer, but I wasn't particularly surprised. I didn't know either.

'Ah, fuck— that's... total bullshit. I do know.' He looked up and we locked eyes. 'I've found it very difficult being around you for the past few days.'

'It hasn't seemed like it,' I interjected.

'Well, I must be good at hiding it then, because it has. It's *confusing* – this. I have no idea what's going on in here...' He tapped his head with two fingers. '*Or* here...' His fingers went to his heart. '*He* seems to have a lot to do with it,' Tommy added, glancing at his crotch.

'So, it was just attraction then?' I ventured.

'Haven't you been listening? And it's never just attraction with you, Ally,' he replied in a hoarse whisper.

'Then what? What is it?'

He pressed his lips together, as if afraid of what might escape, and my coiled insides wound even tighter. 'It's the best and worst thing that has ever happened to me.'

My mouth filled with saliva, and I gulped it down. Oh god, was I about to be sick?

'That sounds cruel, I know,' he continued, 'but it's the truth. And you being here—'

'Did you know? That I was coming?'

'There was talk about an influencer after the actress fell

through. But I didn't put two and two together until you arrived.'

'Did you know I was once married to Julian? Before he told you, I mean.'

Tommy nodded.

'You *knew*? Then why would you accept a job with him? No, why *apply* for the job in the first place?'

'Because— It doesn't matter.'

'It matters to me! There must be a thousand resorts you could work at. But knowing about me and Julian, you came to Aetheria. That's messed up, Tommy. You had to realise there was a chance we'd cross paths eventually.'

He nodded, seeming to accept that my rebuke was justified.

And all that talk before, about the wrath of Ally... Now I truly had something to be furious about, and I could barely muster even a morsel of rage. It's hard to when you're so consumed by hurt.

'You need to leave,' I said, my voice strangled.

'Ally.'

'*No*.'

He came around the coffee table and knelt before me, but I kept my gaze on my lap, refusing to look at him.

'Ally, *please*.' He reached out, capturing my hands in his and it was a thousand sensations at once. 'I'm sorry I said that.'

'Shouldn't you get back to Elsa?' I asked wanly, the fight having ebbed away. I really just wanted him to leave so I could lick my wounds. Again.

'It's not what you think.'

'What do you mean?' I asked, my head snapping up. 'What's not?'

He heaved out a sigh, then dropped my hands and sat back on his heels. 'Elsa and me, we're n—'

My ringtone cut him off and we both looked at my phone, which was face up on the table. It was Claude – only I'd just spoken to her. It must have been something important.

'I need to get that,' I said, reaching past Tommy. 'Hi, what's going on?'

'Have you seen the Divorced Diva Insta account?'

'Not since this morning. Why?' I took the phone away from my ear and put it on speaker, then navigated to Instagram.

'Check the *tagged* tab,' she said wearily. 'It's not good, Al.'

For the typically stoic Queen of the Understatement Claudia to say that, it must have been bad. *Very* bad, and my hand started shaking so severely, I had to tap the screen three times before I got to the post she was talking about. Even then, I couldn't believe what I was seeing.

'Did you find it?' asked Claude.

'Oh my god.'

It was a photo of me and Julian at the restaurant on Friday night, looking very much like a couple in love – he was holding my hand and peering at me adoringly. The photographer – whoever they were – had captured the exact moment before I'd told Julian *no*, so it seemed like I was just as enamoured with Julian as he was with me.

The caption read:

It seems like @TheDivorcedDiva may not be divorced for much longer. Seen this past weekend looking very cosy with her third husband Julian Cushing on his exclusive Greek Island resort. #SecondChanceLove #Reunited #LoveFinds-AWay #AllyAndJulian4Eva

'Yep. Maya got the alert about the account being tagged and called me as soon as she saw.'

I looked at the time stamp. The post had only been up for twenty minutes, and it already had more than two thousand likes. I scrolled the comments, speed-reading to get the gist – everything from incredulity to very, very pissed off. I tapped on the account that had posted it – zero followers and an avatar instead of a profile pic. Suspicious.

'Maya is on it,' said Claude. 'She's working on damage control.'

Tommy craned his neck to see and when I showed him my phone, his brows lifted then knitted together.

'Okay. What do you want me to do?' I asked Claude.

'Talk to Julian. See if he knows anything about it. Maybe he can help get it taken down.'

'Okay.'

'And keep me up to date.'

'Will do.'

I ended the call and stared numbly at the screen.

'That's not good, is it?' asked Tommy.

I turned the phone upside down on the sofa. 'It is decidedly *not* good.' I got up and crossed to the window, scouring the sky for the falcon. I'd started to think of her as a talisman – a symbol of endurance and tenacity.

Sadly, she wasn't about, and my focus shifted inwards, bringing more (fucking) questions: Who took the photo? What do they have to gain by posting it? Did Julian have anything to do with this? Would he really stoop so low?

And the biggie: Why the hell did I say *yes* to Julian in the first place?

'Is there anything I can do?'

I dragged my eyes away from the view and turned towards Tommy. He probably didn't realise he'd been playing leapfrog with Julian, each of them taking turns at the forefront of my mind. With this latest revelation, he'd been knocked to the number-two slot.

'I don't think so,' I replied to his offer.

He stood, shaking out his legs, then jumping up and down.

'Pins and needles?' I asked.

'Yeah.' He stilled, staring at me. He opened his mouth to speak but stopped himself before anything came out.

'Just say it.'

'You're beautiful, Ally.'

'No, no, no, not that. We're not doing that,' I said, waving my hands in front of me. 'Way too messy. Particularly now. All I need is a second photo to surface – "Ally Novak also spotted with her *first* ex-husband!" – and I'm *completely* fucking fucked. The social-media hounds will eat me alive for being the biggest hypocrite on the planet!'

This was not an exaggeration, even though hyperbolising was a favourite pastime of mine.

'I should go,' he said.

'Yes, you should. I imagine Elsa is wondering where you got to,' I added – couldn't resist.

He gave me a lipless smile, his expression pained. There was a lot more for us to discuss, but all that could wait. Or I could use the same tactic I'd had since we split up and avoid him entirely. Avoidance was *definitely* one of my superpowers.

He left without another word, and it was only afterwards that I remembered what he'd said about Elsa. *It's not what you think.*

What *did* I think? I didn't like her. And more to the point, I didn't like her for Tommy. But then again, I wouldn't like *anyone* for Tommy besides me.

But I was *not* going to wish for something that would inevitably hurt me.

Besides, one catastrophe at a time.

Before I worried about Tommy or the European tech billionaire, I had to see Julian about this bloody Instagram post. But I couldn't give the mystery photographer more ammunition, so I went into the bedroom and hunted through everything I'd brought with me, coming up with the perfect disguise.

## 17

Thought of the day...
When life feels overwhelming, start with something small,
then move onto the next small thing.
(And, yes, eating a packet of biscuits one by one counts.)

For the second time today, I stood outside Julian's villa, but before knocking, I listened at the door to see if he was alone. Which I soon realised was silly. Is *Fortress Chic* an architectural style?

I knocked loudly, then waited. And waited. Perhaps he'd gone down to his office or had flown somewhere in that on-call helicopter. I was about to go when the door swung open.

Julian cocked his head at me in surprise. 'Why do you look like a Beastie Boy?'

'That reference dates you, Jules. And didn't they wear baseball caps?'

I pushed past him, but paused in the entry – this would be a quick visit.

He closed the door. 'All right, then why are you dressed like... whatever that is?'

I was wearing baggy trousers, a hoodie, trainers, and giant sunglasses, with my hair piled under a bucket hat – my go-to I-don't-want-to-be-recognised-at-the-airport outfit.

'Because of this,' I said, shoving my phone in his face.

He squinted at the screen; longsightedness gets everyone eventually and Julian was still too vain to wear glasses. Two seconds later, his eyes widened.

'Oh no.'

'That's putting it mildly. Do you know anything about this?'

'Why don't you come in?' he said, heading towards the bar – not a minibar, mind you, but a full-sized, fully stocked bar. 'Drink?'

'No. Just an answer, thank you very much.'

I edged into the enormous room and perched on the end of a sofa. Julian poured himself a slug of his favourite whisky – fifty-year-old Highland Park – knocked it back, then poured another finger.

Finally, he faced me. 'I really am sorry. I got it in my head that—'

'Jules! So, this *was* your doing?'

'No, not exactly. I mean... sort of.'

'Explain better.'

He took a deep breath. 'I should probably back up a bit, start from the beginning.'

'Good idea.'

He came over and fell into the armchair next to me. 'You know the expression *there's no such thing as bad publicity*?' he asked.

'Of course. I know people who've built an entire career around that philosophy.'

'Well, once you agreed to be the face of Aetheria and I told Niki, she was wary.'

'*Niki* was? But she and I have got along just fine. I thought she liked me.'

Apart from that odd exchange in her office earlier, which I didn't mention.

'No doubt she does,' replied Julian, 'but she still found it problematic.'

'Because we used to be married?'

'Yes.'

'But how is that connected to the photo? And why would you allow her to set me up like that?'

'It wasn't a set-up, Ally – that was a genuine moment between us. I only learned about the photo after the fact. Minh took it.'

'Okay,' I said, my anger dissipating by a fraction. 'But you agreed to the post, right?'

Reluctantly, he nodded. 'Niki convinced me it would generate *buzz* – that's the word she used.'

'Well, it's certainly done that. But do you have *any* idea how much damage this will cause – has *already* caused? My followers watch everything I do, hang off every word I say. And when my actions are counter to the core ethos of Divorced Diva – especially my adage that an ex is an ex for a reason – they become disillusioned. In me. In my platform. And that impacts our charity work... God, Jules, you know how hard I've worked.'

'I do – *truly*. And I'm sorry. It was misguided but I only agreed because... well...'

I'd never seen Julian this contrite before – *or* tongue-tied. But that didn't mean he was off the hook. He'd better have a bloody good explanation for what he'd done.

I folded my arms across my chest. 'Well? Go on then.'

'Right. Well, this may come as a surprise, but I'm in a bit of a bind – and not just losing Emma Watson as our spokesperson.'

What came as a surprise was Julian admitting he was in trouble – and so readily. When I'd planted the seed earlier, I'd thought it would take much longer for him to trust me with his problem – if he ever could.

While it didn't disappear entirely, the Instagram-post matter receded into the background. Julian really *was* in trouble.

'Tell me, Jules. You know I'll do whatever I can,' I offered.

'Look, it's complex and all my own doing and I really don't want you caught up in it any more than you already are. Just know that I need Aetheria to be successful. It's my... exit strategy, for want of a better term.'

None of this allayed my concerns. If anything, I became even more worried for him. *Exit strategy?* From what? What were he and Kovalec embroiled in? And where did Dale fit in?

Julian stared into his glass. After a long moment of silence, he tipped his head back, downing the rest of his whisky. He got up to pour some more and brought it back to the armchair, a faraway look on his face.

This Julian was a far cry from his typical affable self and a heavy stone settled in the pit of my stomach.

But what could I do to help? I quickly sifted through every solution that came to mind but there was only one I had any control over.

The Divorced Diva.

Somehow, we had to spin that photo into something positive, then give this PR campaign everything we had. If Julian needed Aetheria to be a massive success – no matter the reason – then I would do everything in my power to make that happen.

'I'll have Niki take down the photo,' he said, interrupting my thoughts.

'No, don't do that.'

He looked up sharply. 'But I thought you said—'

'I know, but I think we can make it work in our favour.'

'How?'

'I don't know yet, but there are very clever people on my team. We'll figure it out.'

'*You're* very clever.'

'I know.'

We shared a smile.

'Why are you helping me, Ally?'

'I care about you – you know that.'

He reached out for my hand, and I gave it to him. 'Thank you,' he said, giving it a squeeze, then releasing it.

'Thank me when it works.'

He smiled wryly and was about to take another sip of whisky when he regarded the glass. He leaned forward and set it on the coffee table, which I took as a positive sign.

'I need to get back to my villa,' I said, standing. 'Lots to do.'

Normally I'd expect Julian to see me out – his ingrained good manners – but he stayed seated, staring into space.

What in the world had he got himself caught up in?

When I closed the door to Julian's villa, the sun was starting to set and I stood on the porch for a moment to appreciate the swaths of colour sweeping across the sky. In the distance, a bird swooped, then rode a current of air upwards. The falcon! I watched her a while longer, her graceful movements a panacea for my frayed nerves, and the stone in the pit of my stomach started to dissolve. She flew out of sight, my cue to leave.

But on my way to my villa, I heard two people speaking in

harsh, hushed tones. I stopped, creeping nearer, and listened in.

'I didn't plan for this to happen.'

'Doesn't matter. You're risking the entire operation.'

It was Tommy and Elsa. But what was *the entire operation*?

'And I don't appreciate being raked over the coals,' she added spitefully.

'*I* was raked over the coals. *You* were toasting marsh-mallows.'

'Hardly – and I'm not the one shagging my ex-wife.'

I inhaled sharply and clapped my hand over my mouth. Our paths were about to cross and I didn't want them to catch me spying, so I did the only thing I could think of – I ducked into the bushes.

And I know how ridiculous that sounds, given how much time I'd already spent amongst the foliage, but I told you this was a bonkers story – and this isn't even the *really* bonkers part yet. My life had become an episode of *The White Lotus*. I half-expected Mike White to pop out and yell, 'Cut.'

Hidden by the leafy branches, I strained to hear the rest of their conversation, but there was only silence. Had they stopped talking or gone the other way? I slunk between the bushes, parallel to the path, and then I saw them – they'd stopped where the paths intersected.

'I'm *not* sleeping with her,' he whispered harshly. 'And you could take some accountability. That was a gross oversight on your part.'

'Just stay away from her,' said Elsa. 'It's only one more day. Do you think you can handle that?'

'I can handle it. You just focus on Cushing and leave Kovalec to me.'

They exchanged angry looks and Elsa stormed off towards the staff quarters.

What the actual fucking fuck was going on?

Once he was alone, Tommy turned, seeming to look right at me. I ducked out of sight.

'I can see you, Ally.'

I stayed perfectly still. Maybe he'd think he was mistaken and go away.

'You're wearing a stupid hat.'

'Hey!' I whispered, popping out of my hiding spot. 'It's not stupid.'

'Will you just come out of there?'

I scrambled out of the bushes, swatting away branches – again wishing I had a machete.

When I made it out, Tommy was looking in the direction Elsa had gone. Maybe he was worried she'd come back and tell him off some more. I was about to ask when he turned and gave me a frosty look.

So, I gave him one back. 'What's that look for, *Tom*? *I'm* not the one who's been lying. So, Elsa's *not* your girlfriend then?'

'I never said she was.'

'You let me believe it.'

His frown deepened.

'So, what is she to you, then? And don't give me the just-a-colleague line – I heard you two talking about "the whole operation". *And* I caught her snooping in Julian's office. Meanwhile, you're trying to get me off the island.' I paused, narrowing my eyes at him. 'You're not just a boat skipper, are you?'

'Look, we shouldn't be out here – together.'

'Where should we be together then?'

'You know what I mean.'

'I really, truly don't.'

Conflicted thoughts danced behind his eyes. But I had my own and Tommy and his non-girlfriend and whatever the hell this operation was *still* hadn't made the top of the list. First, I had to sort this social-media mess. Tommy and his bullshit could wait.

I started to leave, but he put his hand out to stop me.

'Tommy, I swear to god, if you grab me by the wrist again, I'll employ every self-defence skill in my arsenal. And your testicles will *not* be happy.'

He dropped his hand. 'Can I come and see you later?' he asked.

'You can come. I'm not certain I'll let you in.'

And with that, I strode off, head high and so supremely pissed off that my entire body was trembling. I was a one-woman earthquake, and I pitied anyone who crossed my path.

\* \* \*

Once I filled her in, it took Claude less than fifteen minutes to get the meeting scheduled. I didn't care that it was after hours – Project Un-fuck Us All couldn't wait until tomorrow.

At precisely 8 p.m. I logged onto my laptop and started the meeting. Ruby was in her pyjamas, sitting cross-legged on her sofa eating noodles. Maya was at HQ – had she been working late or come back in? Claude was in her home office, still in her work clothes, and her ginger cat Jim was walking back and forth in front of the camera, tail swishing. Ordinarily, I'd have cooed *hello* – I adore my fur nephew – but this wasn't the time.

Niki, seeming chastened, appeared to be taking the call from her quarters. After fucking up so spectacularly, I was surprised she'd had the guts to show up. And a little impressed.

'Okay,' I said, 'so Maya and Ruby, Claude filled you in?'

They both nodded.

'Do you have any questions before we start?'

Twin head shakes.

'How about you, Niki? Any questions?'

'Not a question... I just... I wanted to apologise. I really had no idea that things would escalate the way they did.'

'You're a PR specialist, Niki, with what – eight or nine years of experience?' I guessed, basing my assumption on her age.

Her affirming nod was so slight, I almost missed it.

'So, you *should* have known. Hell, Jim here could have figured it out and he's a cat!'

At the sound of his name, Jim looked right into the camera. I stifled a laugh – I wasn't done with Niki yet. To her credit, she was still looking at the screen, but it was impossible to miss the nervous lick of her lips.

'So, this is wh—'

'I'll remove the post,' she said hurriedly, interrupting me.

'No, you won't,' I said, softening my tone.

She blinked at me, clearly shocked.

'And this is why. While your execution was misguided – at *best* – you had the right intention. And when I checked just now, Aetheria's account has gained a *lot* of followers.'

'Three thousand in two hours,' she supplied.

'Divorced Diva has gained fifteen thousand,' said Maya.

'Oh?' A spark of hope ignited in Niki's eyes – no doubt hope that we would escape this fuck-up relatively unscathed.

'And lost forty thousand,' Maya added.

'Oh, shit.' Niki again, the light of hope instantly extinguished.

'Exactly,' I replied. 'Which is why we're meeting. But we're not going to take down the photo. It's already out there and there's no putting the genie back in the bottle. Instead, we're going to lean into it. Claude,' I said, handing over to my sister.

'Niki, you and Maya are going to find a way to spin this to Divorced Diva's benefit. And Maya's taking the lead.'

'Okay,' said Niki, accepting her fate. 'Just... why do you want me involved?'

'Because it's your mess,' Claude and I replied in unison. We smiled, also in unison. The lessons we learned from our mum popped up at the strangest times.

'I understand,' said Niki.

Ruby unmuted herself. 'Need anything from me?' she asked.

'Probably not,' said Maya, 'but maybe keep your phone on just in case, yeah?'

'Course.' She muted herself again and went back to her noodles.

'Right, so obviously you'll keep us informed,' said Claude. 'Niki, Maya will call you shortly. You can all drop off now.'

'Okay.' She, Maya, and Ruby dropped off the video call, leaving me and Claude.

'Phoo,' she sighed. 'Not what I expected to be doing on a Monday evening. But Maya will sort it. I have every faith in her.'

'Me too,' I said, meaning it. But before I let Claude go, there was one more item on the 'fuckupery' list to address.

'Claude, I lied to you before.'

The number elevens between her brows deepened. 'About what?'

'About the bloke in the photos.'

'Julian, you mean?' she asked, confused.

'No, the blurry bloke. On the boat.'

'Oh.' And then her eyes doubled in size. 'Oh my god. It *was* Tommy!'

'Yes.'

'But why didn't you tell me?' she asked gently.

And even though I'd had my reasons – *good* reasons, or so I'd thought at the time – Claude's gentle tone triggered a pang of guilt. I should have trusted her with the truth from the start.

'I'm sorry I lied but it was all so sudden and unexpected and just really, *really* weird.'

'I understand – I mean, I didn't tell you about running into Gregory until you pressed me – but are you all right?'

I wasn't – not entirely – but confessing to Claude *had* unburdened me. I felt at least a stone lighter.

'I'm all right – or I will be.'

'Okay, good – but I'm here if you need me.'

'Thanks, Claude.'

'Now, what on *earth* is Tommy doing on Aetheria?' Ah, there she was – my forthright sister. 'What sort of engineering project involves sailboats?'

It was an excellent question, but I couldn't tell Claude about the Secret Squirrel business.

'I'm not sure. But if I find out, you'll be the first to know.'

'Sounds intriguing. You're not in any *danger*, are you?' she asked with a laugh.

'Nooo – course not,' I replied, matching her laugh with my own.

We ended the call and the smile fell from my face. 'At least, I bloody well hope not,' I muttered.

I glanced at the time. I'd missed the rest of the sunset, but there were still the lights of Naxos across the way to enjoy. Then my stomach rumbled, as if it had just remembered that I hadn't eaten yet.

'Yes, yes, I hear you.'

I went to the minibar to assemble a plate of nibbles and

pour a glass of wine. I took both out to the porch and had just sat down when a whisper came from the darkness.

'Ally.'

I startled, sloshing my wine down my hoodie.

'Jesus, Tommy!'

He appeared on the porch, wearing all black and an annoying smirk.

'Is now a good time?' he asked.

'As good as any,' I said with a resigned sigh. I bit into a fat olive and stared at him expectedly. 'Well?' I said with my mouth full. 'What do you have to say for yourself?'

## 18

Thought of the day...
The difference between a 'victor' and a 'victim' is two only
letters.
You control your own narrative.

'I suggest we go inside,' he said.

'Do you now?' I popped another olive in my mouth and chewed, watching him become increasingly uncomfortable. When I swallowed, I waved a hand over the aspect. 'No one can see us – it's dark – so why does it matter?'

'Someone might come along.'

'Who, Tommy? There are only twelve people on the island, including us.'

'A slight understatement,' he responded. 'Can we please go inside? Humour me?'

'Fine.' I stood and gathered my portable picnic dinner and led the way back into the villa.

Tommy closed the door softly behind us, then it was just me and him in an enclosed space, landing me in a predicament.

THE predicament. Because soon we'd either be fighting or fucking. And as appealing as the latter might have been (if I completely disregarded our history and the current situation), it was most likely going to be the former. We had a lot of air to clear – emotional smog.

'Now that I'm here, I'm not sure where to begin,' he said, the hesitancy in his tone stripping away a single-cell layer of my built-up protection.

At the minibar, I kept my back to him, busying myself by cutting off a thick slab of Graviera, my new favourite cheese. I took a bite and chewed slowly.

I was stalling, of course, but his very presence had permeated my defences and now that the Instagram post was being handled, I had nowhere to hide.

*Nowhere to hide.*

Years since I'd seen him, living miles apart, our contact limited to text messages... all gone. Obliterated by a happenstance reunion so absurd that I barely believed it myself.

And the fortress I'd constructed around my heart... crumbling. No – not crumbling, *already* crumbled. Dust at my feet.

My throat constricted and the cheese turned to cement, making it impossible to swallow. I reached for a bottle of water, broke the seal, and took a swig. I swallowed hard and gulped for air, my back still to Tommy.

'Ally.'

He'd come up behind me – not touching me – still inches away, but the air sizzled between us. I gripped the edge of the minibar.

'Don't,' I sighed, my ragged voice betraying what lay beneath the bravado. Because when it came to Tommy, almost everything was bravado.

After the demise of our marriage, I spent *years* wrangling

the twin threads of grief – sorrow and fury – diluting their power by 'living my best life'.

And perhaps naively, I'd mastered compartmentalising, convinced that burying my feelings would inoculate me from being hurt. But it only took a handful of days to excavate them, and it was Tommy who was driving the backhoe.

'So, you and Elsa?' I ventured. There was the very slim chance that I'd misunderstood what he'd told me earlier, and I needed to know for sure.

Tommy moved even closer. If I leaned back, just a fraction, I'd feel his breath on my neck.

'She's my partner.'

'Oh,' I murmured, my shoulders stiffening.

'I told you, not like that. We work together – that's all.'

'And what work is that?' I asked, not really wanting the answer. Because, with everything that had happened, I was sure it had nothing to do with structural engineering. Or sailing.

'Ally, look at me.'

The gravelly timbre of his voice sent a thrumming vibration right through me. I swallowed, my breath fractured, and turned to face him, possibly the bravest thing I'd ever done.

'I have so many questions, Tommy,' I whispered, my voice textured with every single one of them.

'I know. And I owe you answers.'

His gaze dropped to my mouth, then returned to meet mine, and every neuron in my brain urged me to close the gap between us. But I couldn't. Not yet. So I said the one thing that would unlock everything else.

'You forgot about me.' My eyes glossed with tears, but I steadfastly held his gaze.

'Never, Ally. I never forgot you. Not for one single day.'

The gasp came from deep inside me, then there was no

more conscious thought of right and wrong and past and present. There was only me and him – my beautiful Tommy, the man I'd forced myself to forget just to stay afloat.

His hands dropped to my waist, pulling me to him, his body firmly pressed against mine. I trailed my hands to his shoulders, my fingers fisting in his shirt.

Our lips collided.

Every nerve ending was electrified as my lips moved against his. Full and soft, yet kissing me with firm insistence, transfixing me. Our mouths melded perfectly, lip to lip, sealing our connection. Our tongues were tentative at first, then engaged in a dance that aroused shivers and sighs.

His arms tightened around me and I unclenched my fingers, slipping my hands around his neck, falling deeper into the kiss and losing myself in him.

Being in Tommy's embrace was everything I'd craved but buried deep. Comfort and adventure, familiarity and excitement, converging in one perfect, breathless, aching moment – exactly how it had once been between us.

But a heartbeat later, the need for him sharpened.

Without breaking the kiss, I tugged at the hem of his T-shirt, aching to touch his bare skin. I slid my palms up his back, raking my nails lightly, and he moaned – a sound that travelled to my core, setting me alight.

He drew back, ending our kiss, but I knew from the look in his eyes there would be another – and so much more.

He roughly grabbed the bottom of my hoodie and pulled it over my head. My hair tumbled onto my shoulders, mussed, but I didn't care. He tossed it on the floor, then reached behind me and undid my bra with a two-fingered snap.

I gasped – I'd forgotten he could do that. He met my eye, his left brow arched sexily.

Still wanting more of him, I reached for the button of his jeans, but he gently pushed my hands away.

'Uh-uh, not yet.'

He hooked one finger under each bra strap, sliding them off my shoulders, and my bra followed my hoodie to the floor. He stood back, his eyes roaming my body then rising to meet mine.

'My god, Ally, you're so beautiful.'

Tommy stared into my eyes, seeing right into me – taking in *all* of me – the bold and sassy Ally who still wanted to change the world, the vulnerable, heartsick Ally who'd kept her distance...

Tears blurred my vision as he reached for my face, running his thumb gently along my jawline. It had always been more than lust between us, something else I'd forced myself to forget because the pain of missing him – of missing *us* – had been too much to bear.

He drew nearer, softly kissing my lips, and shivers rippled over me. He lowered his head, dropping his mouth to my neck, planting soft, tingle-inducing kisses, his lips moving to my collarbone, tracing its ridge. His hands cupped my breasts, his thumbs circling my nipples as they hardened beneath his touch. His lips lowered to one breast, kissing the fullness, his tongue licking, tasting me. He took my nipple in his mouth and I buried my fingers in his hair. Every touch, every kiss, every sensation was shooting straight between my legs.

I wanted him inside me, to be as close to him as possible.

But I also wanted this, this sweet torture.

His mouth moved to my other nipple, more insistent now, sucking and nibbling, making it ache deliciously.

But my need for him grew with each breath until I couldn't stand it any longer.

'I want to see you,' I commanded breathily.

He relented, locking eyes with me as he straightened. Impatient, I undid his jeans, roughly pushing them off his slim hips. They bunched at his ankles, and he toed off his boat shoes before stepping out of them.

He stood proudly, his glorious cock straining against his briefs.

I gently pushed him away from me, then knelt before him. Looking up, a smile alighting on my lips, I reached for his waistband, unhooking it from the tip of his cock. Leaning back on my heels, I slid his briefs to the floor, admiring his tanned, muscular legs, which looked even better out of shorts than they did in them. He shucked off his briefs, kicking them to the side. I rose onto my knees, taking his cock in both hands and stroking lightly.

He moaned loudly.

I held the shaft of his cock firmly in my hands, then lowered my mouth onto it. His sigh was deep and gruff, and I glanced up. His eyes were closed, his head tipped back, and his lips parted.

My mouth glided down the shaft, my lips holding him tightly, then up again, tongue swirling against the underside of the tip. His hands rested lightly on my head, his fingers nestling in my hair as I slid up and down his cock, each time stopping to tongue his most sensitive spot.

He started moving with me, not aggressively, but we fell into a rhythm. I could tell he was close to coming when he said, 'Ally, stop, not like this.'

I released him, then rocked back on my heels and looked up. His eyes had clouded over with lust, and he shook his head as he smiled down at me.

'So tempting but I want to come inside you.'

He held out a hand and I took it and stood. He surprised

me, scooping me up, and I yelped with delight. His hands cupped my arse as he carried me into the bedroom, then laid me gently on the bed.

I was speechless as we held each other's gaze and those dark-brown eyes bored into mine. There was so much between us, tethering us to each other. Desire, yes – *always* – but so much more.

Only I didn't want to think about any of that, and I reached out for him. 'Come here.'

He crawled on top of me and kissed me again, a kiss that was reminiscent of the night before – lusty and hungry. I craved him, his taste, the crushing sensation of his strong body on top of mine.

Torn, I broke the kiss. I wanted more but I also wanted to be closer to him and I was still partially clothed.

'Off?' he asked, tugging on my trousers.

I nodded and he moved down my body to take off my trainers and socks. He crawled back up, stopping at my waist, and waggled his eyebrows.

'Your turn,' he said, his voice low, and my molten insides almost vaporised.

He slid my trousers off, taking a moment to admire my lacy thong. 'Only you would wear La Perla under *that* outfit,' he teased with a half-smile. I didn't want to know how Tommy knew about La Perla – I certainly hadn't been able to afford it when we were married – but it was instantly forgotten when he pulled my knickers off with his teeth.

I giggled, wriggling playfully. Until he ran his tongue the length of my slit, flicking my clit with it and transporting me to another world – another *universe* – as I stilled beneath him.

Tommy had always loved going down on me – and he'd been superbly skilled at it – but this was something else and it wasn't long before I felt myself on the brink. But like Tommy, I didn't want to come like that. I wanted him inside me.

I dragged myself from the euphoria of Tommy's tongue between my legs and propped myself up on my elbows.

'Tommy.' My voice was raw, probably from all the heavy breathing.

He lifted his head, looking at me, then licking his lips.

'I want you. Now.'

'Condoms?'

'Here.' I rolled over onto my side, opened the drawer by the bed, and pulled out a strip of condoms.

'You came prepared,' he teased.

'Always,' I replied, skipping over why I'd packed a dozen condoms for a four-day trip. I tore open a packet with my teeth and took one out.

Tommy had edged his way up the bed, kneeling before me, his erection proud. '*You* put it on,' he pleaded. I rolled the condom onto his cock, firmly holding his shaft. He inhaled sharply but still had the wherewithal to ask, 'Top or bottom?'

'Me on top.'

He rolled over and I climbed on top of him, sliding onto his cock. We sighed in unison at coming together, but before either of us moved, we locked eyes again. He reached for me, cupping my cheek with his palm. 'I've missed you, Ally.'

'Me too,' I admitted, the ache of missing him dangerously close to the surface.

But I forced it back down, desire winning over. I wanted Tommy to take me to the edge and tumble over it with me. I started rocking against him and his breath caught again.

'Put your thumb—' I didn't even finish my request. He knew and he pressed his thumb hard into my clit, his other hand gripping my hips and guiding me back and forth.

I was close and I could tell he was too. 'Hold on for me, baby,' I commanded, and I rode him hard until my entire body was consumed, every molecule of me on fire, then erupting. Head back, eyes shut, I rode the wave of the orgasm, perhaps the most intense I'd ever experienced, and when I finally opened my eyes and looked down, Tommy was watching me, the left corner of his mouth upturned.

'That's so hot, baby.'

I dipped my head to kiss him, my body still thrumming. His lips parted beneath mine, the kiss deepening as I lost myself in the taste of him, the warmth of his mouth against mine. His hand cradled the back of my head and I melted into him, surrendering to the kiss. Eventually, I eased back, breathless, my only thought to give him the same pleasure he'd just given me. 'Now you.'

I started rocking again, leaning forward so my breasts dangled enticingly. He grabbed one in each hand, rubbing my nipples roughly with his thumbs. We looked deep into each other's eyes as we moved together, the years apart falling away until it was Ally and Tommy as we'd once been – bound by hope, by want, by love.

I saw it building in him, the crescendo rising, and at the last second, his eyes fluttered shut, his whole body trembling. 'Ahh,' he cried out. Anyone nearby would have heard him but I didn't care. Let them.

I came to a rest, then climbed off him. He still had his eyes closed when I crawled into the crook of his arm and curled up beside him, my hand resting on his chest.

'That was...' he murmured.

'It was,' I agreed, and he chuckled softly, lifting his hand to stroke my arm.

For a long while, we lay cocooned in the quiet comfort of

each other, shutting out the world and, with it, reality. Or at least, I was.

But the questions began to intrude, breaking the spell. I wanted answers – no, *needed* answers.

*What's really going on with Julian?*

*What is Tommy doing on Aetheria?*

*What does it mean that we've been together twice in two days?*

And he'd said he'd missed me. Was that just the heat of the moment, or had he meant it?

'Ally?'

'Mmm.' My mind jolted back to the room. 'What?'

He chuckled again, then was quiet. 'I wasn't just saying that before. I *have* missed you.'

'Wait, how did you know that's what—'

'I told you, Ally, I know you.'

I wished I could say the same – that I knew him – but the evidence suggested I didn't know him at all. Who even *was* he?

I propped myself on one elbow and peered down at him.

He cracked an eyelid. 'Yes?'

'Why are you here?'

He stroked my arm again. 'Well, I hope that was obvi—'

'Not in my villa. On Aetheria.'

'Ahh.'

'Don't *ahh* me. That's not an answer and considering our marriage ended because you were always off somewhere solving the world's problems—'

'Hold on,' he interrupted. He sat up abruptly, leaning against the bedhead, and pulled a pillow onto his lap. 'Our marriage ended because you wanted it to – you left me.'

'Hah! Like hell I did. It's impossible to leave someone who was never even there, Tommy.'

Feeling exposed under his steely glare, I got up and went

into the other room, picking up my hoodie off the floor. I shoved my arms into it and yanked it over my head, thankful it was long enough to cover everything I wanted covered.

'Ally, please come back.'

I moved into the doorway and stood with my hands on my hips.

'If you can answer *one* question.'

'Go on.'

'What's your job – your *real* job? Are you some sort of spy or something? Fancy yourself as the next James Bond, do you?'

'Well, no, because he's fictitious.'

'Aren't *you* fictitious? A skipper – *really*? I mean, yes, you can sail – very well, I might add – but you seriously want me to believe that you gave up your career as an engineer to live and work here?' I asked, throwing my arms out wide. 'It's a playground for spoilt rich people. And you always hated this kind of excess. You said it was *gauche*.'

'It is.'

'So, what are you doing here then?'

'I can't tell you that.'

'Gah!' I shouted, digging my fists into my thighs.

I didn't care who heard us – before when we were fucking or now that we'd moved onto the fighting portion of the evening's program.

He got up, the pillow falling to the floor. 'I would if I could, but I can't – not yet, anyway. You're already too close to this.'

'Too close? Newsflash, Tommy – I'm caught right the bloody middle of it! So, before you fill me in on what the hell is going on with Julian and Kovalec and all the rest of it, I want you to answer me – once and for all. Are you a spy?'

'For want of a better word, yes.'

'Oh my god,' I gasped – ridiculous, really, given that every sign had been pointing to *yes*. But hearing the truth from Tommy's mouth shocked me to my core.

He sighed loudly, then ran a hand through his hair, mussing it to perfection. He scouted for his jeans, which were on the floor next to me. Still dazed from his revelation, I picked them up and tossed them to him. He caught them one-handed – so many skills, that man – and put them on without bothering to locate his briefs.

'Let's sit,' he said, passing me and heading to one of the sofas.

'Am I going to need a drink for this?' I asked, nerves snaking through my stomach.

'Probably wouldn't hurt. I'll have one too.'

I nodded, part numb, part jittery mess, then poured a glass of wine from the bottle I'd opened earlier. I topped myself up and took both glasses to the sofa, where I sat beside Tommy. I handed him his wine, then tugged at my hoodie until it covered my thighs.

'Okay, I'm ready,' I said.

'Trust me, you're not.' He was probably right, but what choice did I have? I was part of this now and I needed to know.

Tommy took a deep pull from his glass, then set it on the table, his expression pained. 'Fuck,' he muttered to himself.

'You don't know if you should tell me,' I said.

'Oh no, I *know* I shouldn't.' His eyes found mine and he gave me a loaded look. 'Like I said before, you're already too close to this for my liking.'

'You're scaring me.'

'Good. Because all this, what you're caught up in, it's serious, Ally. And I really hoped you'd just do the PR stuff and leave before it all came to a head. But now Julian's told you he's in a bind and—'

'Wait, how can you possibly know that? I didn't tell you about that.' But before he could answer, it came to me. 'You bugged his villa. You've been spying on him.'

He confirmed this with a nod, and I took a fortifying gulp of wine.

'Okay,' I said, 'tell me – *all* of it.'

'I'll tell you what I can, but I should probably start at the beginning.'

'Yes, do that.'

My mind raced to catch up on everything I'd just learned, but hopefully I'd be able to piece it together on the fly. If Tommy was prepared to talk, I wouldn't interrupt him.

## 19

Thought of the day...
Trust your gut.
9 times out of 10 it will be right.
(The 10th time might just be indigestion.)

'Do you remember the ethics professor I had at Oxford?' he began, twin lines of concentration appearing between his brows. 'You met him that one time at the pub.'

'Professor Patel?' I asked, remembering a slightly built, softly spoken man in his late forties.

'That's him. And do you remember the project I was working on after we got married? At Langford Rise?'

'That council estate in South London – the builders cut corners, pocketed the savings, and extorted the council. You exposed them.'

'That's the one. Not really within my purview as an engineer, but too much didn't add up and I wasn't prepared to let it go.'

'You did the right thing. I was proud of you.'

'Thanks, that means a lot. But getting back to Professor Patel... It wasn't just a catch-up that day at the pub. After you went back to the flat, he got to the real reason he'd asked to meet. He was recruiting me, Ally. Apparently, he'd been keeping an eye on me – for years – since our first tutorial together. You see, he's not only a professor; he also helps a particular organisation find people who might be... *suitable*. For the sort of work they do.'

'You mean espionage?'

'Eh... that term's probably a little loaded for my liking. And I'm not *really* a spy – more of an investigator.'

'And you're investigating Julian – you and Elsa?' I asked, even though I already knew the answer.

'Yes.'

'And this business deal... Has Julian done something wrong?'

'Not yet, but it seems like only a matter of time.'

'Oh god, will he go to jail?' I asked bluntly. My hand hovered over my mouth of its own accord.

'That's not up to me. I'm sorry.'

'Is there a way he can avoid it?'

'Like I said, I'm not the one who can make that decision. Nor is Elsa.'

'Okay.'

Only it was very much *not* okay. Whatever Julian had or hadn't done, surely he didn't deserve to go to *jail*?

An idea came to me.

'Is there any way *I* can help? What if I persuade him to cooperate?'

'Ally...' Tommy angled his body towards me. '*Please* stay out of this. There are too many unknown factors and—'

'And Kovalec… He was the one threatening Julian on the phone,' I cut in, ignoring his warning.

'*Ally*,' he said more firmly.

'So, that's a *yes* then,' I shot back. 'And *Kovalec* is your actual target, isn't he? Not Julian.'

Tommy expelled a loud breath, which I also took to mean *yes*.

*Hmm, maybe I can wear a wire – cosy up to Kovalec and get him to confess. Not that I know what he needs to confess to – not yet anyway – but I'm positive there's something I can do.*

But I still needed Tommy to fill in some gaps – well, *lots* of gaps.

'So…' I ventured, only to be cut off.

'I should go.' Tommy stood suddenly and headed towards the minibar where I'd torn his clothes off.

'Wait a minute,' I implored.

I got up and followed, bewildered as I watched him hunt for his briefs. He found them next to the window and shoved them into his pocket, then stooped to collect his T-shirt from the floor, pulling it on before picking up his shoes.

'So, you're flying out tomorrow morning?' he asked, as if it were a foregone conclusion.

'No. I told you, I've extended my stay.'

'Jesus, Ally.'

He huffed, and I bit my lower lip, suddenly too weary to fight any more. What was the point, anyway? If he wasn't going to tell me more about what was going on with Julian, why try to keep him there?

'Well, go on then,' I said quietly, nodding towards the door.

He held my gaze for a long moment, then left without another word.

The door closed and silence descended, thick and deafening. Julian's mess, with all its confusion and contradictions, fell away, and in its place rose a stark and sobering truth: Tommy had been a spy all along.

And his decision to join a secret organisation that sort-of-but-not-really spied on people had left a wreckage in its wake – our marriage.

I sank onto the sofa, a lump rising in my throat as the sting of tears threatened.

All those lies he'd told...

Those trips that had kept him away for weeks or months at a time... He wasn't saving remote villages from flooding or preventing entire towns from crumbling to the ground whenever the tectonic plates collided. He was sneaking around, pretending to be a skipper, and bugging people's villas! I cast my eyes about. Had he bugged mine? God, I hoped not. The thought of Tommy listening in while I pleasured myself...

'Ugh,' I groaned with a shudder.

Then something popped into my mind – the story Tommy would tell the old ladies at the bus stop about treasure hunting in Peru... Was that actually true?

I shook my head, dislodging the notion. Tommy was an investigator, not Indiana Jones! But at least the picture of him dressed head to toe in khaki and wearing that famous fedora was enough to stave off the looming tears. I didn't have the luxury of wallowing in *what ifs*. I needed to focus on the *what the fuck do I do nows.*

'What the fuck *do* I do now?' I muttered.

Well, first there was the Instagram post. I could have missed an update while I was in the throes of passion, so I picked up my phone and checked.

Maya had emailed twenty minutes ago, CCing Claude. I opened it.

Hi Ally,

We've gone with the 'lean into it' approach. I've reposted the original to our feed and shared it to our stories, clarifying that there is nothing romantic between you and Julian and that exes can remain close friends, like you two have. We've already had some comments on the post – mostly support-ive. I'll keep an eye on engagement overnight and come back to you in the morning.

Best,

Maya

PS I think Niki was relieved she got off so lightly.

Niki wasn't the only one who was relieved, and I sent a quick reply to Maya to thank her for her excellent work.

Now, what to do about Julian? He obviously didn't know who Tommy and Elsa really were, but I wasn't about to blow their cover. I was already out of my depth – who knew what mayhem *that* might unleash?

But I could still be there for him – *somehow*... Then it came to me.

The thing about hosting a VIP is that you go above and beyond to make their experience extraordinary. If I knew Julian – and I did – he planned to do exactly that for Ivan Kovalec.

And I wanted in.

But who could get me the information I needed? Tommy wasn't going to share any more intel than he already had – he wanted me as far away from this mess as possible.

Then I thought of the one person who'd be in the know *and* owed me. I picked up my phone and navigated to the itinerary Niki had sent, scrolling to the end where she'd included her phone number. Five minutes later, I had what I needed.

According to Niki, Julian was hosting a dinner for Kovalec

aboard *Ally's Odyssey* tomorrow night. Trudy and Dale were invited, with Tommy and Elsa on board as crew. That didn't add up from a staffing perspective – the yacht had its own crew and surely Niki would have been a better choice as guest services director? But perhaps Julian still had her on the naughty step for the Instagram debacle. I didn't ask, not wanting to rub salt in her wounds. I also suspected that Tommy and Elsa had wangled themselves onto the yacht, which probably meant that something big was about to go down.

All signs pointed to this being no ordinary dinner.

So, first I needed an invitation. I was almost positive that Julian would say *yes* if I invited myself – he might even be grateful for the moral support. And once on board, I'd just have to keep my wits about me then figure it out on the fly. I could do that – I was great at thinking on my feet.

Not the firmest plan, but what choice did I have? Fly back to London and pretend everything was tickety-boo? *Hah!*

I called Julian, and he answered right away.

'Three times in one day. I'm starting to think you might have a thing for me, Ally.'

'Jules, I know about Ivan Kovalec,' I said, cutting to the chase.

'Er... know what exactly?' he asked, a wary edge to his voice.

Bugger – I hadn't meant that to sound sinister. But to be fair, I was new to all this spy stuff.

'That he's coming here, silly – a little birdie told me,' I replied, steering us back to our keep-it-light comfort zone. 'How come you didn't say anything? I mean, *Ivan Kovalec* – that's a big deal, Jules.'

He laughed, a sign that I'd covered my tracks. 'To be honest, I didn't think you'd care. Ivan's a crusty old man who only talks about work.'

'So, you have a lot in common then?' I teased.

'Ooh, low blow.'

'Can I meet him?' I asked, diving right in. 'You must be planning something special?'

'Er, yes, a dinner on the yacht, but aren't you leaving tomorrow morning?'

Double bugger – I hadn't told Julian I was sticking around.

'Oh, I can stay an extra day,' I offered, as if it had only just occurred to me. 'It's a special occasion, right?'

He was silent – probably deciding whether to invite me into the inner circle, where things got... *murky*.

'Actually, you could be of use to me,' he said after a long pause.

'Oh?' I asked, my gut gripping with nervous excitement.

'Well, Dale and Trudy will be there, and you can keep Trudy company if the menfolk end up talking shop all night.'

'Ahh, right. Well, I adore Trudy, so it would be my pleasure.'

'Perfect,' he said with a smile in his voice. 'We'll be flying over to the yacht at 7.30.'

'About that...' I ventured, figuring it was as good a time as any.

'Mmm?'

'Any chance you can change the name, Jules? You did promise ages ago.'

He chuckled. 'God, I'd forgotten about that.'

'You forgot that you named your boat after me? Gee, thanks.'

'No, not like that – it's just... that's her name. I'm used to it. And she's a *yacht*, not a boat,' he retorted, his mild snobbery showing itself.

'*Yacht* then.'

'I'll change the name, Ally.' I took that with a grain of salt, but at least I'd asked.

As I had nothing more to say – I'd got the invite I wanted and asked about *Ally's Odyssey* – I wished him goodnight and ended the call.

For some time, I sat with my phone in my hands, staring at the painting on the wall opposite. It was cobalt-blue geometric lines on a white canvas – a nod to Greek architecture, I supposed. I traced the lines with my eyes, mulling over my situation.

It had only been a handful of days since I'd taken Julian's call and agreed to come to Aetheria. But that had been enough to turn my world upside down. Mostly because of Tommy.

It was *surreal* that he was there. That was the only word to describe it – both real and unbelievable at once.

The sex had been incredible, but we'd always had mind-blowing chemistry. Even after weeks or sometimes months apart, we would come together as if no time had passed, fluent in each other's erotic landscapes, carrying us to another echelon. Like tonight.

Of course, a relationship is far more than sex. And Tommy's job had caused an emotional chasm that widened with each separation. By the time I'd concluded it was over, we were barely speaking.

I cast my mind back to the last night Tommy and I stayed in our flat together, the night before I moved out. We talked that night – *really* talked, as if we were famished for conversation, for each other. At some point around 2 a.m. we were laughing so hard, my stomach muscles were screaming. And I considered – just for a moment – that I could stay and we'd be okay. That we really were in love and we got each other – we *saw* each other, who we truly were.

But then he'd set an alarm, saying he should probably get some sleep as he was flying out the next morning. And that's when I knew I'd made the right decision.

A heartbreaking, gut-wrenching decision that ate me up from the inside. But the right one.

So, our goodbye – the one that ended our marriage – was a silent hug at the door of our flat, me in my pyjamas and Tommy dressed for the next adventure, duffel bag by his feet. We'd held each other tightly and though I fought them off as best I could, my tears had drenched the front of Tommy's shirt. He'd released me, then cupped my face in his hands, pressing a soft kiss to my lips.

Easing back, he'd said, 'I love you, Ally. I'm sorry you don't think we can make this work.' Or something to that effect – an insinuation that it had been my doing alone.

Before I could respond, he'd left, not even casting a look over his shoulder. Claude had come to stay for a few days, making sure I ate and showered and helping me pack up my belongings and move into a flat share across London, closer to her and Gregory.

And now I was in Greece with Tommy, and we'd just had our trademarked super-hot sex – but we hadn't discussed *us*. Not properly.

Not how easily we'd slipped back into Ally-and-Tommy mode that day on Naxos.

Not the still-burning attraction between us.

Not that we'd admitted to missing each other, or blamed each other for our marriage break-up.

And definitely not how getting back together would be a seismic shift – professionally – for us both. If that's what he wanted. If it's what *I* wanted.

And that was the clincher. I *loved* being the Diva – what she stood for, what she'd accomplished, all the people she'd helped.

How would I find anything as fulfilling – and if I did, would I even feel like *me*? There was such a fine line between us – the Diva and me – and yes, sometimes I just wanted to be Ally, but I always wanted to come back to her.

Not that it was likely to matter.

Because on top of everything else was the gigantic lie that had torched our marriage and sat festering for a decade.

And instead of facing it, he'd skedaddled.

Maybe that told me everything I needed to know.

## 20

Thought of the day...
You are the main character in your own life.
Don't let anyone make you take a supporting role.
(No matter how hot they are.)

As I stepped into the ruby-red, silk chiffon Grecian-cut gown, careful not to snag the hem on my strappy gold heels, I was grateful for the foresight to pack it. Yes, I had to contort myself to zip it up, but when I stood in front of the full-length mirror, that was forgotten.

It was *gorgeous*.

And not to toot my own horn too much, but step one of my plan to fix Julian's mess – look fantastic – had a big fat tick against it. In fact, I hadn't looked this good since I attended the BAFTAs last year and that took an entire *team* – hair, makeup, stylist... This was me on my own working with what I'd brought to Aetheria.

Still, I wasn't the spokesperson for an ethical luxury makeup brand for nothing. I knew my way around a palette, and I'd achieved that soft ethereal look Ariana Grande tends to favour. And my hair was in shiny barrel curls that cascaded down my back – like Barbie's.

Ex-wife Influencer Barbie – coming to a John Lewis near you this Christmas. *Hah!*

And if Tommy's jaw just happened to drop when he saw me? That would be the cherry on top.

My stomach aflutter with nerves – understandable, considering I was about to step into a real-life Bond film – I loaded up my gold clutch with the essentials: a compact and lipstick (for touch-ups), my phone (obvs), tissues (always), and condoms (you never know). I closed it with a satisfying *snap*, downed the rest of my getting-ready wine, then went to wait on the porch for Christos to collect me and take me to the helipad.

As I waited in the dusk light, its orange hue setting the sky alight, it struck me how odd it was that *this* was my life. And I sort-of stepped outside of myself and observed her, the Divorced Diva. Well, *me*.

*Here stands the thirty-something, thrice-divorced woman,* David Attenborough said inside my head, *excited, yet nervous about the night ahead. Can she help save ex-husband number three from imminent jeopardy? And what about ex-husband number one? Is there enough between them to warrant another try?*

I lingered on the last thought for several moments, hovering between hope and despair.

Then Attenborough's voice returned: *Should she have slipped some pepper spray into that gold clutch?*

My stomach soured. *Would* I be in danger? Surely not – or Tommy would have said.

Before I could ponder this further, Christos pulled up in the golf cart.

'You look fricking great,' he said candidly.

'Are you supposed to talk to guests like that?' I asked, faking a chastising side-eye.

'God no, but doesn't mean it isn't true. Here,' he said, getting out of the cart and offering me his hand.

I took it and gingerly stepped onto the path (I *was* wearing five-inch heels). Christos led me around the cart and helped me into it, lifting the hem of my dress and tucking it neatly inside. He grinned at me, then jogged around the cart and got in the driver's seat.

'Ready?' he asked.

'Yes,' I replied, even though that worrying question was now playing on repeat inside my head.

*Am I in danger?*

Somewhere between the villa and the helipad, I settled on *absolutely not*. I would be surrounded by people I knew and while Kovalec may have had questionable political affiliations, he was a tech billionaire, not an evil mastermind. *Right?*

'Ally!' Julian strode over, looking very dapper in a dark suit, white shirt, and pocket square – no tie. 'May I?' He offered his hand and helped me out of the golf cart, then Christos drove off at speed.

'You look nice, Mr Cushing,' I said, studying him for signs of nerves. He'd seemed perfectly at ease yesterday, but now I knew more about what was going on, there had to be *some* trace of apprehension?

'And you look *incredible*, Former Mrs Cushing.' He took a step back to eye me up and down. If Julian *was* nervous, he was doing an excellent job of hiding it.

I did a little curtsey, masking my own nerves. 'Why thank you, kind sir.' We exchanged warm smiles. 'Where are the others?' I asked, looking about.

'Well, Christos is collecting Dale and Trudy, so they'll be here momentarily.'

'And what about Ivan Kovalec?'

'Oh, he'll meet us on *Ally's Odyssey*,' Julian replied, emphasising the name of the yacht.

'*Jules*,' I chided.

'Couldn't resist. However, I *will* change the name, I promise. Any suggestions?'

'How about *Midlife Crisis*?' I teased.

'A brutal slur,' he replied, clutching his chest.

'Jules, joking aside, tonight is a big deal for you, isn't it?'

He sobered instantly, a fissure appearing in his otherwise calm exterior. 'Ah, yes, yes it is.'

'Well, I promise to do everything in my power to charm the pants off Kovalec,' I assured him.

'I don't imagine that would take much coaxing – they'll probably fall off the instant he claps eyes on you,' he said cheekily.

I tutted, pretending to be appalled, right as the golf cart pulled up with Trudy and Dale.

Thank goodness – having Trudy by my side tonight helped shave off some of my mounting nerves. She was walking sunshine.

'Ally, what a lovely surprise,' she said, and I shot a look at Julian. I would have thought he'd tell her I was coming but never mind.

I stepped closer for a cheek kiss. 'You look gorgeous,' I told her. And she did in an apple-green swing dress with billowing sleeves. Her hair was up, with curly tendrils falling around her face, and her coral lipstick added a striking pop of colour.

'Oh,' she said, batting away the compliment modestly.

Julian and Dale shook hands, and Dale gave me a friendly smile.

'So, where's this helicopter then?' asked Dale, sending his eyes skyward.

Right on cue, the sounds of a rotor filled the dusk air and a moment later it was hovering above us.

'Way to summon it, hun,' said Trudy with a wink.

When we boarded, Trudy sat next to me and just before we lifted off, she leaned close and said, 'I'm glad you came tonight, Ally. You can keep me company.'

'That's what Julian said. I've got this vision of the menfolk retiring to the library with brandy and cigars while the wives are left to drink sherry and gossip.'

She smirked, then put her headset on and I did the same.

\* \* \*

Dinner was being served on the flybridge, and the crew had gone all out.

Upbeat instrumental music played softly from popup speakers, while blue light from the still jacuzzi cast a shimmering hue across the deck, candles bobbing gently on its surface.

The table – a striking centrepiece – was set with a white linen tablecloth and napkins, fine china with a gold rim, gold-plated cutlery, crystal glassware, and gold candlesticks with off-white tapers that were already lit, adding a warm glow to the ambiance.

A steward circulated with canapés – well, as much as one can when there are only a handful of guests. They were delicious morsels, and I tasted Dimitra's deft hand in each bite. Though, I only had three – a nervous tum, you see.

I was only *pretending* that everything was perfectly normal and Julian *wasn't* about to implicate himself in some sort of (still unknown) nefarious scheme and I *hadn't* insinuated myself into the middle of it.

I wandered over to the railing and stared across the water at Naxos. It may have been a Tuesday night but to the people onshore, it appeared to be a Saturday. Joyous voices, laughter, and music carried across the water, somewhat imposing on the carefully curated atmosphere aboard *Ally's Odyssey*.

Julian *really* had to change the name.

I was about to take another sip of champers, but suddenly remembered that I should keep my wits about me. I lowered the glass, then inhaled deeply, drawing in the warm, briny air. God, I adored being in the Aegean.

The sound of a motor drew my attention. The yacht's tender had pulled up alongside us and I watched as a short, stocky middle-aged man with wiry salt-and-pepper hair disembarked onto a lower deck. He was dressed similarly to Julian in a very expensive, well-fitting suit. Kovalec.

'I should have guessed.'

I jumped, finding Tommy standing beside me. I glanced over, barely moving my head. He was dressed in crew whites and smelled like sunshine and lemons and being on holiday – delicious, but also distracting and I needed to focus.

'Hello, Tommy,' I replied quietly. 'I thought this yacht already had a skipper,' I added with a smirk.

'That's not— I'm working security.'

I hadn't expected that and angled my body towards him. 'Julian has you on security detail?' I whispered. '*Really?*'

'It's a small staff, Ally. Everyone on Aetheria has double duties.' That's what Christos had told me, but *security*? Oh god, maybe this *was* dangerous. 'So, you're here now,' he continued, 'and there's nothing I can do about that. But can you at *least* do your best to stay out of the way?'

Stung, I swallowed hard and squared my shoulders. 'I can be useful, you know. I can talk to anyone – if you need Kovalec to implicate himself... I can do that. I could wear a wire or—'

'Ally, *no*. All of that's taken care of. Just—'

'Ally, darling,' said Julian, 'come meet Ivan.'

*Gah!* I'd have to pin Tommy down later and convince him to let me help.

I gave Tommy a smile – hopefully it wouldn't seem too odd that he and I had been chatting – then headed over to Julian and Kovalec, who openly leered at me. I pretended not to notice.

'Ally, this is Ivan Kovalec. Ivan, this is Ally, my ex-wife.'

Kovalec's eyebrows leapt an entire centimetre. 'That's strange – being on good terms with your ex-husband,' he said accusingly.

'I understand that's true for some people, but Julian's a treasured friend.'

Out of the corner of my eye, I saw Julian beam at me, but I kept my eyes fixed on Kovalec. I'd encountered men like him before – the sort who believed everyone shared their world view. Or should.

He stared at me a beat longer, then broke into false, bellowing laughter. Julian and I joined in out of politeness. When the laughter died down, I excused myself and joined Trudy – far safer waters (so to speak).

'What's he like?' she asked quietly.

'Exactly as you'd expect.'

'Ugh,' she said with a shudder. 'I hope I don't have to sit next to him at dinner.'

We both glanced at the table – no place cards.

I hooked my arm through hers. 'We'll just have to stick together then.'

'Agreed.'

'Can I ask,' I said, 'if you're not here to meet Kovalec, then why?'

'Why did we accept the invitation to dinner?'

I nodded.

'A favour to Julian. Besides, Dale's in the same field and I suspect there's an innate curiosity about one of the world's richest men.'

I looked over to where Dale had joined Julian and Kovalec. They were talking animatedly and Kovalec seemed to be cracking jokes – hilarious ones if measured by the laughter. I peered more closely at Julian, who was facing me, spotting the lines of tension around his eyes. Oh god, he *was* nervous. My stomach knotted again.

I had to talk to Tommy. Whatever was going down, he'd know how best to protect Julian. I just had to convince him to do it.

'Excuse me,' I said to Trudy. 'I need the loo.'

'I'll save you the seat next to mine,' she said.

I left Trudy, depositing my half-drunk champers on a nearby table, then approached the staircase leading to the deck below. With every step, I kept Tommy in my periphery, *willing* him to look in my direction so I could signal for him to follow.

Just as I reached the top of the staircase, I finally caught his eye and with a subtle jerk of my head, I summoned him, then descended.

At the bottom of the stairs, I ducked into an alcove and waited. And *waited*. In tense times, seconds can feel like minutes and minutes like hours. This felt like days, but eventually I saw Tommy's feet on the stairs, then the rest of him.

Wordlessly, I slipped into the salon through the sliding door, keeping an eye out for crew. Seeing no one, I crossed to the day head, an ornate half-bathroom off the salon. I entered, leaving the door slightly ajar.

Tommy came in seconds behind me.

'You're being reckless,' he scolded.

'Yes, yes, your stance on my presence is crystal clear but we don't have time for that. How do you plan to keep Julian safe?'

'Safe? He's not in any *physical* dang—'

'From *prosecution*, Tommy. Surely you can nab Kovalec without Julian ending up as collateral damage?'

'*I* don't have the authority to—'

'Are you being obtuse on purpose?' I asked. 'I mean *you* as in MI6.'

He shook his head. 'I don't work for MI6. I told you, I'm not a spy.'

'Well, whoever then. Can't you make a phone call or something? Make sure Julian's given immunity for cooperating?'

'Ally, I can't share *any* of the details of this operation with you.'

'What if I wore a wire?' I offered again, now desperate. 'Kovalec has already been leering at me. I could probably—'

'*Ally*,' Tommy whispered sharply, cutting me off. 'You don't need to wear a wire – the entire yacht is bugged.'

'Even here?' I asked, looking around.

'Yes.'

'Oh. Wait – how do you know that?'

He sighed, exasperated. 'Where do you think I was all day?'

'Well, I don't know, Tommy,' I snapped. 'This may come as a surprise, but I wasn't sitting about pining over you. I was *busy*.'

The part about being busy was a lie. I'd spent most of the

day inventing ways to distract myself so I wouldn't spiral over Julian's predicament.

'*Regardless*,' he said, clearly having lost his last shred of patience with me (if he had any to begin with), 'there's no need for you to get involved. *More* involved.'

I frowned at him, starting to feel the true futility of my situation.

'In fact,' he said, 'you need to promise me that when Dale, Julian, and Kovalec go inside after dinner, you'll steer clear.'

'Why, what happens then?'

He sighed, clearly weighing up how much he could tell me. 'That's when they're making the deal. Julian's tech in exchange for a *lot* of money.'

'Oh god.'

'So, stay out of it, all right?'

I gulped. 'All right,' I said, my voice small. But I couldn't let that be that. I had to make one last-ditch effort to help Julian. 'As long as *you* promise to ask about immunity for Julian – or at least clemency. *Please*, Tommy.'

His eyes held mine, his expression troubled. 'I'll see what I can do.'

I nodded, my throat too dry to speak.

'Now, you'd better get back or it will start to look suspicious,' he added.

Heart pounding, I left Tommy to rejoin the others. We hadn't even sat down to eat and it was already the most bizarre dinner I'd ever attended.

**21**

In another life, I could have been an actress – a decent one if my performance at dinner was anything to go by.

I convincingly held up my end of the conversation, but my stomach was so tied up in knots, I could only pick at my food. A pity because Dimitra's Cyclades-inspired menu was extraordinary – every morsel I did manage to swallow was delicious.

As the crew cleared the dessert plates – my volcanic lemon soufflé barely touched – Julian suggested that he, Dale, and Kovalec retire to the lounge two decks below for Metaxa and cigars – almost verbatim what I'd said to Trudy earlier.

*And* what Tommy had warned me about. This was it – whatever was going down was about to happen.

As Julian and the other men descended the main staircase, I

looked about for Tommy, catching sight of his retreating head and shoulders on the companionway near the bow.

'Um, sorry, Trudy, nature's calling again,' I said, standing and picking up my clutch. Without waiting for a response, I scurried across the deck and ran down the staircase. Julian had already led the other men to the deck below – I could hear him talking about the cigars he'd imported – but had Tommy followed them?

The deck was clear in both directions. No crew about and no Tommy either. *Fuck.*

'Psst, Ally.'

I spun around and peered into the shadows. Tommy was standing in the alcove I'd hidden in before dinner. 'In here,' he said, sliding open the salon door. He crossed the spacious room, then looked down the corridor towards the bow. Still no one about, so we entered the day head and he locked the door behind us.

'Is there such a thing as the *nautical mile club*?' I joked.

His stern expression didn't waver.

'Sorry, just a joke. I'm nervous.'

'Understandable – you being in the midst of a sting operation. It's not too late, you know. I can have you off the yacht in less than five minutes.'

'I can't leave Julian.'

'Just me.'

'I'm sorry?' I asked, thrown off kilter. 'Did you just—'

'Never mind, it's not important.'

'Then why bring it up?'

He looked away, remorse marring his perfect features.

'And I didn't leave you, Tommy. *You* abandoned *me* – you abandoned our marriage for a *job*.'

I could have left it alone, not said that last part, but he'd brought it up – he'd made the offensive parry.

'This isn't the right ti—'

'Time. I know. It was *never* the right time,' I countered.

I wasn't even sure what I meant by that – the right time to discuss our marriage or the right time for the marriage itself? And then I realised he was probably referring to the person – or people – listening in on our conversation. *The entire yacht is bugged.* I could just imagine Elsa locked away in a cabin somewhere, sniggering as Tommy and I squabbled.

I shook my head, returning to the matter at hand. 'So, what happened when you asked about immunity? For Julian.'

'I'm still waiting on con—'

'But you asked, right?' I interjected. It was a poorly disguised accusation that he hadn't, which I instantly regretted.

'I said I would and I did,' he replied shortly, an undercurrent of hurt in his voice.

God, what was wrong with us?

'Sorry,' I said.

'It's fine.' Only it plainly wasn't.

'So, what are we waiting on then, a phone call or something?' I asked, ignoring how disappointed I was with myself – I should have trusted him.

'*We're* not waiting on anything – *I'm* waiting on—'

Just then, there were three light knocks on the door – two fast, then a beat, then a third. Panicked, my eyes flew to meet Tommy's, and I was about to call out, 'It's occupied,' when he calmly faced the door and repeated the same pattern, then unlocked it.

It opened and Trudy slipped inside the tiny room, then closed the door behind her, locking it again.

*What the actual fucking fuck?*

'Sorry, what's happening?' I asked, completely flummoxed.

'Well, Ally, what's happening is that you have inserted your-self into the middle of our operation.'

My mouth opened and closed several times but at first, no words came out. 'What?' I squeaked eventually. 'So, you're... you're...'

I continued to gawp at Trudy, waiting for everything to fall into place. Only it didn't. It all just tumbled onto the floor in a huge, indecipherable heap.

Trudy placed her hand on my forearm. 'I'll explain what I can later, but for now Tom needs to interrupt that meeting.' She turned to Tommy. 'We got the go-ahead, so get to the lounge and tell Julian his son's on the phone – and it's urgent.'

'But Julian doesn't have a son,' I said, becoming even more confused. 'He doesn't have any children.'

'I know, hun. And so does Dale. He'll understand that something's up and know to keep Kovalec occupied while Julian's out of the room. That'll give me time to brief Julian.'

*So, Dale is in on it too? So much for the cutesy retirees from Ottawa!*

Tommy nodded sharply, then left me alone with Trudy.

'Come on, hun,' she said, 'you should head back upstairs. Unless you *do* need the bathroom.'

'Uh, yes, actually. Do you mind?'

'Not at all.'

Trudy left and I sat heavily on the lid of the toilet, snippets of our interactions flitting through my mind. I'd warmed to Trudy immediately – she'd been so sweet and chatty, if a little nosey at times. But that wasn't her being nosey, I realised. She was getting close to me to protect the operation.

The day on the sailboat... the cooking class with *Yiayiá*... the breakfasts... the afternoon at the spa... her harping on (and on) about Tommy being interested in me... The entire time, Trudy was evaluating me, determining if I was a threat.

Or a distraction.

Which I had been.

'Oh god,' I groaned, dropping my head into my hands as another realisation landed. It must have been *Trudy* who'd raked Tommy over the coals.

Perhaps he was right. Maybe I needed to get off the yacht and out of harm's way. Although, if Trudy believed I was in danger, wouldn't she have suggested I leave? Or even *told* me to?

I took in a long, slow, deep breath and blew it out. Then did the same again. And again. Soon enough, my heart rate started to slow. I stood up and wet a hand towel, patted my neck with it, then dropped it in the basket at my feet. I retrieved my lipstick from my clutch and with as steady a hand as I could muster, reapplied. (Never underestimate the bolstering power of a bold red lip.)

I looked myself in the eye. 'All of this is for Julian. Just stay calm and leave it to the professionals.'

Hah! If only I'd given myself that advice *before* I invited myself to dinner.

After one more bracing breath, I opened the door and peeked out. No one in the salon but when I looked down the corridor, Julian and Trudy were standing close together, talking in terse, muted tones. Julian's face was in shadows, and I could only *imagine* what was going through his head.

Every part of me wanted to rush over and urge him to do whatever Trudy said to avoid being arrested, but there was no possible scenario in which that would help. Instead, I scurried across the salon, out onto the deck, and upstairs to the flybridge. Scott the chief steward was there, checking that the table had been properly cleared.

'Oh, hello,' he said, noticing me. 'I hope you're enjoying your evening.'

'Absolutely,' I lied with a wide smile. 'The crew's been brilliant, and the meal was just incredible.' Translation: *I've barely engaged with the crew and I was too nervous to eat much of anything.*

'Always good to hear,' he said with a grateful nod. 'Can I get you anything?'

I was about to say *no*, but I was suddenly ravenous.

'This is super cheeky,' I said, playing coy, 'but could I possibly have a toasted cheese and Marmite sandwich?'

His mouth twitched, but otherwise he maintained his professional air. 'I'll do my best,' he said with a smile, then left.

I sat on one of the long, built-in leather sofas, my body facing Naxos, and stared at the lights dancing on the water. I could just imagine what was happening in the galley – Dimitra pointing at Scott with a spatula and saying, 'Over my dead body will I make a toasted cheese and Marmite sandwich.' She was a Michelin-starred chef, after all.

'You look like you're a million miles away.'

I jolted, then looked up.

'Not really,' I replied as Trudy joined me. 'I've just asked for a sandwich and I'm going back and forth on whether they'll have Marmite.'

She gave me an odd look but didn't say anything. One thing was evident: the gregarious, effusive, sometimes ditsy woman who I'd befriended was a cover. *This* Trudy had the type of self-assurance that was forged in the fires of leadership – having to make difficult calls, then defend her actions.

Though there was a softness in her eyes, compassion – she wasn't flinty or hard, just different to who I'd thought she was.

'You've known all along who I am, haven't you?' I asked.

She nodded slowly. 'Yes, mostly. Though your connection to Tom came later – after you arrived on Aetheria.'

Tommy had said something similar, and I wondered how it could possibly have been missed. *Ah, that must have been Elsa's cock-up*, I thought. Although, it was moot now and I had other more pressing questions.

'And all those times we talked about Tommy – sorry, *Tom* – you were testing me.'

'I was keeping you close,' she said, not breaking eye contact.

'Right.' I licked my lips. 'Did you ever think about forcing me to leave?' I asked.

'Never *forcing* you, but I was close to fabricating some sort of emergency back in London.'

'Like a photograph of me and Julian going viral?'

'That wasn't us,' she said with a subtle shake of her head.

'I know.'

'No, it would have been more like a burst water pipe in the Chelsea house or something along those lines.'

I drew in a sharp breath. They knew everything. Whoever *they* were. But I was glad they hadn't flooded my house. I loved that house – I still do.

Trudy slid her cuff up her arm to check the time. Something flashed behind her eyes, but she remained outwardly calm.

'I've thrown a spanner in the works, haven't I?'

She regarded me with a measured look. 'Look, we'd always planned on using Julian to get to Kovalec – letting the guppie go free to bag the bigger fish. Your request... it just changed how we executed that plan.'

'Did I cause trouble for him?' I asked, not entirely sure I wanted the answer.

'Julian? No, he pounced on our offer. Once I told him who I was – who *we* were – he seemed relieved and fell right into line. He'll give us what we need.'

'That's reassuring – about Julian,' I said, even though it drove home how close he'd been to being arrested. 'But that's not... I meant Tommy – *Tom*. I don't want him to get into trouble.'

'Oh, I see. That's a little more complicated, because—'

'Excuse me.' A steward arrived, carrying a cloche-covered plate.

I smiled at her. 'Thank you. Just here's fine,' I said, indicating a nearby cocktail table.

She set it down, then left us.

I stared at the cloche, my mind elsewhere. *That's a little more complicated...* That didn't seem to bode well for Tommy – or me.

'You going to...?' Trudy asked, and I came back to the present. She tilted her head towards the cloche.

'Schrodinger's sandwich,' I quipped. 'If I don't lift the lid, there's a fifty-fifty chance of a toasted cheese and Marmite sandwich, and if I do—'

Obviously not one to play games, Trudy lifted the lid and the pungent, delicious aroma of warm Marmite wafted over.

'Fuck me, I'm starving.' I reached for one half of the sandwich and took a huge bite. 'Mmm, heaven,' I said through my mouthful. 'Want the other half?' I offered.

'God, no. That stuff looks like axel grease and tastes even worse.'

After swallowing, I started laughing.

'What's so funny?' she asked, her eyes narrowing slightly.

'Nothing,' I replied through my laughter. 'And everything.'

It wasn't exactly a laugh-or-I'll-cry moment. More of a release – *days* of pent-up tension bursting out.

My laughter lessened, changing to sighs and I looked skyward, catching sight of the most incredible array of stars. 'Oh, wow – *look*.'

'That is beautiful,' she agreed.

I stared at the stars a few moments longer, then watched Trudy, who was still gazing up, a wistful smile on her face. *How often is she able to appreciate something as simple as a starry sky?* I wondered.

'Have you always worked for… whoever it is you work for?' I asked.

She dragged her eyes away from the sky and fixed her potent gaze upon me. 'More or less.'

'And Dale?'

I could tell how seriously she considered the question. Would she answer? *Should* she?

'He joined later,' she said.

It was vague – a mere morsel – but it was enough. They'd made it work, Trudy's career in intelligence. They'd made it work, and Tommy and I had lasted less than two years.

'What happens now?' I asked. 'To Julian, I mean.'

'He's to go to Lyon for questioning. It's in his best interest not to screw us – he'll be arrested if he does – so we're trusting him to show up under his own steam.'

'Oh god.'

'It's… *serious*, what he was planning to do – selling to Kovalec. It could have had terrible ramifications. *Globally*.'

I blanched and she observed me with a scrutinous eye. 'You do know what his proprietary tech *does*, right, Ally?'

Did I? I knew Julian was brilliant and had invented a technological game changer, but beyond that... no. I shook my head.

'Well, you should ask him about it,' she replied, that softness in her eyes waning.

*Fuck, Jules. What were you thinking?*

The sound of the tender's motor cut through the still night air and I half-stood to peer over the railing. Two decks below, a handcuffed Kovalec was being guided onto the tender by Elsa and a man I hadn't seen before. The man took the helm, then drove the tender towards the shore.

'It's done.'

I spun around at the sound of Tommy's voice. God, he looked good in that uniform – even with the sombre expression.

'Greek authorities are meeting Elsa onshore,' he continued. 'They'll transport Kovalec to Athens as planned.'

'Good. Dale and I will be there tomorrow to escort him to Lyon for quest—'

'Um, sorry,' I interrupted, 'but should you be discussing this in front of me?'

'Hah! Hell no,' said Trudy with a wry laugh. Tommy started to apologise but Trudy raised her hand to stop him and he fell silent, his expression inscrutable. 'Look,' she said to me, 'these operations, they can span months, even *years*, and quite often people get caught up in them, like you have – *civilians*.'

'Which means?' I asked, my mouth as dry as if I'd eaten sand. All I could think of was that cliché from spy films: *I could tell you, but then I'd have to kill you.* Was I about to be *disappeared*?

'Which *means*, you will be signing the most iron-clad non-disclosure agreement you've ever seen,' she replied, and I expelled a ragged sigh. 'And Julian's freedom will depend not only on his cooperation, but yours. You understand?'

Incapable of a verbal reply, I nodded – vigorously, so there was no possibility of being misunderstood. I didn't want to be disappeared.

'Good,' she said with a warm smile.

It was near-impossible to keep up with the many facets of Trudy, which was rather terrifying. And I'd thought we were becoming *friends*.

She slapped her hands onto her thighs, then stood. 'Great work,' she said, patting Tommy on the back as she passed by. 'I'll go find Dale and Julian, then we can get the hell outta here.'

When she was gone, Tommy looked over, his mouth stretching into a thin line – not quite a smile.

'Thank you,' I said. 'For helping Julian.'

He shrugged off my thanks. 'Trudy wouldn't have agreed if it didn't suit our purposes. And with Julian as an informant from the start, building the case against Kovalec should go smoothly.'

*Informant*. Julian had been *so* close to ending up in custody with Kovalec. It was horrifying even as a thought experiment, so I ousted the idea entirely. No sense in dwelling on hypotheticals.

Tommy's gaze dropped to my supper. 'Is that...?'

'It is, yes.'

'Could I possibly...?' he asked, looking at me with pleading eyes.

'Yes, yes, of course,' I replied with a soft laugh.

I handed him the uneaten half, and he sat beside me. 'Thank you. I haven't eaten since lunchtime and that was a protein bar.'

He took a big bite, staring out at the view, and I watched his profile for a moment. He truly was the most beautiful man.

*Will he ever be mine again?*

As if he'd read my mind, he looked over and smiled, and my insides turned molten.

Then I took a bite of my half, and we sat together in companionable silence, our knees almost touching, munching on what had been our favourite sandwich, especially on wintry Sunday mornings.

Thought of the day…
Some relationships are irredeemable.
Don't kid yourself, just walk away.
(Or fly, drive, scoot, skip, or scuttle away – just get out of
there.)

The ride back to Aetheria was silent, save for the noise of the helicopter's rotor.

Julian sat beside me, pale-faced, his fingers worrying as if he were rolling something between them. A minute or two into the flight, I couldn't bear it and reached over, laying my hand on top his to still them. He captured it between his and squeezed tightly, then glanced my way. The panic in his eyes was startling. I'd never seen Julian like that.

'You okay?' I mouthed.

He faked a smile and gave me a reassuring nod – only it wasn't reassuring. And what had Trudy and Dale told him about me – about how much I knew?

I looked across at them. Trudy's head was on Dale's shoulder, her eyes shut. It must have been exhausting running a months-long international operation, let alone acting the role of a jovial retiree with a penchant for girl talk.

If I hadn't witnessed it first-hand – her transformation from my gal pal Trudy to Jane Bond super spy – there was no way I would have believed it.

And how much of my experience on Aetheria had been part of the ruse? It was clear that every interaction with Trudy and Dale had been – *and* Elsa – but what about Tommy?

He was sitting beside Dale, his face set in a frown as he stared out the window. I would have given anything to know what he was thinking.

And when was goodbye? When did he need to be some-place else, before or after I returned to London?

I blew out a breath, fatigue slamming into me with full force. It's a lot to be *on* for days on end and it wasn't just Trudy feeling it. Perhaps it would be best if I left Aetheria first thing in the morning and returned to London – back to real life and some semblance of normality.

I just wanted to go home.

But that was ignoring the 800-pound gorilla in the heli-copter – or rather, *two* gorillas: the hot ex-husband and the hot-mess ex-husband. I couldn't leave Aetheria without making sure Julian was okay – that would be abandoning him, and I wasn't about to do that.

And I definitely had unfinished business with Tommy. Even if it was to say a final goodbye – a thought that sent a sharp pang ricocheting through me. I didn't want to say *goodbye* to Tommy – especially not for good – but I also had to prepare for the worst.

I was still in knots when the helicopter landed, my mind zigzagging between twin conundrums. I looked at Tommy, whose unfocused gaze indicated he was still deep in thought, but he didn't – *wouldn't?* – meet my eye. And as soon as Christos opened the door, he jumped out and jogged off towards the staff quarters.

So much for finishing unfinished business. And what happened to the bloke I'd shared my sandwich with just now? Where was *that* Tommy?

Christos offered his hand and I took it, too weary to pull the independent-woman card. Once my feet hit the ground, I looked longingly in the direction of my villa. I was desperate for a hot bath, then to fall into bed. But first, Julian.

'You okay?' I asked again when he joined me.

He stared into my eyes. There was so much behind them that was foreign to me and that scared the fuck out of me. Julian was Mr Confident, Mr I've Got This.

'I will be,' he said quietly.

'Do you want to talk about it?'

'Goodnight!' Trudy's jarring voice cut through the private bubble surrounding me and Julian and we both looked over.

'Goodnight,' we said in unison, like it had been a normal evening out.

Trudy and Dale climbed into the golf cart and Christos drove them away. Would I ever see them again? Now knowing that my friendship with Trudy had been a fabrication – or in part, at least – I wasn't sure I wanted to.

'Want me to wait with you – for Christos?' asked Julian.

I shook my head. 'I'll walk. It's not that far, and it's downhill.'

He glanced at my shoes, then back up, his brows raised sceptically. 'Are you sure?'

'Eh, I'll be fine.' I slipped out of my shoes and picked them up, letting them dangle from my fingers. 'Exhibit A,' I said, showing Julian. 'And you didn't answer me. Do you want to talk about it?'

'How much do you already know?' he asked, a slight wobble in his voice.

'Probably more than you think. But not everything.'

He inhaled through his nose, nodding slowly as his gaze drifted away – reluctant acceptance was my best guess.

'So,' he said, his eyes meeting mine again, 'your villa or mine?'

I emitted an involuntary groan from deep within my chest. It sounded remarkably like *I'm desperate for a long, hot bubble bath* with a little *please, kill me now* thrown in.

'Not to worry,' he reassured me, 'we can talk another time.'

'No – I'm sorry. That just came out. I'm here for you – *really*. Let's go to mine, then I can kick you out when I start to get sleepy.'

'So, five minutes from now?' he teased.

'I promise it will be at least ten.'

He smiled – this one reaching his eyes – then offered his arm. I took it and we headed down the path to my villa.

\* \* \*

A little more than an hour later, Julian had finished explaining his connection to Kovalec. And I won't bore you with all the details. Just know that their respective companies had developed complementary technologies and it was in everyone's best interest to collaborate – which they'd been doing for several years.

*Until* Julian started to worry that *his* tech would be weaponised – seemingly imminent based on rumours about Kovalec's shifting political affiliations. And as Kovalec was about to become one of the bad guys, Julian wanted out before he was dragged down with him.

'So, is that why you invited him here, to end the partnership?' I asked.

Because if that was the case, then why the sting operation? Why not let Julian end his association with Kovalec, then go on his merry way?

'Not quite,' he replied. 'And Kovalec invited himself. He wanted to buy the last piece of the puzzle.'

I gasped, instantly understanding what Trudy had meant. No wonder Julian had been a suspect.

'But you weren't going to sell it to him, were you, Jules?' I asked tentatively.

'God, no! What do you take me for?'

'Well, pardon me,' I said, more than a little cross. 'But all things considered, that's not an unreasonable question. There were actual *spies* here, Jules. Like, people on the island *spying* on you. And you were *this close* to being arrested!' I added, pinching my thumb and forefinger together. 'They think you're in on it – whatever it is.'

'Well, yes, I know all that now,' he replied with a frown. 'I still can't believe that Dale and Trudy were investigating me. I thought Dale and I had struck up a genuine friendship. I *trusted* him.'

'I'm sorry, Jules,' I said, commiserating. *I* was disappointed and the budding friendship I'd lost to a lie was only five days old.

'And Tom – I had *no* idea he was...'

I held my breath, mentally filling in the blank with *your exhusband* and trying to formulate an explanation that wouldn't upset Julian further.

'...*undercover*,' he said, finishing his thought.

*Oh, thank god.* So, Julian *didn't* know about me and Tommy – he would have said something if he did. That meant one less complication to discuss, but I *would* tell Julian eventually. Especially if Tommy and I... Nope, I couldn't go there. I couldn't hope for something that seemed unlikely, if not impossible.

'I thought he was just a skipper,' Julian went on, dragging my thoughts back to the villa. 'And a bloody good one – he came highly recommended.'

Considering the lengths Tommy's organisation had gone to infiltrate Julian's little corner of the world, it was no wonder his sailing credentials appeared legitimate.

'And *Elsa...* You don't suppose anyone else on the island was part of it, do you?' he asked, his eyes returning to me.

'I wouldn't think so, no,' I replied evenly, which was mostly the truth. I wasn't *technically* part of the sting. And it was clear Trudy hadn't outed me, or Julian would have mentioned that as well.

'You shouldn't have any trouble replacing them, Jules,' I continued. 'Once word gets out, people will be dying to work on Aetheria.'

'I suppose,' he replied, seeming deep in thought. 'You know, even if they *had* arrested me, I've done nothing wrong and I've got the build logs to prove it.'

'For?' I asked.

'For the dummy code I was planning on selling to Kovalec.'

'Dummy code?' I blinked at him in surprise.

'Yes, I've been working on it for weeks – back in the trenches, locked away in my villa. It's almost identical to the real code, you see, except for the bugs I've embedded. And at the risk of sounding immodest—'

'You? Immodest?' I teased, injecting a little levity.

He gave me a friendly side-eye, his mouth quirking. 'At the

risk of sounding *immodest*, it would take someone as clever as me a very long time to determine why the code intermittently glitches. And even if they did, it could be attributed to faulty hardware or a random tech gremlin, rather than an issue with the code itself.'

'Wow,' I whispered, simultaneously shocked at Julian's involvement in such a dangerous caper *and* proud of how he'd handled it.

'And what if you *had* sold the dummy tech to Kovalec? Wouldn't that money be tainted?' I asked, wary that I wouldn't like his response.

'Absolutely and I would have donated it – found some cause on the right side of history...'

I was relieved – yet again – but also confused – yet again.

'But I thought it was for Aetheria. You said the island was your exit strategy. Don't you need that money?'

'Nooo,' he replied with a smile. 'I own the island outright. Trust me, I could live to a hundred and never have to work another day. And if I ever *am* in trouble, I can sell *Ally's Odyssey* – that's twenty million quid, give or take.'

'Then I don't understand,' I said quietly. 'What exactly are you exiting?'

'Just... *all* of it – all the superficial bullshit. The jet-setting and wasting time with people who don't matter to me. I want a quieter pace of life. It's all been so frantic for so long. And, yes, it's a situation of my own making, but I'm turning fifty soon and I've realised there's more to life than being a middle-aged playboy.'

I'd never heard Julian refer to himself this way – particularly the undercurrent of disdain – but sensing he was still mid-thought, I remained silent.

'Actually,' he continued, giving me a meaningful look,

'spending time with you... It's highlighted what I'm missing most. Being in love.'

*'Jules...'*

It was part plea, part apology. Because no matter how much I cared about Julian, I wasn't going to magically fall in love with him just because he'd had an epiphany. And notice I said *fall in love* rather than *fall back in love*. That had only happened once and it wasn't with my third husband.

His eyes softened with affection, then he reached for my hand. I placed it in his, hoping to let him down gently – especially after the night he'd had.

But I needn't have worried.

'Don't worry, darling, I didn't mean you. I had my chance, and I blew it. It's my biggest regret, not knowing what I had when you and I were married. But as you said, you and I work best as friends.'

*'Close* friends,' I said, overcome with a rush of affection.

'Definitely,' he replied, and we shared a smile. 'But it's the other thing you said, Ally, and I've been thinking about it ever since. I *do* want to find my someone – and I want to bring her here and make a life together. Well, not the whole year 'round, as I suspect even paradise gets a bit boring after a while,' he joked with a wink.

I sniggered. *I* was tiring of it and I'd only been there five days. Although, my stay had included the wrong post going viral, uncovering a ring of spies, and juggling two ex-husbands.

But I would definitely bring Claude someday. She'd love it – *and* she deserved it.

'Anyway... that's my focus now,' he continued, 'finding the love of my life and making Aetheria *the* destination in the Aegean.'

'Which brings us full circle, I suppose.'

'Indeed. Can you believe it was less than a week ago that I asked you to come?'

'Nope. Feels like forever.'

'So true.' With a heavy sigh, he released my hand and flopped back onto the sofa, his eyes fixed on the ceiling. They started to drift shut.

'Oi,' I said, nudging him. 'You can't fall asleep here, Jules.'

'Mmm?' he murmured sleepily.

'I mean it.' I poked him and he pretended to snore. 'Hey,' I said through laughter. 'One viral photo of our supposed reunion was enough to contend with, thank you very much. Now, off you go...'

I stood up and tugged on his hand and he cracked one eye open.

'All right, all right,' he said, planting his palms on his thighs and standing. He walked to the door, and I followed.

'Goodnight, Jules. Will I see you in the morning?'

'Probably not. I'll be leaving before dawn.'

'Oh.'

'But we'll speak soon, I promise.'

'Good. I want to know what happens in Lyon.'

'Of course. And stay here as long as you like. I know Niki's not your favourite person right now, but she will look after you.'

'Thanks, Jules. And I don't dislike Niki – we all make mistakes, right?'

Something flickered behind his eyes. I'd meant it as an offhand remark, but I could tell we were both thinking about the mistakes that ended our marriage.

A moment later, he blinked, a soft, sad smile crossing his face before he captured me in a tight hug. 'Thank you, Ally – for everything.'

Tears pricked my eyes at the finality in his voice. But I

would see Julian again – and soon. I let go first and he stood back, giving me one more smile before stepping into the cool night air.

That was one ex-husband sorted. Now what to do about the other one?

**23**

_____

Thought of the day...
Just when you think you've cracked the code, life changes
the password.
But that's okay – winging it is a valid strategy.

After seeing Julian out, I rested my back against the door and
exhaled slowly. This was more than physical exhaustion. My
heart was exhausted too.

It would take some time to wrap my mind around Julian's
predicament, his proximity to serious trouble – and, by extension, *mine*. No wonder Tommy had warned me off. And everything he'd said about finding love... My heart ached for Julian,
for the vulnerable man beneath the swagger. I just hoped that
whoever he gave his heart to deserved it. She'd have me to
contend with if she didn't.

And then there was Tommy...

I pushed off the door and wandered into the bathroom to
run a bath. As it started to fill, I generously sprinkled in bath

salts and a sensuous aroma rose from the hot water. I inhaled deeply as I slipped out of my dress and knickers.

I was about to step into the bath when I spied the minibar through the doorway. *A glass of wine wouldn't go amiss*, I thought. It wasn't just the food I'd neglected at dinner; after my first sips of Champagne, I'd stuck to sparkling water.

I was crossing the lounge room stark naked when, out of the corner of my eye, I spied someone lurking on the porch. I shrieked, then ran back into the bathroom, grabbing the first thing I could lay my hands on – a fluffy bathmat – and wrapping it around me.

My heart beating so hard I could hear it over my shallow breaths, I peeked around the doorframe and squinted through the large picture window.

Wearing an apologetic smile, Tommy lifted his hand in a wave.

'You scared the hell out of me,' I shouted.

A muffled, 'Sorry,' came through the glass.

'Well, come around to the door, you muppet,' I said, directing him with a wild wave of my hand.

I swapped the bathmat for a robe – far more coverage – and tied the belt on the way to the door. I opened it to find Tommy standing there, the personification of sheepishness.

'Sorry for scaring you.'

'What were you doing at the window?' I asked.

'Checking to see if Julian was still here.'

'He's gone.'

'Ahh, yep. I figured that out.'

'Before or after you saw me naked?'

'About the same time. Are you going to invite me in?'

I pretended to glare at him, but it was a pathetic effort. Now that the shock had worn off, my heart was about to explode with happiness.

I stood aside, letting him pass, then closed the door.

'You'd think you'd be better at surveillance by now,' I teased, following him into the lounge, 'what with you being a super spy and all.'

He faced me, the left side of his mouth hitched in amusement – that special Tommy smile – and my stomach flipped.

'You would think that, wouldn't you?' he replied, his eyes creasing at the corners. Then he listened out. 'Are you running a bath?'

'Oh, fuck.' I dashed into the bathroom just in time to shut off the bath before it overflowed.

Tommy had followed me and when I turned around, he was looking right at my arse.

'Excuse you.'

'Sorry,' he said. He wasn't, the cheeky bugger.

I shooed him into the lounge, and he backed up, his hands raised in surrender. Then he burst out laughing.

'What's so funny?' I asked, my lips quirking.

He sighed heavily, clasping the back of his neck with both hands. 'Nothing. Everything.' Which was fair – I'd more or less said the same thing to Trudy on the yacht. There are times you just needed to laugh and release the tension.

Tommy dropped his hands, sighing again, only less forcefully. 'Do you mind if I...?' he asked, indicating the minibar.

'No, no, help yourself,' I replied.

I sat on one of the sofas, tucking my feet beneath me, and watched as he checked what was on offer. He'd changed out of the uniform, now wearing well-worn jeans and a light-grey T-shirt that showed off his wide shoulders and slim hips. Fuck, he was sexy.

'Okay to open this?' He held up a bottle of red. 'It's a... mandi... Mandilaria,' he added, reading the label – *badly*.

'Open whatever you like.'

'Are you having a glass?'

'God, yes.'

With a chuckle, he took two glasses from the shelf above and filled them halfway. He crossed the room, handing me my wine before sitting on the other end of the sofa. I watched his graceful movements closely, acutely aware of how easy it would be to fall hopelessly back in love with him. Easy, but dangerous.

But that was something to think about another time – or never.

'What should we toast to?' I asked just as the rim of the glass touched his lips.

'Oh, sorry. Uh...'

'To a successful operation?' I offered.

'That'll do.' He reached over and we tapped glasses, then sipped in unison.

'I wasn't sure I would see you tonight,' I said after a few moments of watching him stare off.

His faraway look vanished. 'I gathered that from your outfit.'

'Which one – completely nude or bath-linen chic?'

'I really *am* sorry.'

I shrugged. 'It's not like you haven't seen it before – and recently.'

He smiled faintly, his gaze dipping to the floor.

'Tommy.'

He looked up.

'You seemed... *distracted* – on the ride back, I mean. And now, come to think of it.'

'Just a lot on my mind. Loose ends to tie up.'

'Does that include me?' I asked, my voice tight. Because if he said *yes* then that was that – we'd go back to how things were before Aetheria, before I was introduced to a skipper called Tom.

'You're not a loose end, Ally,' he said, his voice low.

'Well, I am until I sign that NDA,' I quipped. Only it wasn't funny, and we both knew it – Tommy's thin-lipped smile disappearing almost as soon as it appeared.

He held my gaze for a long moment. 'You're a good person, Ally.'

'Well, we always said we'd try and save the world, right?' I retorted, half-joking.

'I mean it.'

'Oh...' He'd caught me completely off-guard, and my pulse quickened.

He sat forward, his eyes boring into mine. 'You had no idea what you were walking into tonight, but you forged ahead anyway – all to help Julian.'

'I... Thank you.'

'Of course, you're also as stubborn as hell...'

'Hey!' I chided, breaking into laughter.

'Am I wrong?'

'No, but—'

'Maybe I should have said *tenacious*,' he teased.

'Better.'

'Like a dog with a bone.'

'Can we go back to the part where you were being nice to me?'

He didn't answer right away, and the air crackled with anticipation. Were we finally going to talk about *us*?

'So,' he said, breaking eye contact a little too abruptly, 'you and Julian – all good there?'

'Ah, yes,' I replied, grabbing the change of topic like a life-line. Despite what I'd been telling myself, I wasn't ready to dive into the depths of the Ally-and-Tommy mess. 'You know, he wasn't going to sell the real code to Kovalec – he wrote dummy code.'

Tommy's eyes flashed with surprise but only for a moment, then a wry smile tugged at his mouth. 'I did wonder if he'd do something like that.'

'Then why were you about to arrest him for espionage?'

'I wasn't—' He huffed. 'First off, that wouldn't have been the charge. Second,' he said, pinning me with a piercing look, 'I took it to Trudy a couple of weeks ago – the notion that Julian might find a way to disengage without selling out.'

'You did?'

'Yes, but she was sceptical, and I was told not to pursue that line of investigation.'

One thing was clear: Tommy hadn't just helped Julian – he'd gone above and beyond, vouching for a man he barely knew. And sure, the truth would have come out if Julian *had* been arrested, but this was a far better outcome.

And I owed it all to Tommy.

'Thank you for helping him,' I said, suddenly so overcome with gratitude, I didn't trust myself to say anything more.

'Of course, Ally. I'd do anything for you.'

I inhaled sharply and looked away, tears pricking my eyes.

'Besides, he can't have been *all* bad – I mean, you did marry him, after all.'

I looked back at Tommy, my eyes now glossed with tears. 'Are you just saying that to make me laugh?'

He set his glass on the coffee table and edged closer. Taking my glass, he placed it beside his, then took my hand.

'I would much rather have you laughing than crying, so yes.'

A kaleidoscope of emotions washed over me – loss and hurt and wonder and joy, all at once. I could hardly breathe.

'It's very difficult to stay mad at you,' I whispered.

'Why would you want to?' he whispered back.

'Because...' My words drifted away, then abandoned me entirely. Unable to speak, I laid my free hand flat against my chest, right over my heart, and tapped it twice.

'Your heart?' he asked softly. 'To protect it?'

I nodded, tears now running down my cheeks. That first moment I'd seen Tommy on Aetheria, tiny fissures had spidered their way across the landscape of my heart. Now, under Tommy's potent yet tender gaze, those fissures deepened, forging valleys of fear and peaks of hope – both wanting to exert their power over me.

*This* was me naked before him. This was all of me.

Eyes fixed on mine, Tommy didn't speak, just moved closer, drawing his thumb across my cheeks to wipe my tears. He leaned in to kiss me.

I closed my eyes, my lips moving slowly, gently against his. He moved nearer, his other arm snaking behind me and pulling me to him. I slid my hand up his chest and over his shoulder, my fingers getting lost in his hair. I felt his tongue against mine, hesitant at first, and I pulled him further into the kiss, inviting more, igniting a visceral need deep within me.

*God, I want him.*

I broke free from the kiss, shoving him back against the sofa, then climbed on top of him, one knee either side of his thighs. His hands grabbed my arse as I dipped my head and kissed him again, our mouths hungry this time, *wanting*.

Tommy's hands left my arse to tug impatiently at the tie

around my waist. He tossed it aside, then shoved the robe off my shoulders, dropping his mouth to my breast and sucking hard on the nipple. I cried out. He reached for my hips and, fingers wide, slid his hands around to cup my bare arse, giving it a squeeze. I started grinding myself against his crotch, the robe and his jeans between us, his erection straining against the denim.

His mouth left my nipple and I looked down at him. He lifted his chin and I dipped my head for another kiss. His tongue was aggressive, tasting me, duelling with mine.

'I need you, Ally,' he said against my mouth. 'I need to be inside you.'

I needed him too, but I also wanted to stay like that, making out on the sofa.

'*Now*,' he insisted, and with very little effort, he stood, holding me under my arse and carrying me to the bed. He tossed me onto it, making me laugh with glee, then hovered above me and kissed me – *hard*. He propped himself up on his side, parting my robe and running his hand hungrily over my breasts, my stomach, my thighs... everywhere but where I wanted him to touch me most.

I grabbed his hand and shoved it between my legs. 'Rub my clit,' I demanded, and he complied, knowing exactly how I liked it – pressing the pad of his thumb against me and moving in slow but firm circles while two fingers slipped inside me. I was so wet for him and vibrations zipped through me, my nerves electrifying as he took me closer and closer to the threshold.

'Come for me, baby,' he murmured, his lips against my skin. He flicked my nipple with his tongue, rapid and unrelenting, and the orgasm built. Shivers rippled down each limb, my fingertips and toes tingling. Hot yellow light consumed me, crashing about inside me and setting me ablaze. I rose and rose, knowing that when I tipped over the edge, Tommy would be there to catch me.

And he was.

I thrashed against his hand, crying out as the orgasm exploded within me, a supernova of sensation. It was some time before my eyes fluttered open and when they did, Tommy was watching me, a slightly-smug-but-completely-justified look on his face.

'That was...' I whispered.

'Wasn't it just?'

I looked at him, a sly smile on my face. I hooked a leg up and over him, then in one movement, pushed him onto the bed and rolled on top of him.

His eyes widened in surprise.

'Quite the manoeuvre,' he said, obviously impressed.

I waggled my brows a couple of times, then opened the drawer and took out a condom. 'Shall I do the honours?' I asked.

'Be my guest.' He placed his hands behind his head, making his biceps bulge beneath his T-shirt.

'Mind taking that off?' I asked, my eyes dropping to his chest.

He half-sat, his abs rippling beneath his shirt, and pulled it over his head one-handed from the collar. He tossed it aside.

'Quite the manoeuvre,' I echoed, and he grinned.

I moved onto his lower half, undoing his jeans and shoving them and his briefs down to his shins.

'You really do have a beautiful cock,' I said, appraising it as I ran my hand up and down the shaft with a feather-light touch.

He let out a deep, throaty moan. I stopped teasing him, tore open the condom packet, then slid on the condom. He moaned even louder.

'You like that?' I asked.

'You know I do,' he growled back. I was about to climb on top of him when he tutted at me. 'Uh-uh, my turn to be on top.'

'Fair,' I replied, sitting back on my haunches.

Keeping his eyes locked on mine, Tommy sat up, kicked off his shoes, slid off his socks, wriggled out of his jeans and briefs – expertly, mind you, no awkward contortions – then grabbed me, flipped me onto my back, and climbed between my legs.

'Also impressive.'

'Still a few tricks up my sleeve.'

We grinned at each other, then he entered me, and my smile fell away as I wrapped my arms and legs around him, holding him close to me as we became one.

24

Thought of the day...
Careful what you wish for, because what if you get it, but it
doesn't serve you?
(Champagne and cake are the exceptions.)

It was before dawn when I woke, the dull whomp-whomp of
the helicopter off in the distance. Julian had left. *He'll be okay*, I
told myself firmly, heading off any catastrophising before it
took hold.

A hand reached for me under the covers, and I rolled over
to face Tommy.

'Hello,' I said, lacing my fingers through his.

'Hello.'

The dim light cast shadows across his face, making him
look like a different person. I trained my eyes on each of his
features in turn until he looked like Tommy again.

We locked eyes.

'What's going on in there?' he asked, glancing at my
forehead.

I sniggered softly. 'Just thinking about Julian.'

'Ahh.' He pretended to pull away, making me laugh.

'Not like that – come back to me.'

He faced me again, eyes creased at the corners and a slight smile on his lips. My breath caught at how beautiful he was.

*Come back to me.* The words called to me, a siren's song. Is that what I wanted, for Tommy to come back to me?

*Yes.* The voice inside my head was decisive and clear.

But how? The thing that had driven us apart remained – I'd just lived it out in real time. Reality intruded, coiling cold and tight within me.

'Well, that's not about Julian,' he said, his eyes narrowing as he watched me intently. 'You seem sad.' He reached for my cheek, caressing it lightly with the back of his fingers. 'Why are you sad?'

I chewed on my lower lip. Tell him the real reason and spark the conversation we'd been avoiding, or brush it off and enjoy the rest of our time together? But that would have been the coward's way out. And I wasn't a coward.

I sat up, holding the duvet to my chest one-handed and looking straight ahead.

'Ally?'

*Well, in for a penny, in for a pound*, I told myself. If we were going to have this conversation – which was *long* overdue – then I had to go back to the beginning. The beginning of the end.

'When you got the job – this one, as an investigator or what-ever you are – why didn't you... I don't know... *tell* me? Don't you think we'd still be together if you'd just *told* me – I mean, sworn me to secrecy, obviously, but... you let it come between us.'

I was surprised at how measured I sounded, but a version of this question *had* been brewing for a decade. I might've only just learned *what* had driven that wedge between us, but I'd chewed it over plenty of times. And there was something cathartic about finally saying it out loud.

'Oh, right.'

Now Tommy sat up, also pulling the duvet to his chest and there we were, side by side, legs stretched out and both staring straight ahead, our fingers still laced beneath the covers.

A stifling cloud of tension descended, making it difficult to breathe. But I didn't speak, didn't so much as *twitch*, as the thorniest question I'd ever asked anyone hung in the air between us.

Seconds passed, perhaps minutes, then he finally spoke.

'I suppose the short answer is *immaturity*.'

'And the long answer?' I snapped, irritated by his glibness. Didn't he know I needed more? So much more.

He cleared his throat, but I still didn't look at him, sensing that if I did he'd retreat. If he needed more time to order his thoughts, then he could have it. It might be our only chance to discuss this properly, and I wanted the truth.

'Sorry, Ally, but I think that's the long answer as well,' he said eventually. I glanced over and he was looking at me, his face set in a frown. He wasn't being glib; he was being truthful. I gave his hand a squeeze and a small smile appeared for half a second then disappeared. He looked away, then licked his lips.

'After my first assignment – and I really did go to Peru, like I said – but afterwards, when I came home, you were this... this *tether*. To reality, I mean. And you have to understand that my work... It felt surreal doing what I was doing – thrilling, but also surreal. Especially that first year. But I had you and you were real. You were my home. And in a way, there became two of me – Tommy when I was home with you, and Tom when I was on assignment.'

'Tom the spy,' I said, looking straight ahead again.

'More or less.'

'And which one was you – the *real* you?'

'They both were, Ally. That's the thing, you see. I convinced myself I could live both lives. The thrill of the job – travelling someplace new, joining a team, starting a fresh assignment – and the comfort of returning home to London, to my wife.'

I'd figured it was something along those lines, all the times I'd asked myself *why*. He'd compartmentalised to make the separation easier. But I had never considered that it was deliberate – that he'd consciously separated his two lives, taking what he wanted from me, from our marriage, without any regard for the impact on *me*.

And it hit me as I sat there. I'd always recognised the hurt and the sadness... even the longing, which reared its head on occasion, leading to teary bouts of eating too much chocolate and binge-watching *Friends*.

But I had never *truly* dealt with the deep-seated anger I'd been lugging around all those years. Until that moment. Because Tommy's explanation unleashed a fury that had been dormant for years.

'You selfish bastard,' I snarled, flicking back the duvet and climbing out of bed. I headed straight for the discarded robe, scooping it off the floor and shoving my arms into it, then wrapping it tightly around me, my arms folded across my chest. Fluffy armour. I rounded on Tommy, shooting him a look so scathing, so *ferocious*, I'm surprised lasers didn't shoot from my eyes.

He dropped his gaze, his Adam's apple bobbing as he gulped. 'You have every right to call me that.'

'I *know*. How dare you leave me crumbs, then tell yourself they were enough. They *weren't*. And you may have thought of me as a *safe haven*, but you were different when you came home. *Every* time. Moody, sullen, distracted... Even when you were *there,* you weren't. And just as I'd start to get a glimpse of Tommy, of my *husband*, you'd disappear again. And you have the gall to tell me *I* left the marriage! There may have been two of you, Tommy, but one of them was barely a shell. And guess which one I got?'

I whipped around and stalked into the lounge room, pacing its length in front of the picture window as I fumed. Adrenalin pumped through my veins, my heartbeat thudding in my ears.

How *dare* he.

'How dare you!' I shouted into the next room, which made me feel slightly better. But only slightly.

The robe was flapping as I paced, so I scouted for the tie – it was on the floor where Tommy had tossed it. I snatched it up and tied it around me, tightly yanking the ends just as Tommy stepped into the doorway to the bedroom, wearing only a pair of jeans. It had always been my favourite outfit on him – jeans and nothing else. He looked like a model from a Levi's ad. I averted my eyes. I may have been furious with him, but my libido had *not* got the memo.

'Can I say something?' he asked.

'You just did.'

'Can I say something else?'

I stopped pacing and glowered at him expectantly.

'Well?'

He grabbed the back of his neck and stretched it to the side, a gesture that meant, *What the fuck do I do now?* Or in this instance, *What the fuck do I say that won't piss Ally off any more than I already have?*

'How about I make us some coffee, and we go sit out there?' he asked, dropping his hand and nodding towards the porch.

'Fine.'

I strode past him into the bedroom and slammed the door, then quickly got dressed in jeans and a tank top – *with* a bra. Tommy did *not* get to see the girls unfettered.

When I came out of the bedroom, he was holding two coffees. He handed one to me and I took it without saying *thank you*, then went outside. I sat and sipped my coffee, staring out at the Aegean. The coffee was delicious, but I wasn't about to tell Tommy that.

He came out to join me a short time later, having put his T-shirt on (thank god). He sat in the chair next to mine, and we drank in silence. I watched the sky for the falcon and right as Tommy started to speak, she appeared, flying low from one side of the vista to the other.

'Was that a hawk?' he asked. The absurdity of our dour morning being interrupted by a bird – *my* bird, as I'd come to think of her – was nearly enough to make me smile. But not quite.

'Falcon,' I replied. Although, it was only a guess. But I wasn't about to tell him that either.

'Right,' he said. Then he was quiet again, long enough for the silence to become unbearable.

'I thought you wanted to say something,' I said eventually.

'I do and...'

Out of the corner of my eye, I saw him twist his body towards mine. I darted a look in his direction, catching his expression. Unadulterated penitence, damn him. My heartstrings felt a sharp tug, but I returned my gaze to the view.

'I'm sorry, Ally. For all of it. I said before it was immaturity – and it was in part – but you were right to call me selfish. I was selfish and stupid and blind to what I had. There is no excuse, only reasons, and I realise – hearing myself say all this out loud

– how ridiculously feeble they are. How *trite*. It was careless of me to treat our marriage like that – reckless, even – and then to blame you—'

'*Exactly*,' I interjected, facing him. 'You blamed me when I did everything in my power to keep us intact.'

He looked down, staring into his coffee. 'You're right about that too.' He heaved out a weighty sigh. 'But blaming you was easier than admitting I'd failed you, that I'd let my career become all-consuming to the detriment of our marriage. I think it helped me miss you less, convincing myself that *you* wanted the divorce. It definitely hurt less – or at least I pretended it did.'

A stone lodged in my chest. All those years, Tommy had been hurting too. I'd told myself he'd abandoned the marriage because that's what he wanted, that he hadn't loved me enough. But had *I* fought for us – *really* fought for us? And not just compromising, but putting our marriage above all else?

No.

'Wow, we completely cocked that up, didn't we?' I asked.

His head swivelled towards me, and I looked over.

'Ally, none of this was your faul—'

'Just...' I said, raising a hand to stop him. 'What I said a minute ago, about doing everything I could...' I shook my head. 'I didn't.'

'But—'

'No, it's true. I've been thinking about this for the past few days and you weren't the only one who handled it badly. I could have done more – a *lot* more. Why didn't I *say* something when my husband started disappearing for huge chunks of time? *Anything* – a *thousand* different things. "Darling, could you possibly stop leaving me alone all the time? I miss you too much when you're away." I mean, it's not brain surgery, is it?'

'Not when you put it like that.'

'I know that sounds flippant, but I really could have spoken up. *Should* have. Hindsight is such a powerful thing, isn't it?'

'It is. But we were barely in our twenties. Neither of us knew much about anything.'

Our eyes met, and we shared a look of compassion for our younger selves.

'I really am sorry, though,' he added. He extended his hand, spanning the gap between our two chairs. I stared at it, torn. Wasn't this goodbye? A long, tortured, drawn-out goodbye?

*Fuck it.* I took his hand and he smiled briefly, running his thumb over my knuckles.

'So, what now?' he asked, his voice heavy with the question.

'Now, we go back to our lives, right?' I asked, looking over again. He peered into my eyes, his grip on my hand tightening.

'*Or...?*'

I drew in a shallow breath. I wasn't prepared for *Or...?* I wasn't prepared for any of this. I'd been too busy doing my own compartmentalising: Julian needs me... Crisis at Divorced Diva HQ... My new gal pal is the ringleader of a spy network... Tommy is the best shag I've ever had – why not take him for another ride?

Only now there were *feelings* involved – especially *hope*, which lingered in the air like a fart after a takeaway korma. And I didn't dare admit to the L-word, even though it was lurking nearby, ready to pounce.

But what good were hope or love when our circumstances were pitted against us? Tommy's job made it impossible to sustain a meaningful relationship and I was the Divorced Diva, for fuck's sake! The *divorced* part was the primary driver of my entire platform.

What was I supposed to do, change the name?

The Not-So-Divorced Diva. The Once-Divorced-Now-Loved-Up Diva. The Sorry-I-Went-Back-On-Everything-I-Said-About-Divorce Diva.

'You really need to tell me what's happening in there,' said Tommy, dragging me from my thoughts.

'In there?'

'Your head,' he replied, tapping his with a fingertip. 'Your face is telling tales out of school.'

I sucked my lips between my teeth, desperately searching for the best reply when uneasiness crept back in. *Real life is a bitch sometimes.*

'Oh god, I'm not going to like this, am I?' he asked.

'No, but neither am I.'

He dropped my hand. 'But I thought... Never mind.'

'What? What did you think?'

'I...'

'Tommy, what can possibly come of this? Are you quitting your job?'

'No.'

'Great, well, me neither. And if I haven't made it patently clear, my job is being divorced – successfully, blissfully divorced – *and* shouting about it from the rooftops so other divorced people can feel good about themselves and get their lives back on track and never, ever have to feel as small and helpless and lost as I felt when you left that day and never came back. You never came back... *Fuck.*'

A sob burst out of me, sending fat tears spilling down my face. I swiped at them, wishing I was anywhere but on that fucking island with the only man who'd ever broken my heart.

'Ally...'

'Why didn't you come back?' I whispered, my voice strangled.

'You didn't want me to.'

'Yes, I did,' I squeaked, another sob taking hold.

He scooched his chair closer. 'Hey...' He reached for me, wrapping me in his arms and gently stroking my hair, which just made me cry harder.

Tommy wasn't giving up his job and I wasn't giving up mine, and they couldn't have been any less compatible. Simply put, there was no way to make it – *us* – work.

'Shh, it's okay, Ally.'

'No, it's not,' I wailed.

'No... it's not,' he echoed, and my heart split clean in two.

Thought of the day...
There's an old adage that says misery loves company.
That's bullshit.
Misery loves comfort food, binge-watching mindless TV,
crying intermittently, then pretending you're going to be fine.
You *will* be fine, but not for a long, long, long (fucking) time.

I was a walking cliché after I returned from Aetheria. The human version of a cautionary tale. Everything I told my followers to avoid doing, I did.

Wallowing, running through conversations in my head over and over, pining, replaying the sex blow-by-blow, second-guessing my decisions, second-guessing my emotions, second-guessing everything Tommy had ever said and done, indulging future memories that would never happen, more wallowing, more pining, wallowing and pining together...

And what would you even call that? Walling? Pillowing? They sound like sexual positions.

Sorry – I digress...

More than a week passed of me sleepwalking through life. I showed up at work, meaning my body was present, but my mind and spirit were elsewhere – such as the coal cellar or the box room or the cupboard under the stairs. Metaphorically speaking, of course. It wasn't like Claude locked me away for being a miserable git – no matter how much she might have wanted to.

In stark contrast to my zombie-like demeanour, I started dressing like an eccentric, scrounging items from the back of my wardrobe and appearing each morning like Vivienne Westwood crossed with Willy Wonka – and a bit of Elmo tossed in for good measure. Though, to be fair, it was an *adorable* fluffy red shrug.

One morning, I wandered into HQ barefoot, wearing shortie pyjamas printed with ducks. And not regular ducks – *rubber* ducks and each one was in costume. I have no idea where they came from – the pyjamas, not the ducks.

Claude took one look at me, spun me around by my shoulders, and smacked my arse, telling me, 'Get upstairs and take a shower.'

She had a point. It had been two days since I'd bathed, and I was starting to smell a bit ripe. I returned to HQ thirty minutes later, smelling as if Jo Malone herself had gorged on an entire patisserie. But at least I was dressed (semi-)normally in bright-orange wide-leg trousers, a cropped purple tank top, and fuchsia Converse high-tops.

'You should see this,' Claude said as I sat at my desk and stared at a black screen. She reached across and pressed the *on* button and my laptop leapt to life.

'Hmm?' I asked, tearing my eyes from the screensaver – a photograph of one of the towns in the Cinque Terra. Vernazza was my guess.

'This,' she said, reaching across me again – this time to manoeuvre the mouse.

I looked back at the screen and my inbox appeared. Claude clicked on an email and it populated the screen. *I'm Super Famous, I Want Out!* blared from the subject line.

'No,' I said, as decisive as I have ever been. I slammed the laptop shut to punctuate my point.

'Why not?' Claude asked, propping her arse on the edge of my desk.

'A thousand reasons,' I replied – hardly my best effort, but I wasn't hyperbolising. I was positive I could list at *least* a thousand reasons why going on a reality show was a terrible idea.

'Name one.'

'Okay – *bugs*. Bugs the size of a Mini Cooper,' I replied smugly.

'Eh,' she uttered with a dismissive wave of her hand. 'They have mosquito nets for those.'

'Okay, how about not subjecting myself to an array of indignities for no good reason?'

'But there *is* a good reason – *multiple* reasons, actually.'

I scrutinised my sister closely, noticing the faint blueish hue under her eyes. Like me, Claude had access to some of the best skincare products in the world. The dark circles were stress.

'Tell me,' I said, my self-indulgent fugue instantly lifting.

'Well, on top of the winnings going to charity, it's the photo… the one with Julian,' she replied.

I sat back and swivelled my chair to face her dead on. 'But I thought we handled that? Didn't we replace the followers we lost? *Tenfold*.'

'We did, but more than half bounced off within a few days.'

'Oh. Are we in trouble?'

'We're not *haemorrhaging* followers, no,' she replied, 'but…'

She looked over her shoulder and I tipped sideways to see what she was looking at. Maya and Ruby were obviously listening in. Caught out, they startled in surprise, then pretended to get on with something. Ruby even reached for a non-ringing phone.

'*But,*' Claude continued, turning back to me, 'we could still use the publicity – build up engagement... reach a new follower base... At least say you'll consider it.'

'I'll consider it,' I lied.

*No fucking way am I ever doing that. I'd rather eat mashed banana off the floor of the men's loo at St Pancras.*

She flashed me a grateful smile, and guilt piled on top of dread. I knew Claude and there was a strong chance she'd talk me into this. Well, if she was so keen, maybe she should go on the bloody sho—

'Ally?' Ruby's voice cut through my mental rant, and I lifted my head, giving her an inquisitive smile.

'What's up, Ruby-Doo?' I asked. Another post-Aetheria affectation – giving the team stupid nicknames.

'Er...' She looked towards the doorway and I followed her gaze.

'Fuck,' I whispered when I saw who was standing there.

'Right, Ruby, Maya, let's step out for some lunch, shall we?' said Claude with OTT enthusiasm.

Maya popped up, collecting her handbag from her bottom drawer, but Ruby gaped at Claude like a goldfish. 'But it's only 10.30,' she said, clearly confused.

'*Early* lunch then – my treat,' Claude replied, signalling for Ruby to hurry. She finally seemed to twig, jumping up from her chair and following Claude.

Claude patted Tommy's arm as she passed. It was a small gesture, but it meant the world – telling me *and* Tommy that she was happy to see him. Maya scurried into the entry, barely giving Tommy a glance, but Ruby took her time, openly ogling him. Claude must have filled them in earlier – possibly to explain why I was behaving so oddly – because once Ruby reached the entry, she looked back and gave me a silent chef's kiss.

I glanced at Tommy, who was watching the others over his shoulder, seemingly bemused by their sudden exit. He absolutely *was* a chef's kiss of a man – especially in that crisp, white collared shirt and dark-wash jeans. But what the hell was he doing at Divorced Diva HQ?

He turned towards me, still lingering in the doorway. 'Hi.'

'Hi,' I replied, sitting up straighter but remaining behind my desk – a safety barrier of sorts.

He looked around, taking in the high ceilings, the warm light streaming in the windows, the long wall of honour hung with framed accolades and photographs.

'Quite the set-up,' he said with an admiring nod.

'Thank you,' I replied, allowing myself a moment of pride.

Seeing HQ through Tommy's eyes was a pinch-me moment, a reminder of how much we'd accomplished in a relatively short time – a far cry from when it was just me and an Insta-gram account.

Only Claude seemed to think we should be doing more – something to worry about later, when my one true love wasn't standing in the middle of our office.

He wandered over to the wall, peering at the commenda-tion we'd received from the Lord Mayor of London for our work with a women's shelter.

'This is incredible, Ally,' he said, his eyes coming back to me. 'I had no idea—'

'That it wasn't all lipstick and sex positivity?' I asked, raising my brows impishly.

Banter was so much easier than giving my heart a look-in, especially with it hammering in my chest and screaming at me to run away.

Tommy gave me a self-deprecating smile. 'Touché.'

The screaming eased off a little, Tommy's easy good humour a potent foil for my internal disquiet.

'I don't suppose you get that sort of acknowledgement in your line of work?' I asked, genuinely curious.

He perched on the edge of Maya's desk and folded his arms, his biceps straining against his shirt. Very distracting.

'Er, no. Nothing like that – usually just some vague headline about something mildly significant happening someplace no one's ever heard of.'

I nodded. 'Like a tiny resort island in the Aegean Sea.'

'Exactly.'

*Why are you here? Why are you here? Why are you here?*

'You're probably wondering why I'm here,' he said. Now *I* was the goldfish.

'How do you keep doing that?' I asked. 'Reading my mind?'

'It's not mindreading. At least, not this time,' he said with a slight smile. 'It's just what I would be wondering.'

'Oh, so, what *are* you doing here then? Are you on assignment?'

He shook his head. 'No, I, er... I took a leave of absence.'

'Oh,' I said, my eyes wide with surprise.

'Yes. It's been back-to-back assignments for some time now and... well... I needed a break.'

'A break,' I repeated – not a question, just affirming that's what he'd said. But what the hell did that mean? Was he talking about a long weekend? A month? A *year*?

And there was something else bothering me. 'So, what did Trudy say about that? Isn't she your boss?'

'Sorry? Oh, no. She just led the Kovalec assignment, but I doubt we'll work together again. It's a large network.'

'Ah – so same for Elsa?'

'Yes.' I perked up at his reply and Tommy gave me a knowing smile. 'I know you didn't like her.'

'Well, no. But to be fair, I did spend the first few days thinking she was your girlfriend. She could have been the loveliest person in the world, and I still wouldn't have warmed to her.'

Ordinarily I wouldn't have been so forthright, airing my jealousy like that, but I'd already laid the rest of my cards on the table back in Greece.

'Mmm,' he murmured, giving nothing away.

'It was her, wasn't it, who vetted me?' I asked. 'Only she didn't go back far enough – she didn't find the connection to you.'

'How did you know?' he asked, his eyes curious.

'Just something Trudy said – *and* that you were genuinely surprised to see me.'

'I was. And pleased.'

I laughed. 'You didn't seem pleased. If I recall, you were adamant that I leave.'

'Well, that wasn't *me* per se. I promise, I was very glad to see you, Ally.'

My eyes lingered on his as I tried to decipher what he meant, emotions battling inside me.

Hope was prodding me to get out of my chair and go to him. But fear was stronger – hurt as well – both weighing me down like anchors. So, I stayed put. And silent. This was Tommy's show – whatever line in the script came next, it was his.

'God, I really thought this would be easier,' he said, which did nothing to break the rising tension, only added to it.

Thought of the day...
'No' is a complete sentence.
(And 'no bloody way – you're out of your mind' is a
completer sentence.)

Thought of the day...
Prepare for difficult conversations – know what you want to
say and how you'll say it.
(Practise on your pet. If you don't have one, a potted plant
will do.)

Thought of the day...
If you're caught up in chaos of someone else's making, it's
not your job to untangle the mess.
(Repeat after me: Not my circus, not my monkeys.)

My heartbeat pulsed loudly in my ears, and I swallowed the enormous lump in my throat. Was this worse than never seeing him again? It felt worse. And I started wishing, more than anything, that he would just go.

Then he pushed off Maya's desk and crossed the room in three long strides. Kneeling before me, he took both my hands in his, sending a forceful current rocketing through me.

'Ally, I'm sorry, but I can't do this – I can't spend the next decade, or the one after that, or the one after that making the same stupid bloody mistake I made when I let you go.'

'What?' I whispered, my mind racing to catch up.

'I love you. I've loved you from the moment I saw you dancing on that table at the Turf Tavern.'

'Britney Spears – "Womaniser",' I said, the memory flooding back.

'Yep. You only knew half the words but that didn't stop you from belting out the whole bloody song. You were fearless and beautiful and when I finally struck up the nerve to talk to you – which was a *least* an hour later – I discovered that you were warm and funny and so fucking clever about pretty much everything that I felt like a right numpty next to you. I was certain you wouldn't want anything to do with me.

'But miraculously you did, and we fell in love and got married – despite everyone warning us not to – and then I completely fucked it up.'

'But it wasn't just y—'

'It was mostly me. And I want to fix that. If you'll let me.' He looked down, shaking his head. 'Seeing you on that island... it brought everything back and I thought I could handle it, be professional and just get on with the job but... I couldn't bear the thought of being so close to you and not being *with* you, you know?'

I nodded. Because I did know. It had been torture.

'It was torture,' he added, and I laughed at the uncanniness.

'What's funny?' he asked with a gentle laugh.

'Just... you read my mind again.'

We shared a smile.

'Do you think we could try again?' he asked, tightening his grip on my hands. 'Do you *want* to try again?'

How could he ask that? Of *course* I did, but as full as my heart was, reality loomed, casting a deep shadow and giving me pause.

'But, Tommy... *how*?' I lifted my gaze and looked around at HQ to make my point.

'I have no fucking idea,' he replied, and my eyes shot back to his.

'Well, at least you're being honest about it.'

He shrugged, breaking into a smile. 'We're smart people, Ally. We'll figure it out. But you still haven't answered my question. Do you *want* to?'

I looked into Tommy's eyes, seeing right into his soul, the soul of a man who had been my everything – my love, my best friend, my *home*. And I saw what I'd longed for – possibility and hope and dreams coming true.

But most of all, I saw love. True, happily-ever-after, Hollywood-ending love.

I was overcome with choking sobs and tears filled my eyes, spilling onto my cheeks. With a vigorous nod, I barely managed to gasp, 'Yes.'

'Oh, thank god.'

Then he captured my face in both hands and kissed me. And it was the most perfect, passionate, pure kiss that ever was.

I'm serious – Westley and Buttercup had *nothing* on us.

# EPILOGUE
## NINE MONTHS LATER

Thought of the day…
Trust your heart. It's almost always right.
And if it isn't, then at least you won't spend the rest of your
life wondering,
'What if…?'

'Well, this doesn't suck,' I say, turning my head towards Tommy. He's stretched out on a sun lounger, a twin to mine, his eyes closed behind his sunglasses.

He lifts my hand to his lips and gives it a soft kiss. 'It decidedly does not.'

I look down to the beach where aquamarine waves lap at the purest white sand I've ever seen, and palm trees sway gently in the breeze. Seriously, this view is ridiculous. It looks like a screensaver. On cue, a squadron of pelicans flies overhead, and I chuckle to myself.

'What's funny, my love?'

'Nothing. Just a pinch-me moment,' I reply, looking over.

He lifts his sunglasses, and we lock eyes, sharing a smile

before he slides them back into place and continues soaking up the sun. My gaze drops to his chest, then to the ridges of his stomach, then lower where a muscular V points to his groin.

I look in all directions. The beach in front of our bungalow is technically private but the staff are never far away, always at the ready to meet any request we might have. Still... we *could* chance it. I scooch down my lounger and roll onto my side, then slip my hand from Tommy's grasp and lightly trail my fingertips over his pecs.

'Mmm,' he murmurs.

I follow the contours of his abs with whisper-soft touches, then slide my fingers under the waistband of his board shorts. He grabs my hand with a laugh, halting my seaside seduction.

'Oh, *please*,' I beg, and he looks over. I stick my bottom lip out, pouting dramatically.

'There is nothing I would enjoy more than making love to my beautiful wife on this beautiful beach, but you know we're waiting on a call. It could come any time now.'

'*I* could come any time – if you'd *make* me.'

'*Ally...*'

I huff with frustration. 'What if we're quick?'

'I'd rather not rush it,' he teases with a wink.

I snigger, conceding. Besides, pent-up sexual energy makes for wonderful foreplay.

My phone rings, drawing our attention, and I check the screen. 'It's Claude.'

'Make it quick,' says Tommy, and I nod.

'Hiya,' I chirrup.

'Why did I let you talk me into this?' she asks – no preamble, which is typical, but it sounds like she's in a tizz.

'If you remember correctly, *you* said it would be good for Divorced Diva.'

'That was when *you* were the Diva, not me.'

I cover the handset and whisper to Tommy, 'She's having a wobble.'

He nods in understanding.

Claude has had many wobbles since we made her the new face of Divorced Diva. The choice was a no-brainer, really. If it couldn't be me – and it couldn't, not after Tommy and I remarried and I acquired a new... er, *role* – then why not the still-divorced woman who knows Divorced Diva inside and out?

We began with a glow-up to find a look that suited her *and* the brand. Claude's always been a natural beauty but she's even more gorgeous now, something she's still getting used to. Particularly when people flirt with her.

With regards to the work itself, we eased her in by sending her to Aetheria for a week. Niki took Claude under her wing, showing her the ropes and ensuring she was pampered even more than I'd been.

Claude even got to meet *Yiayiá* and they hit it off, just like I knew they would. *Yiayiá* was good for her, encouraging her to be bold, to take life by the horns – something she's still working on. But I've seen a lot of light in Claude's eyes since she returned from Greece. She's getting back to who she was *BG* – before Gregory.

And while on Aetheria, Claude befriended Julian's new girl-friend Camille, who is (shockingly) age-appropriate at forty-seven. I like Camille too, by the way – being with her makes Julian a better man.

And everything else? We're making it up as we go and I am still around if Claude needs me.

'*Seriously*, Al, what the bloody hell am I doing?'

'You are embracing the new, Claude, moving forward with

your life. *And* you're growing our brand. I'm sure it will be lots of fun.'

The last part is an abject lie – *I'm Super Famous, I Want Out* is my idea of hell on earth.

'But I'm not even famous!' she wails.

'Well, you will be after this,' I quip.

'Ugh,' she groans.

Right, so cajoling her isn't working – tough love it is.

'Listen here. You are Claudia Jane Novak and you are clever and kind and brave. You excel at anything you set your mind to, Claude, and you'll absolutely *smash* it, okay?'

'If you say so,' she replies with a sigh.

Not exactly a rousing cry of self-confidence, but I don't get the chance to push further as my phone notifies me of another call. 'Look, I've got to go, Claude. We love you. You'll be brilliant.'

I end the call before she can reply – the last time I'll speak to my sister for at least six weeks while she's in the wilds of Borneo – then switch to the secure line and accept the incoming call.

'This is Mrs Jones,' I answer, giving my assigned pseudonym.

'We're expecting hail by sunset.'

'And a typhoon, I hear – with hundred-mile-an-hour winds,' I say, responding with the corresponding code phrase.

Tommy's eyes meet mine as I listen to – and memorise – our orders. A short time later, the call ends abruptly without a *goodbye*.

'Well, Mr Jones, we're on.'

Tommy stands up and offers me his hand. I take it, and he helps me off my sun lounger, then dips his head, landing a soft kiss on my lips. 'Let's go, Mrs Jones.'

We share a smile, then return to our bungalow to change clothes and gather our equipment.

It's showtime.

\* \* \*

## MORE FROM SANDY BARKER

The next brilliantly funny romantic read from Sandy Barker is available to order now here:

https://mybook.to/SandyBarkerNewBackAd

# ACKNOWLEDGEMENTS

I've dedicated this book to all the hopeful romantics out there – especially romance readers, because without you, I wouldn't get to do this wonderful thing: being an author.

As always, there are quite a few people to thank.

First, to my editor at Boldwood Books, Emily Yau – thank you for trusting me to turn a slightly bonkers plot into a love story and for being so vigilant in helping me tell it. Your thoughtful insight and direction are greatly appreciated (even though you made me kill a few darlings). I learn from every book we work on together.

To the rest of the team at Boldwood – Niamh and Katia, marketers extraordinaire; Emily Reader, copy editor; Jennifer Kay Davies, proofreader; and everyone else who works tirelessly to support my publishing journey – thank you. And to Nicolette Chin, super-talented narrator – thank you for bringing Ally and her band of merry misfits to life.

To my agent, Lina Langlee at The North Literary Agency – this is our fourteenth book together! Thank you, thank you, thank you for being my partner in publishing for nearly seven years – can you believe it? – and for embracing Ally, especially helping me to smooth out her rough edges.

To my author besties, Nina, Andie and Fi – I couldn't do this without you, and I wouldn't want to. And to my romcom gal pals, Simonetta, Sharleen, Leonie, Laura and Frankie, I so appreciate you and your unwavering support. Thank you to my other wonderful author friends – near and far – whose work inspires me and whose unwavering support humbles me.

Thank you to authors Veronica and Laurie at Australian Book Lovers, because your adage to 'read more Aussie books' is so important and you do so much to support our community. And to the book lovers who share their love of romance reading online and in person – I've gotten to meet so many of you this past year and your generous support is greatly appreciated.

A special thank you to one of my dearest friends, Maria Papathanassiou, who reviewed the Greek language, culture and cuisine – confessing afterwards that she read the whole book, not just 'the Greek bits' and that she wouldn't mind Tommy for herself. I love you, Bella.

And to my family and treasured friends – thanks for proudly displaying my books on your shelves, and for bragging about me to everyone who'll listen. Special shout out to my mum who reads my books as I write them, encouraging me and telling me when I'm taking too long to get to the sexy bits.

And to my favourite person, Ben – I can't imagine ever getting this far without you by my side. Thanks for the cheering, the hugs, the bubbly (even for tiny milestones like finishing a tricky scene) and for making life such a grand, fun, awesome adventure.

Lastly, dear reader, thank *you*. I hope you enjoyed Ally's excapades (see what I did there?). Next up is a super fun adventure set on the Isle of Capri.

Till then, happy reading...

Sandy xxx

# ABOUT THE AUTHOR

**Sandy Barker** is a bestselling romance author. She's lived in the UK, the US and Australia. She has travelled extensively across six continents, with many of her travel adventures finding homes in her books.

Download your exclusive bonus content from Sandy Barker here:

Visit Sandy's website: www.sandybarker.com

Follow Sandy on social media here:

f facebook.com/sandybarkerauthor

instagram.com/sandybarkerauthor

BB bookbub.com/profile/sandy-barker

# ALSO BY SANDY BARKER

**The Ever After Agency Series**

Match Me If You Can

Shout Out to My Ex

The One That I Want

Someone Like You

I Knew You Were Trouble

My Big Greek Island Ex-Scape

# Boldwood

Boldwood Books is an award-winning fiction publishing company seeking out the best stories from around the world.

**Find out more at www.boldwoodbooks.com**

Join our reader community for brilliant books, competitions and offers!

Follow us
@BoldwoodBooks
@TheBoldBookClub

Sign up to our weekly deals newsletter

https://bit.ly/BoldwoodBNewsletter